Johnny picked  shards of broken glass from the floor, and used it as a mirror to look around the corner and into the suite . . .

The older Vietnamese scientist stood silently over the fax machine, motionless as a deer, watching the strip of thermal paper with the access codes being pulled in slowly, line by line.

Codes the Yakuza mustn't get!

Johnny dropped the glass and lunged out of the bathroom at the same time that the Yakuza in the doorway stepped forward, right thumb held high.

Johnny grabbed the paper, just as Shinji whipped his thumb in a tight circle. The filament cut through the air without a sound, cut through the fax machine and the table that held it; cut through the paper just as Johnny pulled it loose.

The paper was sliced clean—all he had was one image.

The old scientist held the other two; and with a sudden swift motion, he dove for the hibachi.

Shinji's thumb jerked upward; the filament flashed and flew—and the old man's hand holding the paper fell, severed, onto the glowing bed of coals. . . .

JOHNNY MNEMONIC

A NOVEL BY TERRY BISSON

BASED ON THE SHORT STORY
AND SCREENPLAY BY **WILLIAM GIBSON**

POCKET BOOKS
New York   London   Toronto   Sydney   Tokyo   Singapore

This book is a work of fiction. Names, characters, places and incidents are products of the author's imagination or are used fictitiously. Any resemblance to actual events or locales or persons, living or dead, is entirely coincidental.

An *Original* Publication of POCKET BOOKS

POCKET BOOKS, a division of Simon & Schuster Inc.
1230 Avenue of the Americas, New York, NY 10020

ISBN: 0-671-52300-7

First Pocket Books printing June 1995

10 9 8 7 6 5 4 3 2 1

POCKET and colophon are registered trademarks of Simon & Schuster Inc.

Printed in the U.S.A.

For David Hartwell,
just because

ONE

—◼—

"I'm here!" said Johnny, talking to himself as much as to the face that was resolving itself on the vidphone.

Here! Beijing. City of light and air, so different from run-down, played-out, used-up America and the dark and twisted Sprawl. Above Beijing's boulevards, glasteel towers soared into alluring formations, their video-generated curves augmented by holo-enhanced "cakering" that glowed by night and shimmered by day. It was beautiful. Johnny liked cities. Which was good, since he had never seen anything else, except in pictures.

"Here? Where's *here,* Johnny?"

"Just here, Ralfi. Beijing. I'm in a cab. Downtown, Agnes Smedley Boulevard. You got me on a car phone. I'm on my way to the hotel."

"Did you get it?"

"Get what, Ralfi?"

"The upgrade." The agent's carefully sculpted face looked worried; but Ralfi always looked worried. Johnny didn't know whether to be touched or amused. Casually he answered, "Sure . . ."

1

The cab stopped suddenly with a sickening lurch. Johnny almost slid off the seat, catching his briefcase with one hand and stopping himself with the other against the grimy vidphone screen. At the same instant a hand slapped against the rear window of the cab. Blood smeared down the glass. Things were definitely getting wilder. Johnny leaned over to peer through the thick side window.

A jerking line of demonstrators, their faces hidden behind surgical masks—either for dramatic effect or some other reason Johnny didn't want to fathom—was surging onto the boulevard from one of the side streets. Steel drums boomed under a forest of sticks and banners. The front line of demonstrators wore helmets, and two rows of police were falling back as they advanced, as if in a ritual dance that both sides knew well.

Most of the banners were in Chinese but others were in Arabic, Russian, Spanish and English; they read STOP NAS! NO NAS! WHERE'S THE CURE! The demonstrators had the zombie-like gait, the twitching limbs and the angry stares of those already afflicted with the disease. One, a woman carrying a child wrapped in a shroud, was pushed onto the hood of the cab. The driver honked; the woman dropped the child and either slid or was pulled off the other side. Johnny couldn't tell.

"What's all that racket?" Ralfi asked. "What's going on?" He looked alarmed, as if he were with Johnny inside the cab, instead of half a world away.

"Some kind of demonstration," Johnny said.

"Anti-American?"

Johnny snorted. "You wish. As if anybody cared anymore. No, it's about NAS; you know, Nerve Attenuation Syndrome."

"There, too?"

A demonstrator clambered over the hood of the cab, followed by another; others pushed into the sides.

2

The cars behind started to honk, their horns and sirens (legal in Beijing) raising a wail over the beating of the steel drums and the howl of the crowd.

"Everywhere, Ralfi. Read the fucking papers. But don't look so worried. We have our job here; it's under control."

Ralfi couldn't help how he looked. He had only two expressions: sad and worried. He was a small, dapper man whose face had been surgically modified to imitate some forgotten movie star from the forties of the last century. It was a Singapore botch job; the surgeons had overdone the drooping eyes, giving him a permanently troubled frown. But Ralfi's worry was genuine, this time: "This is a big one, Johnny. You sure you can carry it? I could send out this new guy who's fitted with the latest . . ."

"Ralfi, stop it!" said Johnny. As if to reassure his agent, he adjusted his tie and sat up straight, seeing himself reflected in the vidphone screen over Ralfi's image. The dark suit, the conservative tie—

"I got upgraded with the MDA-18 this morning," he lied. Convincingly, he hoped. "You don't have a thing to worry about."

The cab was rocking back and forth as the crowd vented its anger on the foreign object in its midst. The driver rolled down his window and began to shout obscenities in an obscure northern Chinese dialect.

Suddenly a hand reached through the window, and the driver pulled his head back and hit the "close" button. From the back seat, Johnny noticed with approval the gleaming top edge of the window glass, sharpened for just such emergencies.

Apparently, so did the owner of the arm. It was jerked back just before the glass reached it.

The cab rocked harder, the air shocks howling in protest.

"Even with the upgrade, I'm worried," said Ralfi. "I'm not sure."

The cab rocked harder. The drums were getting closer. The screams of the crowd were getting louder.

"What's going on?" Ralfi's eyes grew wide as the cab rocked from side to side. It was, Johnny thought, as if the agent could feel it inside the vidphone monitor.

"Everything's under control, Ralfi," Johnny said. *Everything's under control.* He crooned it to himself like a mantra. He had once spent eleven months in Bangkok perfecting the trick of getting cooler as things got hotter. A trick of the breath and of the spirit, it was his Zen, his religion. It was Johnny's protection and his weapon, all in one.

"What time is it there? Are you going to be late?" Ralfi whined. "How far are you from the hotel?"

Johnny crooned his mantra: "Everything's under control, Ralfi." He dipped the international cash card Ralfi had loaned him into the slot on the back of the seat; the meter went off. He pulled two bills from his pocket and gave them to the driver; he got a smile in return. He picked up his briefcase and reached for the door handle—

"Where are you going?" Ralfi protested.

"I'll walk," Johnny said.

"Walk!? But, but . . . ?"

Ralfi's *but*s were lost in the din of shouts and screams, bullhorns and steel drums, police sirens and cracking billyclubs as Johnny slid open the door of the cab. With only a second's hesitation, Johnny straightened his tie once more, composed his features into a perfect blank, and plunged into the maelstrom.

"But . . ."

As the cab door slid shut, the driver reached back and slapped the top of the vidphone, turning it off and consigning Ralfi to oblivion.

Johnny walked through the crowd like a hot knife through butter, a tall European, or almost-European,

4

in a dark business suit. Conservative faux-leather briefcase. Eyes straight ahead. Benign smile, nodding his thanks to those who gave way before him. His studied, formal politeness was as effective as a police escort, even in the midst of chaos; so effective that he made it for almost a block before getting stopped.

The demonstrator leaped in front of him from the side of an overturned car. He was holding a sign that read:

STOP NAS NOW! NO MORE DELAYS!
RELEASE THE CURE!

He was screaming in Chinese through a surgical mask. The mask was stained with blood and spittle. Smiling and nodding, Johnny tried to pass to the right but the man blocked his way.

He tried to pass to the left but the man blocked his way.

Johnny looked down. The man's feet were swathed in filthy bandages. In the half-light of evening they were as quick as ghosts, stitching their way from side to side on the pavement in a macabre dance, the death shuffle of those in the last stages of NAS.

Bowing politely, Johnny stepped back, feeling behind him with one hand. He felt warm metal; he looked back and saw that it was the hood of a police cutter, nosing through the crowd like a blue shark. As he vaulted up and over the narrow hood, he looked through the windshield and saw two rows of riot cops filing out the back of the cutter like paratroopers, masked in black lucite, eagerly slapping their palms with heavy plastic stunclubs.

Time to get scarce, Johnny thought as he hit the street on the other side of the cutter. Running.

The crowd was running, too. Screaming. There were shouts, groans, the sickening *crack* of dense plastic on bone.

Johnny dropped the smile; it was no longer necessary. He ditched it behind somewhere, on the street, like a trick hat, a piece of a disguise. He loosened his tie. The crowd was moving faster and faster, and now he was moving with and not against them. He looked at his watch, then up at the ideograph above the street a few blocks ahead, under it the words BEIJING RAMADA.

Barely late, he thought. He slowed just a fraction, and started moving toward the edge of the stream; but that proved more and more difficult as the crowd began moving faster and faster. A man with a bullhorn jostled him, shouting in incomprehensible Mandarin. A young Chinese girl in a crimson blouse rushed past, impossibly pretty but already marred by the wild eyes and frantic hand movements of the NAS-afflicted. Was she trying to catch his eye? Under her blouse Johnny caught the slight swell of a breast that reminded him of . . .

But Johnny didn't want to be reminded of anything. He had a job to do. He had reached the edge of the street; he pulled back against a wall and searched through his pockets for the matchbook with the room number on it.

Just then the girl in red went down, so suddenly that a pursuing riot cop almost tripped over her. The street was filled with running feet, but instead of following his compatriots the cop stopped to feed. He looked down at the girl, stood over her in regulation stance, raised his stunclub, and—

Without thinking, Johnny lunged forward and blocked the blow with his briefcase.

The cop turned, expressionless. Johnny looked into the black lucite faceplate and saw nothing there but himself reflected: a blue-suited businessman holding a briefcase up like a shield. The girl scrambled to her feet and ran, looking back over her shoulder with

6

regret, as if to say, "Thanks for helping me; I wish I could do the same for you. . . ."

The cop turned and followed the girl, and Johnny breathed a sigh of relief. *Let her fend for herself. I have other—*

Suddenly he felt a hand grab his collar from behind, then violently spin him around. He fell to his knees. He looked up and saw another cop looming over him. This cop's face was also, of course, a blank, but Johnny could almost imagine the smile behind the lucite mask as the stunclub was clicked into shock mode and the little red light on the tip began to flicker as the cop brought it down, tauntingly and slowly, toward Johnny's face.

Too slowly.

Johnny's hand was already out of his suit coat pocket, his thumb already on the button of the tiny tube of *Victimize* ("Turn perps into victims with one push of the button"). He thrust it up, under the cop's face mask, and pushed.

The cop's hand let go and Johnny scrambled to his feet. Johnny knew he had gotten the cop on the intake when the cop didn't scream. The cop dropped his stunclub and fumbled with his helmet, trying to get it off while the other cops rushed past, still chasing the crowd.

The cop wouldn't scream for at least sixty seconds, Johnny knew.

Then he would scream for quite a while.

Meanwhile, Johnny slipped around the corner and across the street, toward the brightly lit hotel entrance. He dropped the spray tube, useless now, into a trash can, and fished a matchbook out of his pants pocket. As he entered the revolving door, he unfolded it to check the number scrawled on the inside cover: 2571.

* * *

From the twenty-fifth floor of the Beijing Ramada, the world's second largest city was a sea of lights, like the Milky Way beached on a dark planet; except for the analog audio of a few far-off sirens it seemed a hi-res video display of pure information, digital, a landscape of light and dark, without the grayscale complications of flesh and blood.

The complications are what we live for, thought the young Vietnamese scientist as he shifted slightly, so that he could see his wife and baby behind him, reflected in the glass: a warm image of family life superimposed on a vast, cold, uncaring world. He shuddered as he thought of how much he loved them, and how much he was risking for an abstract "humanity."

His wife was breast-feeding their infant daughter, who had finally stopped crying.

The young scientist would have given anything not to have brought them here. But there was no choice.

He turned to the older man, also Vietnamese, standing beside him. Both were dressed conservatively in dark blue suits, cheaply cut and frayed, identifying them as research scientists, perhaps even academics.

"The courier is late," the younger man said.

"Be calm," the older replied.

Calm! The young man retreated from the window and surveyed the hotel room behind him. What he saw made him even more nervous. To him, they were not people but muscle.

The four Koreans sharing the suite had been hired for their lethal, not their social, skills. They were killers. Their leader, dressed in a SpeedRacer T-shirt and sweat pants, was as large as a sumo wrestler; he had disarmed the smoke alarm and was frying shrimp on a charcoal hibachi set up on the coffee table. His male partner, also in T-shirt and jeans, was channel-surfing on the TV, flipping desultorily past news reports of the riot in the streets below. He finally settled on a Japanese superhero cartoon. A rerun.

The two other Korean bodyguards were women. One was short-haired and muscular, in a bathrobe that she didn't bother to close over her colorful tattoos and drab cotton underwear, cleaning her 9mm Glock semiautomatic pistol with a Q-tip. The second leafed through a month-old copy of *Glamour* that she could just as easily have been in, with her perfect hair and makeup. She wore a Victoria's Secret robe, with other elegant secrets underneath—among them a .357 magnum.

"Why is he late?" the young Vietnamese scientist whispered to his partner. "We should have put it out on the global net while there was still time."

"No," said the older man. He had the sharp face and soft demeanor of an Uncle Ho. "It would have been suicide. They are monitoring every fragment of transmitted data. A courier is the only way."

"So we hire a criminal with a silicon chip in his head?"

"A highly skilled smuggler," said the older man. With a hand on the arm he attempted to calm his younger, more agitated companion. "Besides, it was *she* who chose him, just as she chose us. You must remember that."

The young man was still nervous. "He's late."

"Americans have a different sense of time. . . ."

The courier was not the only one who was late.

A few blocks away, in a limousine trapped behind the riot police's mopping-up operation (an English expression that was becoming more literal yearly as NAS demonstrations became more violent around the world), six conservatively dressed "businesspeople" waited in traffic.

At least they seemed like businesspeople, in their identical gray suits. Five were men and one was a

9

woman. They sat wordlessly, with blank faces and seemingly infinite patience; only the fingers drumming on the gym bags held in their laps betrayed their tension in the slowly creeping limo.

The man in the right front seat looked at his watch, then out the window at the traffic jam, then up through the sunroof of the limousine at the spectacular lighted towers, Beijing having long ago replaced New York as the skyscraper capital of the world. Many of Beijing's skyscrapers were post-postmodern constructs sprouting holographic virtual upper floors that changed with the seasons; dramatic by day, they were even more beautiful at night.

Not that the man looking up, or the five with him, had eyes for beauty. They were professionals, operatives for the world's largest, most whispered about, most feared and most profitable criminal organization. The Coca-Cola of crime.

They were Yakuza.

The man in the right front, looking up, was the youngest and at the same time the hardest-looking of the six. He was a Japanese-American, as neatly tailored as the others, but he sported a ponytail over the back collar of his understated, expensive gray suit.

The limo crept a few more feet, around a corner, and he found what he was looking for. A neon holo, floating high above faux-crenelated towers: BEIJING RAMADA.

The hotel was still several blocks away, but not too far to walk, even hauling the heavy gym bags the other five Yakuza held on their laps.

The man with the ponytail was just about to give the order to get out when the limo began to move, slowly at first and then quickly gathering more speed.

He looked at his watch and nodded, to himself as much as to the others.

He almost even smiled.

* * *

The first thing Johnny noticed, stepping out of the revolving door, was the smell: the curious, oddly familiar hotel mix of plants and food, shoe polish and tobacco. Then the noise: the pleasant flutter and scurry, rattle and hum—the controlled chaos of travelers coming and going.

One whole wall of the Beijing Ramada's lobby was taken up with television monitors, scanning leisurely from channel to channel as sensors picked up how many eyes were on each screen: thus the guests in the lobby indirectly and collectively controlled the display. No one was watching but a five-year-old boy and a grizzled veteran in a worn but carefully pressed People's Red Army uniform. Thus half the monitors showed news footage of the NAS riots, and the other half showed a Japanese superhero cartoon, a violent rerun with fake blood that seemed to Johnny, as he stopped just inside the revolving doors, even more horrifying than the real stuff in the streets.

Johnny didn't have a problem with real blood; real blood you could mop up. Fake blood was forever.

As he scanned the lobby looking for his contact, Johnny felt an unexpected glow of well-being and warmth, a feeling he always felt in hotel lobbies. He somehow associated it with his childhood—irrationally, he knew, since he remembered nothing of his childhood.

He soon noticed the well-dressed Chinese man standing by a potted fern, reading *Let's Go China, 2020.*

Last year's edition, as arranged.

Johnny walked over, bowed, and in a low voice accompanied by a polite smile, said:

"Let's have it, quick. I'm running late."

The man smiled back and handed Johnny a white paper bag. In Chinese and English it read, *Dunkin' Donuts.*

Johnny looked inside and frowned; then smiled

11

even more politely, and said, "You promised me an *MDA-18*. I paid for a fucking *MDA-18*."

The Chinese man shrugged, still smiling. "They promised me. Look, pal, that's a Pemex Doubler. It should do the job."

"Should—!"

"The guy who supplied it said that should give you almost the same capacity as the MDA-18."

"*Almost!* It's not even close."

The Chinese man reached for the donut bag. "Look, if you don't want it . . . ?"

Johnny sighed and folded the top of the bag over. He bowed punctiliously. "It'll have to do."

The Chinese man bowed just as politely and closed his *Let's Go China*. As he was about to walk away, a sudden, subtle change in the light made both men turn and look behind them.

The monitors on the wall were all changing, one by one. Instead of echoing the same images, they were each presenting part of a single, larger image; they were single pixels in what gradually appeared as a low-resolution image of a young black man wearing dreadlocks and mirror shades.

"J-Bone," the Chinese man said, a little distractedly.

"Who?" asked Johnny.

"Loteks," the Chinese man said. "Video guerrilla stuff."

"Guess those dudes are worldwide," Johnny said. He had heard of them but had never paid much attention. Now, despite himself, he was impressed. The video guerrillas known as the Loteks had the uncanny capacity to break into any programming, network or cable, satellite or fiber-optic, with their anti-establishment message. *But what's the point?* Johnny wondered. *What do they gain by it?*

"Snatch back your brain, Zombies," said J-Bone's

12

voice, in a rough rap cadence with an African-American accent. "Snatch it back and hold it!"

Then his face, distorted with rage and passion, was replaced by the peaceful image of a dolphin, seen first on each individual screen, and then gliding across all the screens as one image in perfect, choreographed silence.

Gliding, gliding . . . then gone.

The news and the cartoon was back. Default mode.

The buzz was back; the rattle and hum. The crowd in the lobby picked up where it had left off. They had clearly seen all this before; the Loteks' intrusions were obviously part of the normal TV matrix everywhere.

Johnny looked around and saw that he and an old man in an old Mao suit were the only ones watching; even his contact was gone, spinning out through the revolving doors. The noise in the lobby resumed full volume, like a glass filling with warm bright water.

Johnny headed for the bank of elevators. Suddenly a child's head popped over the back of a couch; it was a black-haired Asian five-year-old, too well-dressed to be a street urchin (besides, they weren't allowed in hotel lobbies). The kid looked at Johnny gravely as if, somehow, he saw in him a kindred soul.

Without thinking, Johnny ducked his head behind a fish tank. He could imagine the child's astonishment at his distorted, enlarged face. He winked. He wriggled his fingers like an octopus—

The soft *ding* of the arriving elevator brought him back to reality.

No time for play. Had there ever been?

The kid waved goodbye. Johnny stepped onto the elevator and punched twenty-five.

Johnny waved back, two-fingered, as the doors slid shut.

Johnny set down his briefcase and opened the donut bag.

The Pemex Doubler was about the size of a deck of cards; transparent green plastic with gold circuitry embedded inside, and an orange stripe down the outside. There was an LCD display at one end, and a short extension with a male phone jack at the other.

With a rueful shake of his head, Johnny hefted the tiny device. Would it be enough? Only one way to find out. He pushed back the hair over his left ear, exposing a small, surgically implanted female phone jack.

The elevator display over the door read 3.

Then 4.

As he inserted the male end of the doubler into the female jack wetwired into his skull, Johnny's eyes closed briefly in a short, sharp spasm of pleasure—or was it pain? Or apprehension? He didn't have the time to sort it out for himself, even if he had been so inclined.

Work to do.

The elevator display read 6.

The LCD display on the device read: RAM UPLOAD READY. Then: RAM UPLOAD BEGIN.

Then it read 224.

As the numbers on the display over the elevator door got higher—8, 9, 10, 11—

—the numbers on the LCD display got lower—181, 164, 123, 110.

Johnny rode with his eyes closed, his mind a careful blank. This was a simple procedure, the addition of temporary RAM, but he didn't want to risk a crash or a lock-up. It could be painful or dangerous if interrupted; plus, there was no time . . .

18, 19, 20—

—98, 76, 63, 44.

It was almost pleasant. Uploading cold RAM didn't hold the thrill of jacking through cyberspace, but Johnny felt a certain peace, rare for him. It turned his consciousness inward. It was like wandering through an empty house after everyone had moved out. It was the abandoned house of his own memories. In the places where the furniture had been removed he could almost sense the ghosts of what-had-been . . .

21, 22, 23—

—28, 19, 05.

Even the regrets were gone, and there was a strange sense of peace, an unfamiliar but pleasant sensation for a man who lived, as he did, so close to the edge. . . .

00

25

Ding.

Just in time. Johnny unjacked the Pemex Doubler and dropped it back into the donut sack. The door opened. He stepped into the carpeted hallway and dropped the donut sack into a potted plant by the elevator as the door slid shut behind him.

He checked that his hair was back in place.

He straightened his tie.

He adjusted his smile.

TWO

———■———

On the TV in suite 2571, the riots were still going on. The channel-surfing bodyguard with the remote groaned and switched back to the Japanese superhero cartoon. The tattooed woman continued cleaning her Glock. The sumo-charcoaler turned his shrimp on the grill. The older Vietnamese scientist stood at the window watching the gleaming lights of the city; the younger stood beside him watching the reflection of his wife and child in the bedroom.

The fashion plate turned another page of *Glamour*.

The doorbell rang.

All four Korean bodyguards jumped to their feet. Weapons appeared, ancient but effective. (And intimidating.) Gunpowder/projectile guns.

The sumo-guy walked to the door, surprisingly light on his feet; a sawed-off ten-gauge in his hand. The fashion model joined him, a miniaturized .357 almost visible under her open robe. Behind them, on the couch, where the other two waited, they heard the satisfying *snick-snack* of oil and steel.

The sumo-bodyguard opened the door.

Johnny stood holding his briefcase out before him like a pizza box. "Double cheese, anchovies?"

He didn't seem surprised or disappointed when nobody laughed. He stepped into the room, around the poised but restrained bodyguards, where he was confronted by the younger of the two scientists who had left his station by the big picture window.

"You are Mr.—?"

"Smith," said Johnny.

"You are late, Mr. Smith."

"Right." Johnny reached toward the room-control panel on the wall. The sumo-guy tensed as if to stop him, but was held back by a flicker in the eye of the older Vietnamese, who stood perfectly still, his back to the window.

Ignoring the bodyguards, Johnny pushed a button and the window blinds closed; the city disappeared as if it had never been. He pushed another button and a ceiling fan started rotating with a low hum. Johnny seemed absorbed, like a kid playing with a new toy.

"Question," he announced to the young scientist.

"Yes?"

Johnny edged the top of a rheostat, dimming the lights. The Koreans looked at one another, then at their employers.

Johnny ignored them. "You don't look like the kind of people I usually work for," he said.

"We are—uh—new at this," the scientist answered.

"No shit." With a single contemptuous sweep of his hand, Johnny indicated the four bodyguards. *"Them,* you could have gotten out of a vending machine. But *you—!"*

He looked closely at the young man, then at the older man by the window.

"You *two—"*

17

The older scientist stepped forward. He spoke in soft, formal, clipped tones, with a slight French accent. "Please. No more questions. We approached you through the correct channels. We paid half in advance into the Swiss account, exactly as your agent instructed."

"Yeah," said Johnny. "I know all that. What I'm saying is, I guess I expected players. You two look more like . . ."

He hesitated, dredging up an ancient image.

". . . Missionaries."

The old man held out a sealed envelope. "Please. Everything is taken care of. Here is your ticket. Suborbital to Newark. First class, as arranged."

Johnny put the envelope into the inside pocket of his suit. "First let's see what you want to upload," he said.

The older scientist nodded to the younger, who went into the bedroom.

Johnny set his briefcase on the coffee table, next to the brazier, and clicked open the locks. He opened the briefcase, took out a small electronic device, and closed the briefcase again. He crossed to the door he had entered and attached the device to the door frame with two-sided tape. A tiny red light on the side started blinking.

"Motion detector," Johnny said. "In case the natives get restless."

The blinking light was echoed by an even smaller red light on a beeper-like device on Johnny's belt.

The younger scientist came back into the room carrying a tiny black box. His wife with the baby watched from the bedroom doorway; he shooed her away anxiously. When she was out of sight, he opened the box and pulled out a CD-ROM disk the size of an antique U.S. buffalo nickel.

18

"So that's it," Johnny said. "How much am I carrying?"

"Three hundred twenty gigabytes," the young scientist said nervously.

"You mean megabytes."

The older scientist spoke from across the room. "Gigabytes."

Johnny tried not to betray his surprise and concern; he wasn't entirely successful.

"Are you sure you have enough storage capacity?" the older man asked.

"More than adequate," said Johnny. *Didn't even blink,* he thought. *Almost convinced myself.*

"It's extremely dangerous if you don't," the older scientist said. "If the upload volume exceeds your storage capacity, synaptic seepage will kill you in two or three days. Plus, the data will be corrupted; a coherent download will be impossible."

"You don't need to tell me my business," said Johnny coldly. "Are we uploading or not?"

The older man nodded. "As soon as you're ready. Your agent will contact you in Newark and arrange the meeting for the download."

"Perfect," said Johnny. "Let's boogie."

Or bust, he thought to himself.

He sat on the sofa in front of the coffee table. He wiped his palms on his knees. Inconspicuously, he hoped. He opened the briefcase on the coffee table in front of him. The two scientists and the four bodyguards stood watching, fascinated—until the sumo-bodyguard sent the fashion model and the TV addict to the door with a practiced flick of his tiny eyes.

Johnny opened the briefcase and took out a roll of Lifesavers.

A credit card.

A pair of sunglasses in a hard black case.

Johnny closed the briefcase. The two Vietnamese

scientists looked at each other, until the younger man spoke:

"You were supposed to bring the upload device!"

Johnny looked up with a shy smile as he took the glasses out of the case and set them aside. Then with practiced hands, he snapped the "case" into two unequal pieces, connected them with a gold rod that pulled in segments from the smaller piece, slid the "credit card" into a slot along the edge of the larger piece, then inserted the "roll of Lifesavers" into the end of the unit, locking it in place with a half twist to the left.

The older man looked on with a thin smile, his confidence in his courier growing steadily.

Johnny pulled a thin cable from the bottom of the assembled upload device and, pushing back his hair, inserted it into his wetwired temple jack. He set the upload device on the table and picked up the TV remote from the couch where the channel-surfing bodyguard had left it.

Pointing the remote first at the upload device and then at the TV, Johnny reprogrammed it by punching in a few numbers. He handed the remote to the younger of the two scientists.

"This remote is keyed in now," he explained. "Watch the counter on the upload device—here—and when the counter approaches zero, click on any three frames off the TV. They'll meld with your data and I won't know what they are. Those three images are your download code. Got it?"

The young man nodded.

"You'll get a hard copy—here. Fax a copy of that to your connection in Newark or wherever"—Johnny pointed with the remote to the hotel fax machine by the phone on the end table—"and when I get there, they feed in the three-image code and download, delivery done. Okay? *Capiche?* Got it? *Comprendo?* Understand?"

The young man nodded.

"Good. Now give me your shit."

The young man handed Johnny the CD-ROM, and Johnny slipped it into the top of the "Lifesaver" roll. It spun, then stopped.

320000 appeared on the counter.

Johnny pointed toward a button on the top of the upload device. "Press that to start the upload, okay?"

The young man nodded.

"It'll stop on its own. We hope." Johnny smiled. He put some drops in his eyes and put on the sunglasses, looking around the room one more time before dropping the mirror shades over his eyes.

Then he leaned back on the couch. "Hit me," he said, popping a tooth protector into his mouth.

The young man pressed the button; the tiny bright disk became a silvery blur.

At that precise moment, another silver blur, twenty-five floors straight down, was "inserting" six figures in identical gray suits into the hotel. A hush fell over the lobby as they came through the revolving door, one after the other; then the rattle and hum resumed as everyone pretended not to notice who, or rather *what*, had just entered.

Yakuza. Those it is never wise to notice.

The leader of the six, the young Japanese-American known since his college days (SF State, '07) as Shinji, gave two curt nods. Two of his men peeled off and stayed in the lobby; one by the revolving door and one by the elevator bank. While giving these orders Shinji never slowed; he headed straight across the lobby, his neat ponytail swinging from side to side, rhythmically.

It was almost as if he were enjoying himself.

An American walked by Shinji's side, matching him

step for step. A Japanese man and woman, as identical as twins, which, in fact, they were, walked two steps behind.

From behind a potted plant a black-haired five-year-old boy watched, spying. Though he was intrigued, he wasn't tempted to play with these four. Something about them said they weren't a lot of fun. Perhaps it was the identical gym bags that all but Shinji carried; bags that clinked and rattled every time they brushed against a knee or a thigh.

The four stopped as one at the elevator. Shinji pressed the button with his thumb; or rather, with the metal cap on the end of his thumb.

The Yakuzas' faces fell into wait-mode. All except for one.

"Shinji . . . ?" asked the American.

"What is it, Henson?"

"These guys upstairs: they *Viet-ching* or what?"

"No," Shinji said. "Scientists. R&D guys from Pharmakom."

"R&D?"

"Research & Development. Defectors . . ."

Ding. The wait was over.

"Defectors." The American's eyes brightened.

"Forget that," said Shinji. "Tokyo wants the data. Remember *that*."

The elevator doors opened. The four stepped in.

The doors closed.

Navigating cyberspace is one thing; mainlining it is another. As a "cowboy," inserting himself into a program, Johnny was in control. He could articulate his consciousness through the virtual reality of the electronic matrix as naturally as a fish swims in water.

But mainlining, receiving an upload—or "taking a dump," as the indelicate current expression had it—

was more like being a leaf on a raging stream, rudderless, powerless, directionless, lighter than nothing—a speck in a rushing flood of digital information.

It is the opposite of inserting yourself into a program; you are inserting raw data into yourself. And it comes all at once—in a howling, uncompiled, uncodified, unformatted, unpartitioned, incomprehensible rush of raw files and naked subroutines, protocols and archives, macros and heaps and sequences: a data storm, undifferentiated and unhierarchical; a digital cyclone that is scary as hell even to hardwired veteran cybernetic couriers like Johnny, but terrifying to novices or first-timers.

Johnny was terrified.

His fear in itself told him something was wrong, terribly wrong; that knowledge terrified him even more.

Pyramids and formulas flew by, howling; circles and proofs and sharp-featured squares, ungeometric, neogeometric and supergeometric; shapes that shifted and equations that screamed; icons and elements in every color of the rainbow—plus several that had never made reality-release; molecular models in three and four dimensions and more; beziers curves and TIFF towers, custom characters and CDEV codes in Arabic and Japanese, numeric and English, ascii and Greek . . .

Johnny tried to quell or at least control his terror but it grew as the tsunami of data grew, faster and faster, overpowering even his practiced relaxation techniques. Too many things were happening too fast, it was too much, the wave was too tall, too dark, too cold, too thick. . . . It was an unassimilable flood of data, murderous yet still increasing, towering over the tiny spark of his consciousness.

Johnny knew his only chance was to let go, to go under and ride it out, let it take him. He let go . . .

23

He went under . . . into what was boring into him, folding inside himself, inside the green and black and roaring . . .

He screamed. It didn't help.

Then his scream screamed.

. . . And screamed and screamed his scream and screamed his scream and . . .

"You think he's okay?" the young Vietnamese scientist asked. He was standing over Johnny, who was lying rigid on the sofa, his feet out before him, his heels beating a tattoo on the floor; his eyes clamped shut. His face a death mask.

His low groans filled the room.

"I guess." The older scientist shrugged. "He does this for a living; he must know what he's doing. How much is left to go?"

The upload device on the table was counting down. The counter display was racing, a blur from which the younger Vietnamese scientist could only occasionally pick out a number that was gone as soon as, or even before, it was recognized:

0011386
0011074
0009963
0008352

This is the opposite of communication, he thought as he watched the numbers race by. *Information as quantity. All humanity's hopes jammed into . . .*

"Shouldn't you be getting ready to click on the images for the download code?" the older man asked.

Snapping out of his reverie, the younger man looked up at the TV across the room, then back down at the upload device on the coffee table.

0002651
0001301

"Quick!" said the older man.

The younger man pointed the remote at the TV screen. The Japanese cartoon figure was drop-kicking a bad guy from this world into the next.

Click.

As the image was booked the channel changed automatically from the cartoon to a middle-aged Chinese man holding up a bottle of pills. The young scientist absently noticed that the man was nude; male nudity in commercials was still a novelty in China. Speaking in Mandarin, he began to explain to viewers the advantages of New Super-Rogaine Hair-Care Shampoo, when suddenly, amazingly, his body began to morph into a woman's face. The camera drew in on her features; a European or American face with brown eyes, soft but commanding, *yin* and *yang* earrings; a woman in her fifties . . .

Click.

The face disappeared and the image was booked, even though the younger scientist hadn't meant to hit the remote.

"Did you see *that?*" he asked.

"See what?" The older scientist was watching the counter roll down toward nothingness.

000034
000024

"It was *her!*"

"Hurry, we need one more. Get your third image."

The younger man aimed the remote at the TV without even looking to see what was on the screen.

Click.

"That's three." The younger man looked at the courier on the sofa, who was still vibrating all over, like a reed in the wind.

He looked at the tiny display on the upload device. Instead of numbers, it read

25

On the sofa, the courier stopped shaking. The Korean bodyguards looked relieved. The display read

320 GB
DOWNLOAD
COMPLETE

"Got it?" asked the older Vietnamese.

"I think so," answered the younger. He put down the remote and was surprised to see that his hand was shaking; he hid it in his pocket. He saw his wife, white-faced, in the doorway to the bedroom, and he smiled at her. It was going to be all right.

On the coffee table, the upload device whirred and extruded a twelve-inch-long strip of thermal paper. The younger scientist tore it off. He looked at it, shook his head, and placed it, face down, on the table.

"The access code. Three images."

The numbers on the elevator, meanwhile, were getting larger.

. . . 4 . . . 5 . . . 6 . . .

There was a clinking sound as three gym bags were set down on the floor of the elevator.

. . . 9 . . . 10 . . . 11 . . .

There was the soft sound of zippers as three bags were unzipped.

. . . 15 . . . 16 . . . 17 . . .

There was the soft *click-click* of plastic as three high-powered air guns were assembled: futuristic, clear lucite guns that looked almost like kids' toys; that is, if killer kids carried toys.

. . . 22 . . . 23 . . . 24 . . .

There was the soft whisper of cloth as bulletproof vests under gray business suits were checked.

No one spoke. Only Shinji, seemingly unarmed, stood and watched the numbers fly by.

. . . 25 . . . *Ding.*

"Mr. Smith."

Johnny was in still, dark water. He couldn't breathe. Had he drowned? Gone under? Too bad.

Too goddam bad.

"Mr. Smith."

Johnny opened his eyes. Darkness. This, then, was Death.

Goddam Death, then.

"Are you all right?"

But why all the racket? Johnny lifted his sunglasses. There was the younger of the two Vietnamese scientists, bending over him, looking concerned.

The upload. It had worked.

"Did you get your code clicked in?" Johnny asked.

The young scientist nodded, pointing toward the paper face-down on the coffee table next to the upload device.

"Good. Fax it to the other end. I don't want to see it."

Johnny pulled the jack out of his head and smoothed his hair back down into place. He looked around the room. The four Korean bodyguards were looking at him as if he had just awakened from the dead.

Hell, maybe he had.

He looked at his watch. The upload had taken only six minutes.

Six minutes for enough data to choke a brontosaurus, Johnny thought. His head felt as if it would burst. It was worse than a headache: A headache was a feeling. This was physical in a far more alarming way.

He wiped his nose and was surprised to see a thin smear of blood on the back of his hand.

He hid his hand. "Where's your bathroom?"

"Bathroom?" asked the younger scientist.

"Toilet," said Johnny, standing. "Loo, head, john. I always have to use the bathroom after I goddam kill myself, okay?"

"Okay," said the scientist. "Over there. Through that door."

Ding.

The elevator door opened on 25, and four figures filed out into the thickly carpeted hallway.

Three of them didn't bother to hide the plastic weapons they carried, as bright as new Christmas toys.

The fourth, Shinji, was unarmed, or so it seemed. He stopped and studied the sign on the wall.

←2526–2550
2551–2575→

Shinji turned to the right and started down the hall. The three others followed.

The American, Henson, peeled a piece of gum from behind his ear and put it into his mouth.

He was the only one who was grinning.

Breathe In.
Breathe Out.
Palms together.
Breathe In.
Breathe Out.
Better, thought Johnny, watching himself in the bathroom mirror. He separated his hands; they were still shaking, but less visibly. His meditative exercises were bringing his heartbeat back down toward normal.

Control, thought Johnny, as he looked at his reflection. Except for the thin trickle of blood from his left nostril, he looked normal.

Almost. For now.

28

"Jesus!" he said to himself. "What the hell have I done. Too much data . . . 320 gigs. *Way* too much."

He splashed water on his face.

"How long did the old man say, a day or two? 'Synaptic seepage,' oh shit . . ."

But there was no backing out now. The deal had been struck. The data was uploaded. The money was too big to pass up. Johnny was used to running on the edge. This was just a thinner and a higher edge than usual. Maybe if he moved fast enough and downloaded it soon enough, everything would be all right. . . .

He reached into his pocket and patted the plane ticket, for luck. Suborbital. Newark only four hours away.

He heard a gurgling. He turned away from the mirror and noticed for the first time that there were two doors into the bathroom, one from each of the suite's two rooms. The other door was open a crack and he could see a woman on a bed, breast-feeding a baby. She was sitting half-turned away so Johnny could see the soft curve of her full breast. A sweet scene; it brought him back to earth.

With two fingers, Johnny waved, at nobody, since the woman hadn't seen him and the infant was too preoccupied with the breast. With one foot, he shut the bathroom door.

He adjusted his tie and brushed his hair and tried to find his smile. Time to go back out and face his employers again.

The three Yakuza stood back with their weapons drawn and charged, as their leader placed himself in front of the door marked 2571. Shinji unscrewed the cap off his prosthetic thumb and held it between his teeth.

A thin loop of silver filament extruded from the open end of the thumb. The filament was far thinner than a spider's web; it didn't catch the light as much as tweak it, altering its path only slightly. It floated like smoke, like a sound, weighing only slightly more than nothing.

It shone in the air like an angel's halo, an almost-lasso less than a molecule in thickness.

Shinji extended and spun the filament like a whip, then drew it back. He held his thumb out toward the door as if he were measuring it or giving it the high sign.

The Yakuza on either side of Shinji were all grins. Although they had seen this many times, it was always fun to watch.

What's taking him so long? the younger Vietnamese scientist wondered, glancing toward the bathroom where Johnny had disappeared a few minutes before. *Quit worrying,* he told himself. *"So farce, oh good,"* as the Americans liked to say. The first stage was done, successful.

Now to destroy the evidence.

He popped the nickel-sized CD-ROM out of the upload device. He picked it up with a pair of enamelled chopsticks and held it over the charcoal fire. The sticks would burn, but they would last long enough to do their job.

While he held the CD-ROM over the hot coals, he looked around the room. The excitement of the upload was over, and the room was back to normal. The channel-surfing bodyguard had reclaimed the remote and was back into his cartoon, his antique ballistic Tek-9 on the sofa beside him. The sumo-guy was noisily finishing off his shrimp, his sawed-off matte-black ten-gauge lying across his lap. The fashion model was still slowly turning her *Glamour* pages, as if she hoped that by turning them deliberately enough she would, somehow, learn to read. Her

Victoria's Secret robe was open, revealing her miniaturized, pearl-handled .357 magnum in its black lace shoulder-holster/bustier combo. The tattooed lady was still cleaning her Glock. The floor near her chair was littered with Q-tips, gray with gun oil.

The older Vietnamese scientist was across the room, turning on the fax machine. In his hand he held the twelve-inch sheet of thermal paper with the three codes.

The chopsticks were starting to singe.

Shinji flipped his thumb and the filament flashed down, toward the doorknob.

Soundlessly, the knob and lock fell forward, bringing with them an oval piece of wood, scooped from the solid oak of the door like ice cream.

The lock assembly hit the carpet with a soft thud.

Henson kept one hand free, ready to push, but it wasn't needed.

The door to 2571 swung slowly inward on its own.

The older Vietnamese punched in the fax number of the contact in Newark, waited, got the READY TO SEND signal on the fax machine's tiny display.

He punched SEND.

The thermal paper with the three images of the download code was off-sized, so he aligned it in the feed slot until the machine started its slow pull. *An old-fashioned line-by-line fax,* he thought, as the machine started the stuttering pull. *Almost as old as I.* Born in the precise center of the last century, he had fought as a teenager with the patriots who had rid his country of the Americans. *Then sold it back to them, piece by piece,* he thought with a sigh.

Still, he had no regrets. He had learned patience in the war, and vigilance as well. Had learned to listen for every falling leaf, every breath; learned to sense danger a few seconds before it struck. At seventy, he still had that capacity.

That was why he was the first person to look around when the door swung silently inward.

Johnny was about to step out of the bathroom when he heard a small sound—behind him? No, below him.

It was on his belt. The red light.

The motion detector.

He looked around the corner of the door and what he saw made him retreat quickly into the bathroom and close the door behind him, pulling it shut gently so as not to make a sound.

He needn't have bothered worrying about the noise.

As the bathroom door was softly clicking shut, the sawed-off matte-black ten-gauge went off, both barrels in quick succession, followed by the blast of the pearl-handled miniaturized .357.

The .357 blew a small hole in the ceiling and a larger one in the rug of the Lotus Blossom Honeymoon Suite upstairs, terrifying but leaving unharmed the newly-weds who had won a trip to the capital in the Ulan Bator lottery. It would be their last visit.

It wasn't that the aim of its owner, the fashion model, was poor. It was just that by the time she got her shot off she was already falling backward, one side of her face—the better side, her boyfriends had always told her—already gone, transformed by the double load of double-aught into a bright spray of blood and bone on the wall behind her lyre-backed chair.

It wasn't that the sumo-guy had meant to shoot her. It was just that the rain of plastic pellets that set him spinning backward had caused him to fire wildly just before they plastered him against the picture window. The matte-black ten-gauge fell to the carpet just as the sumo-guy crashed through the glass and into the chill night air, and fell, still spinning, like a small planet nudged out of its orbit, to the faux cobblestones of the newly antiqued outdoor shopping mall twenty-five floors below.

The channel-surfer had better luck, or so it seemed at first. At the first shot, he dropped the remote and picked up his Tek-9 with one swift motion. By the time his compatriot was crashing through the glass, he was squeezing off three bursts in quick succession, one for each of the three Yakuza who stood along the front wall, firing their plastic air pistols. And his aim was perfect—for the center of the body, the heart and lungs.

Unfortunately, for him, the techtite vests of the Yakuza effortlessly deflected the rain of 7.62 Xpndrs, and the channel-surfer's three bursts did little more than concentrate the attentions of his adversaries, so that they were able to focus their fire on the couch, enveloping him in a small cloud of blood and Dacrofluff couch stuffing.

It was over in 6.8 seconds. The tattooed lady never even got her Glock put together. She lay on her back in a scattering of Q-tips, seemingly unwounded, except for the bubble of blood rising from her lips, which looked, in death, as if they had been rouged for the only time in her life.

Fifty-eight years earlier, as a young guerrilla, the older Vietnamese scientist had learned the secret of standing perfectly still in a firefight, thus rendering himself almost invisible.

The younger scientist crouched over the hibachi, watching the CD-ROM soften and sag and drop into the fire, to be finally consumed. Relieved, he closed his eyes, awaiting the shot that would do as much for him.

Henson, the American Yakuza, stepped forward and raised his air gun toward the back of the younger scientist's head.

Firefights were fun. But execution-style was awesome.

Shinji stopped the American with a shake of his head. The defecting scientist had destroyed the CD-ROM. That meant he had done something else with the data.

Perhaps a courier.

Shinji pointed with his chin toward the closed bathroom door; Henson crossed the room and reached for the knob.

Air pistols make little noise—only a whisper—followed by the soft *dik dik dik dik* of multi-barbed plastic darts stitching their way through flesh. From inside the bathroom, Johnny thought the fighting had all been one-sided. Judging from the *boom*s, he thought the Korean bodyguards might be on the winning side.

He watched the doorknob turn, thinking it would be a friend, or at least a temporary ally. But just in case, he switched out the light.

The door opened a crack. A hand reached through, and stubby, scarred fingers searched for the light switch. Something gleamed in the sliver of light from the other room. An Upper Montclair High School ring.

Johnny had caught a brief glimpse of the Yakuza entering the suite. One of them had been American.

Johnny let the fingers find the switch before slamming the door. Hard.

He heard the muddled *crunch* of cartilage and tendon, and the sharper, more satisfying *snap* of bone.

He flung the door open and pulled the American in, flinging him in one easy motion through the sliding door into the shower stall. The Beijing Ramada was an old-fashioned hotel; the door was glass.

Johnny left the light off. He picked up one of the shards of broken glass from the floor, and used it as a mirror to look around the corner of the door into the suite.

It was a less than pleasant scene.

The fashion model was sprawled on the floor behind her lyre-backed chair, her Victoria's Secret robe flung open, immodestly revealing her lingerie for one last time.

The half of her face that was still there was still.

The channel-surfer lay back on the sofa, the red of his blood slowly turning gray as the furniture stuffing, blown into the air, settled onto his corpse.

The sumo-guy had disappeared altogether; the glass was gone from the window and a cool, high-altitude breeze wafted through the drapes. The ten-gauge lay on the floor, pointing toward the fashion model. Sirens wailed far below.

One of the Yakuza was turning the tattooed lady over with his foot. The back of her robe had been shredded by darts and the green and black deer-in-the-willows scene on her back had been overwritten in red, a crude and final stencil.

Two of the Yakuza stood over the younger Vietnamese scientist, who was huddled over the brazier, his eyes closed. The other Yakuza, the one without a gun, the one with no tip on his thumb, was in the doorway, looking toward the small table that held the phone and fax machine.

Johnny followed his eyes.

The older Vietnamese scientist stood silently over the fax machine, motionless as a deer, watching the strip of thermal paper with the access codes being pulled in slowly, line by line.

Codes the Yakuza mustn't get.

Johnny dropped the glass and lunged out of the bathroom at the same time as the Yakuza in the doorway stepped forward, right thumb held high.

Johnny grabbed the paper just as Shinji whipped his thumb in a tight circle. The filament cut through the air without a sound, cut through the fax machine and the table that held it; cut through the paper just as Johnny pulled it loose.

The paper was sliced clean—all Johnny had was one image.

The old scientist held the other two; and with a sudden swift motion, he dove for the hibachi.

Shinji's thumb jerked upward: the filament flashed and flew—and the old man's hand, the one holding the paper, fell, severed, onto the glowing bed of coals.

The paper was just starting to burn and the old man was just starting to smile as the Yakuza's third swing of the filament sliced him in half, on an angle, from his right collar to his left hip.

He slipped to the floor in two pieces, still smiling.

Johnny dove for the door as a rain of darts *dik-dik-dik*'ed into the wall behind him. He rolled through, into the hallway.

Shinji grabbed the burning paper and pulled it off the brazier. With it came the severed hand, and he tossed it aside as he beat out the flames.

Too late—only half the paper was left. One of the three images.

The courier had escaped with one, and the other was lost in the fire.

No matter. There were ways to retrieve data even without the codes. The first step was to find the courier.

"Follow him!" Shinji said, nodding toward the hallway. The two Yakuza sprinted out of the room, into the hallway.

Shinji knelt before the younger Vietnamese scientist, who gradually opened his eyes, surprised and a little dismayed to discover that he wasn't dead.

"Where's he going?" Shinji asked, almost gently.

"Wh-who?"

"You know who. The courier. Where's he taking the data?"

The young man summoned up all his courage and shook his head. "I can't tell you that."

From the next room a baby's cry was heard. The young Vietnamese looked horrified.

For the first time that evening, Shinji actually smiled.

"Oh, yes, I think you can," he said.

Down.

Down.

Racing down the stairs, leaping over the railing, jumping from the center of one short flight of concrete steps to the landing of the next, descending each floor with three long gravity-augmented strides, Johnny half-ran, half-fell down the dusty, echoing back stairwell of the giant luxury hotel.

Down.

Down.

Down.

As he ran Johnny popped a capsule into his mouth, biting down on the gelatin so that it would take effect more quickly.

As he ran he tore off his tie, clipping on a soup-stained black bow tie with his right hand, as his left vaulted him over the railing to the landing below.

As he ran he massaged his scalp, with his fingers spread like a comb, releasing gray streaks of color that he dispersed backward.

As he ran he pulled a small square package from his pocket and shook it open, into a raincoat; from the pocket of the raincoat he pulled a hat.

37

As he ran the pill swiftly took effect: Each time he leaped over a railing, Johnny could see the skin on his left hand getting deeper in color, liver spots appearing, changing tone and texture . . .

Ding.

The elevator door opened and the two Yakuza burst out, their hands in their coats. Man and woman.

Killer twins.

They surveyed the lobby swiftly, spoke curtly to the Yakuza who had been left to guard the elevator, and crossed toward the revolving door.

Across the room a five-year-old boy looked up from his game, making faces at the fish in the tank. He was bored. He usually liked new people.

But not these new people.

He went back to his fish.

The killer twins walked across the lobby in lockstep, scanning the crowd like one animal with two heads and four eyes; looking behind every potted plant, behind every newspaper. The lobby fell silent, pretending not to notice them.

Yakuza. Those it is never wise to notice.

They spoke a curt word to the Yakuza waiting by the revolving door and watched hotel patrons file in and out. There was only one other entrance to the lobby, a stairwell, and the Yakuza by the elevator had his eye on it.

Now all they had to do was wait.

The Yakuza were the most powerful crime organization in the world. Everyone in the lobby knew who they were. Everyone knew they were looking for someone and everyone hoped it was someone else.

Everyone in the lobby avoided eye contact with them, even those who filed past them into the revolving door that led to the street.

Even the little old lady with the Scottish terrier.

Even the mother with the crying baby.

38

Even the little girl with her Mao doll.

Even the stooped, gray-haired old Chinese salesman, chopsticks sticking out of the pocket of his raincoat, whose liver-spotted hands pulled his hat down over his thinning hair as he shuffled out into the siren-haunted Beijing night. . . .

THREE

—■—

WELCOME TO THE FREE CITY OF NEWARK said the sign over the customs entrance. A smaller sign underneath said the same thing in twelve languages, four of them misspelled, one of them dead.

To the observer this might, indeed, seem the city of the dead. The arrivals were all skeletons as they passed through the scanner, grinning skulls carried aloft on clacking bones, femurs and tibias and scapulas still able, somehow, to haul their own luggage into this howling land of suffering and darkness . . .

But wait.

One of the skulls looked wrong.

"Excuse me, sir."

Johnny's heart skipped a beat as he was stopped by the customs officer manning the scanner.

He composed his face into a mask, slowed his breathing as he slowed his steps, gathering himself into a simulacrum of nonchalance, as always when a crisis loomed. He stepped out of line. He was a businessman again, a blue-suited corporate, one of seven hundred debarking from the just-landed Beijing-Newark suborbital.

"Is there a problem?"

The officer showed Johnny his image, caught as a still on the small screen at the scanner station. It was a skeleton carrying a ghost briefcase and an overnight bag. The case and the bag read empty, but inside the skull a dark object rested, eerily resembling a robotic fetus curled up in a cranial womb.

"This implant . . . ?"

"It's all right," Johnny said. "Government approved. Dyslexia prosthesis."

"You have a permit, of course."

"Of course."

Johnny handed the officer a plastic card. The officer swiped the card through his machine and concentrated on the display.

Johnny tried to ignore the vicious, pounding headache that had been getting steadily worse the entire four hours of the flight.

"Sir—?"

Johnny jerked awake, trying to look bored and helpful at the same time.

"Here's your card back. It checks out okay. But there is a problem . . ."

"Problem?"

"The scanner shows a seepage—looks like your implant may be disgorging. Better get it checked."

"Oh. Sure."

"As soon as possible. Those things can be dangerous. I have a *compañero* whose . . ."

"Thanks, *gracias,*" Johnny said over his shoulder as he hurried off down the corridor.

It was a kid's room. A little girl's room. A pink and white powder-puff of a room, hung with frilly curtains and festooned with toy and trinket shelves, crammed with stuffed animals, video games and interactive dolls—all the colorful gadgetry associated with the well-cared-for twenty-first-century child.

Everything in the room said joy, love, laughter. Hope. Everything but the black-draped Shinto shrine in the center of the floor.

And the man on the bed.

He sat awkwardly, knees together and expensively manicured hands on knees. He was too big, too powerful; he looked out of place in the low, fluffy, pink bed in his expensive Italian suit. But he was not thinking of himself or how he looked. He was thinking of his daughter, Mikiyo.

Indeed, he was watching her. Mikiyo sat on the floor under a sun-flooded window in the corner, an eight-year-old girl with raven black, straight hair, wearing silk pajamas, a girl as delicate and beautiful as a ceremonial Japanese doll. As he watched she shimmered like a creature made of light, and her voice rang as clear and untroubled as memory as she scolded her stuffed toy:

"Now, Mopmop, if you and Shirley can't play nicely, I'll have to separate you!"

It was a happy scene. Which made it all the more odd that a tear rolled slowly down the hard face of the man on the bed.

There was a knock at the door. It was a low, timid, deferential knock, and the man picked up the remote that lay on the bed beside him.

He pointed the remote at the child in the corner and suddenly she was gone, along with her stuffed toys and the window that had shed its golden light upon her.

The man set the remote back down on the bed. It at least was real. So was the tear he wiped from his cheek as he turned to face the door.

"Come in."

A woman stuck her head in the door. Her gray hair was pinned up in a conservative, no-nonsense American bun. "Sorry to disturb you, Mr. Takahashi, but . . ."

"I know, Mrs. Sutton." Mr. Takahashi rose, smoothing the bed coverlet where he had sat.

"I know," he repeated, his face darkening as if he had just tasted something unpleasant. "Shinji has arrived."

Takahashi's office was huge and almost bare, as befit the head of North American operations for the world's largest, most reputable, most feared and most profitable criminal organization. One wall of the office opened to a small formal garden with raked sand and artfully placed stones, suggesting the unhurried serenity required for world-class decision-making.

It was from the garden, opening on the other side to his private home, that Takahashi entered his office. His features had already lost their temporary softness and they hardened even further when he saw the man standing beside his desk, arrogantly leaning against it.

Shinji executed a slight, deliberately insolent bow as Takahashi walked past him to stand behind his desk.

Takahashi didn't offer his visitor a seat.

"You look well enough," Takahashi said. "Asia seems to agree with you."

He rested his gaze pointedly on the younger man's capped prosthetic thumb.

"And I see you have found a way to turn your shame into an asset."

Shinji replied coldly, as if matching loss for loss: "My condolences, Takahashi-san, on your recent sad loss."

Takahashi didn't answer. Instead he shuffled some

43

papers on his desk. When he looked up, he spoke in Japanese:

"I've seen the report from Tokyo. Pharmakombinat Industrie of Zurich have engaged us to recover their missing data."

Shinji nodded and answered in Japanese:

"Our operation in Beijing met with limited success. The Pharmakom traitors are dead . . ."

"But the mnemonic courier escaped," Takahashi said. His tone was one of reproach. "With the data. He is coming here, to Newark?"

Shinji smiled distantly as if recalling a pleasant memory. "We have been given reason to believe so."

"Why was I not informed of this fact at once?"

"It took a certain amount of time and, let's say, effort to obtain that information, Takahashi-san. And I did not wish to disturb you in your grief. Children are so special. It must be terrible to lose a child, an only child, especially one so young, and so I assumed you were unavailable . . ."

Shinji spoke softly and deliberately, in formal Japanese, as if lashing the older man with the blame that great sorrow and loss can carry with them.

"We are Yakuza," Takahashi replied tersely. His face was cold, his eyes were stones in ice. "I am always available. What is the nature of the data we are to recover?"

"I am not at liberty to say."

"Because you do not know."

Shinji looked away, and Takahashi smiled. A direct hit.

"I have been charged with recovering the head of the mnemonic courier," Shinji said. "Cryogenically preserved."

"Preserved?"

Shinji nodded. "For the data. The defectors wiped the Pharmakom mainframe, then also destroyed the pirated CD-ROM. If we lose the courier, Pharmakom has lost the data forever."

Takahashi turned away, looking toward his garden as if using its images of peace and serenity to order his thoughts. The situation was worse than he had thought. When he turned back to face the younger Yakuza, he spoke in English once again.

"Newark is mine, Shinji. You were insolent when you trained here under me, and you are insolent still. You will report only to me, understand? If the mnemonic courier is in my territory—if you have not managed to lose him altogether—*I* will be responsible for the recovery of the data. I understand you managed to salvage at least part of the courier's download code?"

"Only one of three images."

"Better than nothing." Takahashi held out his hand. "Give it to me."

Shinji stared at the older man, as if calculating the disparities of age, status, power and cunning between them. He shrugged, coming up short, and pulled a singed, folded sheet of thermal paper from the inside pocket of his gray suit.

Takahashi's hand waited. Motionless.

Shinji handed the paper to Takahashi, executed the slightest of bows as if to confirm that his insolence, if not his dignity, was intact, then turned to leave.

"My secretary, Mrs. Sutton, will see you out," Takahashi said to his visitor's departing back.

Takahashi waited until he was alone before unfolding the paper and spreading it out on his desk. It was charred on one side, sliced clean on the other. The image was from the *Beijing Evening News*, of NAS rioters and police battling in the streets.

He pressed a button on the vidphone on his desk,

and his secretary's face appeared on the monitor. "Yes, sir, Mr. Takahashi?" she said.

"Get me Karl Honig."

"Honig . . . ?"

"The man they call Street Preacher. Church of the Retransfiguration."

"Yes, sir." The screen went blank. After a pause, the image of a lamb, resting on a hillside, came up. Soft voices sang:

"'Onward Christian Soldiers, marching as to war . . .'"

The lamb stood up, bleated once, and began trotting toward a shepherd with a crooked staff.

Takahashi drummed his fingers on his desk impatiently.

The shepherd, a long-haired generic Jesus in a striped biblical robe, picked up the lamb as the singing swelled and faded. Then the generic Jesus morphed into a smiling man—steel teeth in a cheap suit with too many pockets—holding a child.

The child was smiling moronically, as if it had been drugged.

The man spoke:

"You have reached the Church of the Retransfiguration. I am Pastor Karl Honig. If you wish to make a tax-deductible contribution to our worldwide ministry, please press one.

"If you wish to speak directly to me or to a member of my staff, please press . . ."

But before the message could finish the pastor was suddenly gone, replaced by an image of a young African-American man. It was the same face that had hijacked the TV monitor array in the Beijing Ramada hotel lobby. The image was accompanied by the *thump! hiss! thump!* of the music known as techno-neo-rap:

"Hey, make your own images and get your life back! The human race is waitin' and the . . ."

Takahashi stabbed at the buttons on the vidphone, but J-Bone's face persisted, along with the music. Finally he yanked the cord loose. The screen finally went blank.

The outer door to the office opened, and Mrs. Sutton's worried face appeared. "I'm sorry, sir. I really don't know how that happened."

Takahashi's voice was filled with suppressed anger. "Our lines are triple-shielded, we have our own satellites, but *still* my private line is invaded by these idiotic, insufferable Lotek anarchists!"

"I'm sorry, sir, I—"

"Never mind. Send the tech team in here immediately. Hook this back up. Get Honig on another line as soon as possible. I'll be—in my daughter's room."

"Yes, sir."

Takahashi nodded, and the door closed. Twilight was falling as he walked, head bowed, across his interior garden. He stayed on the path, carefully avoiding the perfectly raked sand.

Some landscapes *look* bombed-out; some *are*. Newark had the distinction of being both. The city had already been in ruins when the inner city fighting heated up just after the turn of the century, and bombs went off in buildings that were already deserted ruins, lending a ruins-on-ruins look to the landscape that had intensified in the succeeding decades as refugees from the fighting in New York and Philadelphia had moved in and taken over the shells of the buildings, patching together water, gas, even bootleg electricity fed in from Queens and Connecticut through cables strung in the old Path train tunnels.

That electricity accounted for the lights Johnny saw, high in the ruined fangs of broken towers, or shimmering under what seemed to be piles of shattered brick.

Newark was a hellhole, or rather, a string of hell-holes, linked by shattered pavement and punctuated by the charred skeletons of former office buildings. As the taxi penetrated deeper and deeper into what had once been the industrial belt around the center city, the cabbie drove slower and slower. Ditches, shell craters and improvised sunken graves potholed the road; even the steel-banded tires of the taxi were no match for the razor-sharp six-inch-high "jacks" that had been salted on the roads over the years by roving bands of auto-strippers.

Now that the traffic was gone, the strippers were gone, too; but their booby traps still remained.

"That's why I gotta go slow," the cabbie explained, either to himself or to Johnny, who had been trying to get the ancient backseat cellular vidphone to accept a dollar token.

"Huh?" Johnny sat up and looked over the seat.

"Potholes," the driver said.

He hit a particularly vicious bump and Johnny's dollar went in. There was a *ding* and a dial tone.

"Oh, yeah, right," Johnny said. "Whatever."

Meanwhile, he thought, punching in the numbers, *I gotta get through to Ralfi. Fast.*

His head felt as if it were about to split, to burst open like an overinflated tire. The howling of the taxi's long-dried-out shocks and the screams of the tortured springs reverberated agonizingly between his ears.

Fast!

"Hello?"

"Ralfi, it's me."

Ralfi came up on the dusty, stained screen set into the back of the front seat. He was a small, dapper man whose surgically augmented movie-star visage usually bore an expression wavering somewhere between worry and disgust.

48

Disgust was now primary. Johnny half-expected Ralfi to pull the handkerchief from his pocket and wipe off the inside of the filthy screen.

"That you, Johnny-boy? I'm not getting good video."

"It's me," Johnny said. "Fucked-up phone."

"Alone, you say? Where are you, kid?"

"Somewhere in Newark. Heading for the delivery." Johnny peered out the window at the shattered darkness punctuated by distant fires and uncertain lights. *Newark, all right.*

"You feeling any better?" Johnny could hear the beat of retrodisco behind Ralfi's voice, which meant the agent was calling from his "office" in a booth at the Drome.

"Worse. Much worse. Ralfi, I'm way overloaded, man. You wouldn't believe how much."

"Johnny, you told me you got upgraded, or I wouldn't have—"

"Yeah, yeah. Whatever. I got the goods, Ralfi. I just want 'em out of my head! Fast. Did they get the download codes okay?"

"Don't worry, Johnny-boy, they say they can extract easy, with or without the codes. Delivery is confirmed, and that means you get rid of the data."

"Who is this 'they,' Ralfi? What's going on, man? This is starting to feel like a blown deal to me. I don't even know who I'm dealing with, and I'm going to be completely exposed when—"

"Johnny-boy, Johnny-boy. Has Ralfi ever let you down? I would have come with you except I'm all tied up here at the office." Johnny heard giggles and a faraway scream of hilarity or ecstasy. "All you have to do is get to the address I gave you. They'll take care of it from there."

"Okay," Johnny said. He cradled his head in his hands; he was afraid if he let go of it, it would burst.

"Just make the delivery, okay?" Ralfi said. "Then come by the Drome and we'll have a drink. Celebrate, Johnny-boy."

"Celebrate. Sure. Later."

Johnny hung up. He took the thermal paper from his pocket and stared at the single image as the taxi threaded its way through the potholes and between the ruined buildings, deeper and deeper into the heart of darkness that was twenty-first-century Newark.

"Bye, Johnny-boy," Ralfi said. He hung up the phone on the hook at the center of the table and looked around the Naugahyde booth that served him as an office.

"Too bad about Johnny," he said to the two bodyguards who sat with him in the booth. "Good kid."

The two shrugged in perfect unison. "Never liked him," said one. "Me neither," shrugged the other.

Yomamma and Pretty didn't like anybody except each other, and they didn't like each other all that much. They had been man and woman once, though nobody except themselves could remember which had been the man and which the woman. Now they were both women—Ralfi's amazon gladiator muscle. Yomamma was black and Pretty was white, but they both had augmented jade-green eyes and, except for the tone of their skin, they could have been built out of the same kit: steroid-spectacular biceps, V-2 rocket breasts, hips like sugar-cured hams and thighs twisted with muscle like bridge cables. There hadn't been enough meat left over for brains.

Pretty and Yomamma sat on either side of the little "talent agent," flanking him in the booth. A man as well-known and as little-liked as Ralfi wouldn't last long in the Drome without protective muscle.

50

The strobed dance floor was filled, but it was hard to tell which of the patrons were swaying to the band, which were zoned out on recc drugs, and which were in the earlier—or later—stages of NAS. It might have been a scene from Hell, if Hell were a place people lined up to get into; if Hell were filled to capacity every night with nubile young women who wore their pubescent sexuality like plumage, men whose suits came from better neighborhoods than their brains, and every nuance of gender, age, race, class and station in between. The only thing the denizens of the Drome had in common was their underworld status: The club was a market and meeting place for a world outside the law, where those who lived on the margins of the night came to seek diversion, jobs, revenge, sex, drugs, contracts, money or just amusement.

At the bar, a young woman watched as Ralfi hung up on Johnny. She had been watching Ralfi all evening, even while the man standing next to her whispered earnestly down the front of her half-open leather jacket, as if there were a mike hidden between her small breasts. He towered over her, his broad shoulders slumped with fatigue, a computer nerd on steroids with a leaven of concern in warm brown eyes that flashed behind his thick, horn-rimmed glasses.

"About these *episodes* you've been having, Jane—I want to get you back to the shop for some tests. Hey! Are you even *listening* to me?"

"No more tests, Spider. You and me aren't playing 'doctor' anymore, remember?"

He straightened up and looked hurt. "Hey, that's not what I—"

But Jane was paying no attention. Her alert violet, darting eyes were on Ralfi and his amazon bodyguards in the half-circle booth at the far side of the dance floor.

"Look at those two!" she said disgustedly. "The lap dancers from Hell. They're old, Spider. Thanks to you, I'm twice as fast as they are."

"It's not your *speed* I'm worried about, Jane. I'm worried about your *nervous* system. Hey, where you going?"

But she was already on her feet, walking away—a small, quick figure in skintight black jeans and black leather with short, spiked hair.

"Another beer?" asked Hooky, the bartender, deftly spinning a longneck onto the bar with his stainless-steel prosthetic.

"Nah!" said Spider, watching her dejectedly. "I've had enough."

"On the house, Spider," said Hooky.

As Jane walked toward Ralfi's booth, hands reached out to sample her as they would any attractive figure, male or female, who essayed the meat market that was the Drome's dance floor.

Then the hands pulled back. Without touching. Jane seemed slightly dangerous. She walked like a fighter, with a menace and a strut that belied her size. She seemed all speed, even when she moved slowly. Her hands were at her side, fingers extended as if she were drying her nails. Her bright violet eyes were on her target, who was already on the phone with another client.

Jane waited until Ralfi hung up again before taking the last steps to the booth.

"No way!" said Pretty, standing to ward off the half-pint intruder.

But Jane caught the larger woman's shoulder, and using speed instead of strength, spun Pretty off-balance back down into the booth, where she hit the cushion with a *whoof.*

Before either Pretty or Yomamma could regroup and respond, Jane was leaning over the table. Her face

52

was inches from Ralfi's, whose perfectly sculpted jaw had dropped open in surprise.

"Your hired muscle's aging on you, Ralfi. I coulda *done* you." Jane straightened up, her point made. "Time you hired somebody young. Somebody fast."

"You crazy little . . . !" Yomamma hissed. "Street trash bitch . . ." Pretty finished. They started to their feet as one, but Ralfi held them back with a back-handed gesture.

Ralfi was intrigued. "Somebody like you?"

"Yeah."

Pretty started up again. "You going to be shittin' out of a plastic bag when I . . ."

Ralfi restrained Pretty with another gesture, then turned his surgically amplified smile on his guest. "Have we met?"

"I know you," said Jane. "You're the agent for all the best combat artists in town. Well, I'm the fastest thing going, now that Spider's jacked my system."

"Spider?"

Jane pointed with her chin back toward the bar where Spider was watching. He shrugged his massive shoulders and lifted his bottle in greeting.

After responding with the coolest and faintest of nods, Ralfi turned back to Jane.

"You're fast, huh? Let's see. Hold out your hand."

Jane held out her hand, palm up, then palm down, showing off the thin scarification lines, almost like tattoos, where Spider had gone in, regrouping and augmenting her tendons and nerves.

"Well?"

"Fine," said Ralfi. He took a sip of his drink. "Just hold it steady right there."

Jane looked at him, a flash of alarm in her face.

"You *can* hold it steady, can't you?"

"Sure."

"Fast is one thing," Ralfi said, smiling first at Yomamma and then at Pretty. "Steady is another."

They were all starting to grin.

Jane's hand was starting to tremble. She stopped the tremor by striking out and grabbing Ralfi's wrist.

"See?" she said, as if that was what she had intended all along.

Ralfi didn't answer. Instead, he stared at Jane coldly until she released his hand. Then he shook his head. Slowly.

Yomamma and Pretty laughed in perfect unison.

"You're damaged goods, baby," said Yomamma. "Your friend Spider's jacked you up, all right," said Pretty. "So tight she shakes," said Yomamma. "Another month or two, you'll be like *her*," said Pretty.

Both women pointed to the bar, where a trembling victim of NAS was trying to raise her drink to her lips. It slopped down the front of her silver dress.

"Sorry, but I can't use you," said Ralfi. "Not for muscle. But maybe . . ."

For a moment Jane thought he was trying to be kind; then she saw the cold glint in his eye, and heard the tone in his voice as he continued. "Maybe you could be kind of cute, though, if somebody cleaned you up."

Ralfi reached up and cupped his hands over the front of Jane's leather jacket without actually touching her. "Ever consider something less actively physical?"

Yomamma said, "Yeah, like on your back?" Pretty added, "Or on your knees?" They both laughed.

Jane backed away, restraining her rage. "I'll get a gig, Ralfi," she said. Then she turned and walked away into the harsh strobed beat of the crowded dance floor.

"Bastards!" she whispered.

FOUR

High above the dark tangle that was the ruins of Newark, in the steel bones of a building whose skin had long ago crumbled into the red dust of the below-grade brick sold for housing projects and inner city schools, two figures moved—climbing, dropping, hanging and strolling on the naked steel beams spanning yawning chasms as casually as if they were sauntering along a sidewalk on the ground.

Far *more* casually, in fact. This high, abandoned upper realm was their turf, uncontested, unlike the surface, with its tangle of bureaucratic officials, corrupt cops, and roving bands of desperados.

Up here, they were the desperados; here, they ruled. None challenged them.

The older, the larger and clearly the leader of the two figures, was dressed in a layered costume of what might appear to the untrained eye to be rags, carefully chosen for color and dramatic effect—a Triple Fat Goose jacket over a sheepskin vest; a tank top over a T-shirt; a flannel shirt tied like a skirt over baggy pants; and, under it all, Timberland boots with the soles strapped on with bungee cords; and the whole decorated with beads, totems, trinkets and colored scraps like flags. For a hat, he wore a scarf, tied on backward. Around his waist, on an ancient army web belt, he carried a collection of flashlights, screwdrivers, wrenches, wedges and prybars: tools dedicated to the arts of breaking and entering, repair and salvage, recycling and refurbishing. Tools appropriate to a culture of re-creation, in which the discards of an earlier age created the matrix, the subsoil of a new; a culture in which the high had become the low, the low high, the first last, and the last—at long last—first.

A culture, in other words, that was proudly and distinctively human.

Over the leader's shoulder was slung that most human of accoutrements, a weapon—in this case, a spring-loaded crossbow, a postmodern melding of firearm and slingshot, an ingenious adaptation of found technology of the sort that had given this loose clan of mostly lost boys their name: Loteks.

The leader stopped at the end of a swaying steel I-beam and looked down. Though his origins, his accomplishments and even his last name were shrouded in obscurity, his face was well known. He was J-Bone, the acknowledged leader of the Loteks, the media rebel whose face and taunts were familiar around the world, wherever he and his crew decided to momentarily hijack the airwaves and insert their subversive message of autonomy, anarchy and freedom.

J-Bone was anywhere from eighteen to thirty, clearly an adult. The Lotek hurrying to catch up with him, though armed and dressed in imitation of his leader, was just as clearly a kid. Toad was almost thirteen, but held onto the precocious innocence of a nine-year-old as if it were his most prized possession.

He was a favorite of the entire Lotek crew, though

none of them would have admitted to such a conventional and suspect sentiment.

"Yo, J-Bone!" he called out, adding for effect: "Maximum leader, sir!"

J-Bone signalled with one subtle backward flick of his brown hand for Toad to (1) shut up, and (2) catch up.

"Watcha clockin'?" Toad asked in a stage whisper when he reached J-Bone's side.

J-Bone was peering through a monocular he had taken from his belt. "Cab arriving down at the old paint factory."

"Lemme see?"

J-Bone handed the boy the monocular; he wanted to view the larger scene, anyway.

The taxi pulled up at the rim of a crater where the factory's main entrance had once been.

The door opened and a man carrying a briefcase got out. He closed the door behind him and handed something through the cab's front window.

The cab sped off, in reverse, spinning its wheels.

"Give," J-Bone said, taking the monocular back. He saw that the man was approximately his own age, somewhere between childhood and thirty. White, or mostly. Dressed in a blue business suit that seemed, somehow, like a disguise.

As J-Bone watched, the man hesitated at the edge of the shallow crater, scanning the horizon with what appeared to be a practiced look. He swiped at his nose, leaving a dark streak across the back of his hand. Then, with a shrug of his shoulders, he walked toward the dark shell of the factory.

"Keep the change," Johnny said. He needn't have bothered. The cab was already gone, wheels spinning as it backed up in the dirt, turned around, and roared off into the night.

How do I get out of here? Johnny wondered. Then he wiped his nose and saw the blood. *First thing is, get rid of this load.* His head was pounding, and the pain was worse with each passing moment. *Then, if I'm lucky, maybe they'll give me a ride back across the river.*

Johnny shrugged and started across the shallow crater toward the factory, where he had been told his contact was waiting. With each slow, deliberate step, he breathed in calmness, breathed out panic; breathed in alertness, breathed out ego. By the time he reached the entrance he was as ready as he could make himself.

There was a light coming from under the door.

Johnny crept around to a window and tried to look in, but it was too high. To the left, another window was covered over with corrugated steel.

Behind him was scattered trash and the rim of the crater. Directly overhead loomed the sagging steel skeleton of a skyscraper, one of a pair that had fallen together in a precarious tangle.

Johnny straightened his tie. Time to go in.

Almost.

First he took a device like the one that had saved him in Beijing and stuck it to the door frame with two-sided tape. He armed it: The blinking of its red ready light was echoed by the smaller light on his belt.

He knocked.

The door opened suddenly, as if whoever was inside had been waiting with one hand on the knob.

"You're Johnny," he said.

Johnny stepped back. "You're the contact?"

He didn't like the looks of it. The man who had opened the door was a punk with spiked blue hair, wearing razor-toed cowboy boots, and brick and asphalt-blend camouflage. The kind of free-lance street muscle the Yakuza often picked up for dirty assignments.

"Sure hope so. Come on in."

58

Johnny stepped in—a long step, so that the punk was now between him and the door, which seemed to suit the punk just fine.

The room had once been an office. Now it had a faintly medical look, with a folding table spread with white plastic under a bright light. At one end of the table was a tray filled with none-too-clean surgical tools, and a small cabinet with a handle on the top, its glass door frosted with carbon dioxide mist.

Johnny recognized it from his days of looting organs from accident scenes and bootlegging them to donor banks. It was a CryoCarryAll, a cryogenic organ transporter.

Johnny took one step back.

From the shadows, another man took one step forward.

At first Johnny thought it was the Invisible Man, from the old movie. The man's entire face was swathed in white bandages, except for two holes revealing tiny eyes, and a long slit for a mouth.

Johnny recognized him—or at least his Upper Montclair High School ring—from their brief encounter in Beijing. It was the man he had thrown through the glass into the shower stall. Shinji's right-hand man, Henson.

He was holding a chrome saw. His smile appeared through the bandages like an open wound.

"The doctor will see you now," Henson said, savoring his little joke as he tucked the saw under his arm and pulled on a pair of rubber gloves.

Johnny turned to the punk who was blocking the door. "You lied."

The punk looked genuinely surprised. "Of course I lied."

Johnny's hand brushed against the sender unit on his belt. The door exploded inward, sending the punk flying into Johnny—who ducked and used the punk's flying momentum to toss him over his shoulder into

Henson. Johnny dove through the shattered door frame into the night.

Johnny hit the slope of the crater rolling, and rolled all the way to the bottom. He was searching for the best route to scramble up the far side when a burst of fire stitched a line of miniature craters halfway up.

"Don't get in a hurry, Johnny," Henson called.

Johnny hid himself behind a pile of 55-gallon oil drums. The far side of the crater, his only escape route, was too exposed, bathed in the light from the blown-away door.

He peered out between the drums. Henson was in the doorway, silhouetted in the light. He was screwing a laser-sighting device onto a 7.62 automatic with a folding stock.

"We got all night, white meat," Henson taunted.

He screwed a silencer onto the muzzle.

"Don't really need this because no one's around to hear us, Johnny," Henson explained. "But I like to use it anyway."

He stepped out of the door and started down into the crater.

"I'm the quiet type."

"Yo, J-Bone, look at—"

That was as far as Toad got. J-Bone's big hand was across the kid's big mouth in half a second as the two of them knelt to watch the tableaux taking place fifty feet below.

First the stranger had entered the old factory. The door had blown open. Then a shadow had flown out, followed by a burst of full-auto fire. Now a bandaged man who looked like the Invisible Man stood in the doorway fitting a laser heat-seeking sight onto a gun.

Then a silencer.

Now Invisible was striding down the wall of the crater toward the garbage and 55-gallon oil drums piled at the center.

"Mmnm mhmm mnmhm!" said Toad.

"If you'll shut up, I'll let go," whispered J-Bone. The kid's eagerness annoyed him at the same time that it appealed to him. He had been the same way.

He let go and the boy stood, peering down over J-Bone's shoulder.

"Which one we for?" Toad whispered.

"We don't frankly give a hot damn," whispered J-Bone. "Not our fight."

He hefted his spring bow and, for good measure, checked the miniature one-shot air bow strapped to his wrist like a deadly bracelet. If need be, J-Bone knew, he could kill either of them. Swiftly and silently. Loteks didn't need guns, semis, autos or otherwise.

. . . Although that heat-seeking laser sight would be a handy tool.

The visitor in the blue suit hiding behind the oil drums didn't have a weapon, it seemed. J-Bone was looking straight down at him as blue suit picked up a length of steel pipe and tossed it against the side of the crater, to the left of Invisible.

The pipe rang against the rubble. The Invisible Man whirled toward the sound, gun at the ready—but the gun didn't fire. *Sought heat but didn't find it,* thought J-Bone. *Neat. Handy.*

"Groovy!" whispered Toad, his eyes big with excitement.

"Get back," said J-Bone, reaching back to cover the boy's mouth again.

But Toad was too fast this time. He dodged back playfully, and leaned out over the other side of the beam, so he could watch. And as he did, his foot hit the monocular, knocking it off the beam.

It fell straight down, barely missing the Invisible Man, who whipped the gun around, searching, then up—

Where it found heat.

And fired.

61

A burst of four shots in a sixth of a second. Four 7.62-caliber steel-jacketed slugs. Two of them rang out against the underside of the steel beam. Two of them passed straight up into the night; one of these passed through Toad's lower jaw and brain en route.

The boy was already pitching forward when his elder, his mentor, his leader, looked back and saw what had happened.

"Aaaaiiieee!"

The scream was J-Bone's. Toad was dead before he even began to fall.

Johnny saw it all from his hiding place behind the 55-gallon drums. He couldn't see Henson but he heard the shots ring out against the steel beam overhead. Looking up, he saw the shape falling, tumbling, faster and faster, until it hit the muddy side of the crater with a sickening *splat* and rolled down toward the center.

Then Johnny saw a second shape, like a swift shadow, following, swinging down through the beams and broken window frames of the skeletal building almost as fast as the first one had fallen.

Johnny ducked back into his hiding place just as the second figure hit the ground running. Instead of fleeing, as Johnny had expected, the second figure— this one as clearly a man as the other had been a boy—ran into the open and knelt by the body, cradled the boy's shattered head, and raised an anguished moan:

"Toad, Toad, shit . . . !"

"Do me one favor, man."

J-Bone held Toad's head cradled in his arms. He heard the voice just as he was closing the boy's eyes for the last time.

He looked up and straight up the barrel of a laser-sighted, silenced, full-auto 7.62. At the other end of the weapon was the Invisible Man—just two eyes and a sneer like a slash.

"You weren't on the menu," said the mouth. "But I want you to do something for me."

"Do?" J-Bone was still stunned.

"Yes, you, you low-life motherfuckin' Lotek. I want you to say 'bye.'"

The Invisible Man's eyes darkened and his sneer widened, as if delighted at his own joke. But before he could laugh or fire, the top of his head collapsed inward with a dull wet sound like a ripe watermelon cracking open, and he pitched forward onto the mud.

Behind him, swinging a waterlogged two-by-four like a Louisville Slugger, J-Bone saw the man in the blue suit—the man who had been hiding.

And behind him was yet another man, a spike-haired punk in cowboy boots and cammies, his clothes singed as if by a blast. He was holding an antique AK-47 he looked eager to use.

"Just hold it right there," the punk said. "Raise your hands, both of you."

J-Bone was glad to oblige. He raised both hands slowly until they were pointing directly toward the punk.

And tightened a muscle in his wrist.

Zing!

The bolt from the air bow on his wrist went straight through the punk's left eye, leaving the right eye circling insanely as he fell forward into the dust, now reddening with blood.

"Sorry about your friend," Johnny said. He picked up Henson's gun and snapped off the heat-seeking laser sight and tossed it into a puddle beside the punk's body.

Then he unscrewed the folding stock and tossed it into the puddle.

Then unscrewed the silencer and tossed it, too, into the puddle.

He was left with an automatic pistol, which he wiped clean and tucked into his belt.

The Lotek leader watched silently, then asked, "You tooling up for an evening of this? How come you didn't carry a gun in the first place?"

Johnny shrugged. "If they think you're technical, go crude . . ."

". . . And if they think you're crude, go technical," finished the Lotek. "I know." It was an old saying, a proverb of the street. Something they had in common.

The Lotek leader took off one of his jackets and laid it over the dead boy's face. He knelt over him for a long moment, breathing what might have been a prayer or a curse or a farewell. Then he stood and wiped one eye with a sleeve. "Anyway," he said, "whatever you're up to, you and I are even, understand?"

"Sure." Johnny shrugged, then asked: "Who are you, anyway? You look familiar."

Instead of answering, the Lotek looked at Johnny as if measuring him. Then he reached down into the puddle and retrieved the heat-seeking laser sight. He wiped it off and put it into his pocket, extending his hand.

At first Johnny thought it was for a handshake. Then he saw that the Lotek was pointing toward the horizon, beyond the ruined skyscrapers, to an ancient iron drawbridge festooned with cables and crammed with shacks and walkways, like a giant insect nest.

"I'm J-Bone," he said. "I run Heaven. Up there."

FIVE

—■—

Home holograms are evocative but sometimes the memories they unleash are too strong. Takahashi also had home movies, videos, photo albums, all the memorabilia of a child that a doting parent assembles. And sometimes when the longing was too strong, when the sorrow threatened to overwhelm him, he found he could assuage it a little by showing the video he had made almost five years earlier, of Mikiyo building a sand castle on the beach, a tiny girl creating a tiny world with her tiny hands.

An impermanent world. Perhaps that was the lesson that made this video almost soothing; perhaps someday he would be able to see her life as just another transient fragment of life's beauty, just as fleeting but no more heartbreaking than the sand castle, the waves turning the blue-green pages of the sea, the clouds passing far overhead on that long-ago Sunday afternoon on the Jersey shore.

Takahashi's broad, harsh features ("the face that hired a thousand killers," his enemies and friends alike called him) softened as he leaned back and watched Mikiyo's image on the wall screen across from his desk. It was late afternoon of another business day for Yakuza of North America. While his secretary, Mrs. Sutton, was placing an important but difficult and time-consuming call, he took the opportunity to retreat again into the reverie of a happier time. . . .

But what was this? He had watched this video many times, and never before had he seen a figure approach across the sand. Was this another video intrusion by the Loteks, the media guerrilla scum that danced in and out of the electronic matrix around the world?

Takahashi picked up the remote from his desk and hit PAUSE, but nothing happened. Mikiyo kept building her sand castle and the figure kept approaching. It was as if she had walked straight out of the sea.

Except that she was fully dressed. A middle-aged woman, somewhere in her late forties or early fifties; European, Asian, or a little of each; startlingly beautiful, dressed in a simple but elegant linen and silk business suit.

Walking in high heels across the sand. Leaving no tracks behind her.

Takahashi hit OFF; he tried FAST-FORWARD; he tried REVERSE.

The woman knelt beside Mikiyo, who seemed not to notice her; then she stood again and stepped forward until her face filled the wall screen. She was wearing striking *yin* and *yang* earrings.

"How sad," she said. "The loss of a child . . ."

Takahashi hit the remote again but the picture stayed on. The woman looked toward him, as if she could see out of the screen as readily as he could see into it.

"Who are you?" Takahashi asked. "What are you?" He set down the remote and opened a drawer to find the pills the doctor had prescribed for depression. No one else in the organization knew he was taking them.

"I understand your loss," the woman said. "I have also experienced, in my own way, the loss of a child."

Without taking his eyes off the screen, Takahashi counted out two of the pills, added a third for good measure, and swallowed them, washing them down with a swig of Evian from an open bottle on his desk.

"You are an illusion," Takahashi barked, as if saying it somehow solved a problem. "You are an hallucination!"

The woman looked from him down to the sand castle and the footprints of the little girl, which were already being washed away by the receding waves.

"Of course," she replied. "An illusion. Like life itself. But let us hallucinate together, Takahashi. There is something I want to share with you—as an executive and as a parent—something you will understand."

Takahashi hit the remote again. "No! Get out of here! Leave me alone!"

"You will understand for the same reason I understand you, Takahashi. I was like you; I *was* you. Rigid. Powerful. My will flashing like lightning between all the world's megacities. My name a cold wind in the corridors of power. . . ."

Mikiyo was forgotten—Takahashi was furious at this intrusion into his private sanctuary. "You are sent by my enemies!"

The woman shook her head. "Say rather that I am sent by conscience. In the name of memory."

"Memory?"

"Where I am, Takahashi, there is only memory. All is memory. Memory and the play of conscience, an endless reckoning of the score."

"Hell . . . ?"

The woman laughed. "A tale from humanity's childhood. Though if there was never such a thing as Hell before, surely we invented it. You are in your own hell, Takahashi. I know you. Your purpose is lost. At the very center of all your power there is only an emptiness, a hollowness carved in the shape of an absent child. . . ."

Suddenly she was gone. Mikiyo, or Mikiyo's image, was back, playing on the beach. Mrs. Sutton walked into the office and put some papers on Takahashi's desk.

"No luck, sir," she said.

"Luck?" He looked up at her, dazed.

"I still haven't been able to get Reverend Honig on the phone," Mrs. Sutton said. She saw the image of Takahashi's daughter on the wall and looked away, masking her concern.

Takahashi picked up the papers and pretended to look through them. "Oh. Street Preacher. Well, keep trying. Very important."

Either by accident or design, the loudspeakers that filled every room of the Drome with the relentless neo-rap beat of megalopolis nightlife were left out of the restrooms. So whenever Ralfi needed to get away for a few moments of quiet reflection, he headed for the men's room.

And right now he needed to think. He was in trouble. A delivery promised to the Yakuza had gone wrong.

The men's room was empty. Good. Ralfi stationed himself in front of the urinal, unzipped his pants, and—

Suddenly he was grabbed from behind in a hammerlock. His expensively reconstructed face was flattened against the cold porcelain tile of the wall. Ralfi thought it was a robbery, until he heard his assailant's voice.

"They were waiting for me, Ralfi! Two of them."

"Johnny—is that you?"

"They were Yakuza, Ralfi. But you *knew* that."

"Johnny-boy! Please . . . !"

"You set me up. Didn't you, *friend?*"

"Johnny, it's not my fault. There's been a screw-up, but it's not my— Ow, you're *hurting* me!"

"I mean to hurt you. I'm going to *worse* than hurt you, Ralfi. Your ass is dead if you don't figure out a way to get this batch of product out of my head before—"

Thwack!

Ralfi felt the grip relax as the voice went silent. He pulled free and turned, and saw Yomamma standing over Johnny's crumpled body. She was holding a high-heeled pump in her hand.

"Not on the head!" Ralfi groaned. "Tell me you didn't hit him on the head!"

Yomamma shrugged and slipped her shoe back on, balancing on one foot like a pelican. "I saw him follow you in," she said. "Zip up your pants, Ralfi. Say, I haven't been in one of these for years."

"Not since you had a dick, huh?" Ralfi bent down and checked Johnny's scalp. No blood, and he was still breathing. "Now let's get him into the back room, okay?"

Yomamma lifted Johnny as easily as if he had been a rag doll. Ralfi followed her out of the men's room. They carried him to the bar, picking up Pretty on the way.

The bartender was skillfully opening three beers at once with his skeletal stainless-steel prosthetic. "Dead?" he asked, barely looking up.

"Just a bum who had one too many, Hooky," Ralfi said. "Can we deposit him in your back room for a while?"

"Sure."

Ralfi signalled across the room to a table of burly, gray-suited Japanese men, who nodded when they saw what Yomamma was shouldering.

The dance floor was already filled, even in late afternoon, but the early revelers stepped aside and

69

made way as Yomamma carried Johnny across the floor, with Ralfi and Pretty following close behind. Injuries were as common as deaths at the Drome, and no one paid any attention.

No one except the spike-haired young woman in black leather at the other end of the bar.

She watched as Yomamma carried Johnny into the back room.

She watched as Ralfi and Pretty followed.

She watched as the gray-suited men got up from their table and went into the back room, closing the door behind them and leaving one of their number stationed outside as a sentry. He didn't bother to hide the Chinese-made Shansei "broomhandle" .45 in his belt.

Jane turned back to the bartender. "Hey, Hooky. What's the deal with all the Yakuza action? Is Ralfi in their pocket now?"

Hooky shrugged. "I don't ask those kinds of questions," he said. "If you were smart, you wouldn't either, Jane. Want another beer?"

"Nah." She paid and got up to go. "Gotta keep my fightin' edge."

At first Johnny thought it was ICE, the impenetrable cybernetic armor that protects a program from penetration by cowboys like himself when they are jacking through cyberspace.

But in cyberspace your head doesn't hurt.

Then he saw Ralfi's head hovering over him like a bad planet.

Was he in the hospital? Maybe Ralfi was going to take care of him after all.

"What'd they upload, Ralfi?" Johnny asked, still dazed. "The goddam Library of Congress? My head feels like it's going to explode."

Ralfi looked sad, then concerned, then almost managed embarrassed. "Your friend here tells me he can take care of that."

Another face joined Ralfi's. It was Shinji. He wore a cheap transparent raincoat, unbuttoned, over his trademark gray Yakuza suit.

He was holding a Makita saber saw.

Johnny tried to sit up but he was held down by a leather strap around his arms and upper body. His legs were free and he kicked them futilely. "Ralfi, you lying sack of shit!"

"What am I supposed to do, Johnny? Argue with the Yakuza?" Ralfi looked extravagantly sad. He stepped aside so that Yomamma could set what she was carrying onto the table by Johnny's head.

Craning his neck to look around, Johnny saw a CryoCarryAll portable organ freezer. Exactly the size of his head.

"Oh, shit," he said.

Shinji flipped his ponytail back out of the way and began buttoning his transparent raincoat. "We'll need a bucket," he said.

Jane latched herself into a stall. She waited until she was sure the ladies' room was empty, then stood on the toilet seat and stepped up onto the tank.

Her fingertips could just reach the ventilation grid above her head.

She pushed on it; it gave. It had never been screwed down. *Thank God for shabby construction,* she thought. She slid the vent grid to one side, flexed her fingers, stood on her toes—and gave a jump.

Her fingertips caught the T-bar frame. Spider's enhancements were subtle, but they made the difference. Speed and timing accomplished as much as strength. Jane was up and into the cooling-vent passage in one swift, easy motion.

She set the grid back into place behind her and

started crawling through the narrow shaft, toward a dim, distant light.

Pretty wiggled her pretty butt for the entertainment and enlightenment of those in the room behind her as she rummaged through the janitorial supplies in the closet.

She straightened coyly, holding up a filthy plastic bucket.

"It's not sterile," she said.

"It will do," said Shinji. "Put it here, beside the table."

"Can we talk about this?" Johnny asked. Coolly, or with the illusion of cool, he hoped.

"Talk?" Shinji held up the Tokarev 7.62 automatic pistol Johnny had taken from the American Yakuza, and placed it on the table between Johnny's feet. "I notice you didn't bother talking to Henson."

"I have one image of the access code," Johnny said. "You have the other two parts. Let's download. I'll give you the data. Glad to get rid of it. Everybody will be happy."

Shinji tried the saw. It was powered by tiny fuel cells. It whined on and off.

"You don't understand," Shinji said. "We have only one. And clients don't just want the data, anyway. They want everything it's ever been stored in."

"Yeah, but—"

"That way, there's less danger of information decay. And they won't have to worry about somebody going in later with an unerase nanobot, or a memory restorer. These days, you see, dead men can tell tales."

"There's gotta be a way to work this out!" Johnny said, his cool by now completely departed.

"There is," said Shinji. He took a small blue rubber ball out of his pocket and jammed it into Johnny's mouth.

He opened the little door on the CryoCarryAll. The air was icy cold, like after-shave, on Johnny's face.

A new and final kind of cool.

From where Jane was perched, across two of the lightweight alumisteel supports holding the cheap ceiling vent in place, it looked like an opening scene on her favorite real-life TV show, "Operating Room."

Except that the "patient" was wide awake, rolling his head from one side to another in silent panic. He had a blue rubber ball in his mouth.

You'd think he would close his eyes, Jane thought. But he opened them wider as the "doctor" (in a clear plastic raincoat over a gray Yakuza suit) revved the saw once or twice, drawing an imaginary line across the "patient's" neck.

"Hurry it up, willya?" and "This is kinda disgusting," came two familiar voices. Jane leaned down and saw Ralfi and his twin Amazons in the corner of the room. Yomamma had her eyes closed. Pretty was watching avidly.

"Don't rush me," said the Yakuza with the saw. "I don't want to make a mess."

Jane didn't bother to think. Snap decisions were her forte. She drew her knees to her chest and dropped straight down onto the vent, which gave way smoothly, giving her time to grab the T-frame for a swing, and get her boots pointed dead center at the temple of the Yakuza in the raincoat with the ponytail and the whining saw.

"What the fuck!" said Ralfi, as he saw Shinji go down, hard. Pretty and Yomamma both dived for the intruder, who had landed on her feet and was spinning already—drop-kicking Pretty backward, into the door, where she made contact with a sickening *crack* and slid to the floor.

73

"Two down," said Jane. She started for the table, where Johnny was thrashing his head from side to side, trying to spit out the rubber ball, trying to get away from the open door of the cryo-unit, which was freezing the side of his face.

But Yomamma was already there, at Johnny's side. She pulled a pearl-handled boxcutter from the bosom of her low-cut dress, pressed it to Johnny's neck and slid the button on the side forward.

The blade peeped out. Johnny was suddenly still.

Jane pulled out her own weapon, concealed in her belt: a telescoping car antenna with a razor-sharp steel fang welded to the end.

The blade bobbed like a fly rod over Yomamma's face, centimeters from her heavily mascara'ed eyes.

Yomamma was unimpressed. She held her box-cutter at Johnny's jugular. "I'll slit his fucking throat, bitch."

Jane cocked her head to one side, as if curious. "So? The Yakuza was going to cut his head off."

Ralfi, mopping his forehead in the corner, saw the standoff and decided it was time to regain control. Mustering all his courage, he stepped between the two women.

"Jane-Jane," he said, "what say we pay you for a night's work and you just walk away, okay?"

"Ten grand," said Jane, folding the antenna.

Johnny groaned. He had finally managed to spit out the blue ball. "Twenty grand!"

"Don't listen to him, Jane," Ralfi said, edging closer to the table. "He's a dead man. Besides, I can make it thirty, if . . ."

The rest of Ralfi's words were lost, as Johnny lashed out sideways with his foot and caught Ralfi precisely between the legs. Ralfi doubled over in agony, and as he did, Yomamma dove for Jane with the knife.

Jane flicked her antenna back out, then up, neatly

severing three of the five major tendons in Yomamma's wrist.

"Aiiieee!" Yomamma howled in pain and rage, dropping the boxcutter.

"Forty," yelled Johnny.

"Fifty," said Jane.

"Done!" said Johnny. Jane caught Yomamma's knife before it hit the floor, and sliced through the strap that bound Johnny's arms in one swift, fluid motion. *Good work, Spider,* she thought. *I'm as fast as you wanted me to be.*

Meanwhile Shinji, on his knees, was unscrewing the cap on his thumb.

Johnny rolled off the table, hitting hands-first, and heaved upward with his feet. The table flew across the room, catching Shinji in the side just as he was about to swing the shining, molecule-thin lethal filament that flashed from the end of his thumb.

The Tokarev 7.62 fell from the table to the floor.

The door flew open and the Yakuza guard burst into the room, pulling the Shansei "broomhandle" .45 from his belt, a look of surprise on his face that deepened to wonder and then to almost comic dismay as he tried to focus on Jane's Ninja throwing spike that had appeared like a sudden steel blossom between his eyes.

He fell backward. Ralfi, about to step across the fallen Yakuza body, paused when he saw the second throwing spike poised in Jane's hand.

Meanwhile, the 7.62 still lay on the floor.

Pretty and Johnny both dove for it, but Johnny had an unfair advantage, because Pretty was slowed by Jane's kick, which both flattened her nose and cracked loose two of her recently reseeded teeth.

"Freeze," Johnny said, hefting the pistol.

Ralfi froze. Shinji froze. Pretty froze.

With his free hand Johnny closed the door of the

cryo-unit. The pistol was like a magic wand. When he waved it, Ralfi and Shinji huddled closer together.

Behind him he heard a noise. It was Yomamma pulling another boxcutter from the top of her boot. That girl never gave up. He heard another noise. It was Jane cracking Yomamma's good wrist.

"It's okay," Johnny said. "I got the gun."

The cracking sounds continued. Johnny looked behind him and saw Jane, in a frenzy, beating Yomamma unconscious with a broken leg from the table.

"Hey!" Johnny reached back and touched Jane's shoulder, all coiled rage. "Cool it. Time to go."

"Oh . . . yeah . . ." Jane came to herself and left Yomamma, bleeding but mercifully unconscious on the floor.

She stepped to Johnny's side and they backed toward the door. One step. Two. Johnny opened the door with one hand and let Jane through, then slipped through behind her.

Just as he was slamming the door behind him, he heard the high singing sound of Shinji's filament cutting past his head. He ducked—and fled, following Jane onto the crowded dance floor.

"Damn!" said Ralfi, who had been about to follow Johnny. He spat at Shinji: "Watch what you're doin'. You coulda killed *me* with that thing!"

Shinji looked at the tiny, sad-eyed talent agent thoughtfully, then shrugged. He flicked his forearm, up and down, twice.

Ralfi's mouth opened as if he had just thought of something further he wanted to say. But nothing came out. He slid to the floor in three neat, almost equal pieces.

Well, not so neat.

SIX

—■—

Getting into the Drome was never easy. If it had been easy, people wouldn't have wanted to go. They stood impatiently under the marquee in front, a restless, bobbing herd like cattle assembled for slaughter. All sexes, all ages, all jealous of whomever was let in and all hoping to be the next to join the elect. The doormen, one white and one black, whose identical loincloths and chaps concealed some intricate and interesting weaponry, appeared to be in charge of selecting who was to be let in:

"You!"—pointing over the crowd to a tall, bearded man in a tuxedo, at the back of the shifting mass, with an evening-gowned woman on either arm; "You!"—giving the nod to a bright cluster of men in drag passing a bottle of single malt; "You!" to a wide-eyed teen in a half tank top, eager to lose her innocence and about to have her enthusiasm rewarded.

The selection process appeared to be regulated by whim, but it was in fact part of a system in which the needs of the rich and powerful, who used the club for their own purposes, were carefully looked after. A manager of the club, hidden in a window in the O of the Drome marquee, continually scanned the crowd for video and music celebrities, Yakuza and other crime notables, influential politicians and special, invited guests. These were marked with an infrared pointer only the doormen, through their coated contacts, could see.

It was all regulated by the velveteen rope, pinned and unpinned by the doormen like the gateway to a heaven of excess: . . . *Abandon all moderation, ye who enter here* . . .

The velveteen rope was naturally designed to keep people out, not in. In fact, surfeited patrons left the Drome by another door, to protect the illusion of total desirability. So the doormen were as surprised as the people milling on the street when two figures, a man with a 7.62 full-auto machine pistol and a woman with short, dark, spiked hair, burst out the door in the wrong direction, leaping over the rope and disappearing into the crowd, which parted before them like a miniature Red Sea.

"Hey, man! Watch where you're going!"

"Sorry . . ."

"Oooofff! Dude!"

"Excuse me . . ."

Johnny broke free of the crowd, into the street, and stopped short. *What now?* He had a gun, a headful of smuggled data that was killing him with synaptic seepage . . . and nowhere to go.

And no time to think about it. "Move!" Jane said, slapping his butt as she flashed past. Johnny followed across the street. Horns honked and brakes squealed as she jumped a cab's hood and scrambled under the wheels of an elevated tour bus. The prospective patrons in front of the Drome applauded. They thought it was all part of the show. They thought everything was part of the show.

Jane darted into an alley between darkened buildings and stopped. Johnny followed.

The alley was dark, narrow, cool. Johnny's footsteps resounded off the brick canyon walls, but slower, and yet slower. His head was bursting and he was running out of wind. At the far end of the alley, Jane was already stopped, bending over a trash pile under a poster of the latest NAS poster child, a little girl with china blue eyes.

The blurb under the picture read:

Nerve Attenuation Syndrome.
It's not your problem.
Yet.

Johnny slowed to a jog and then to a walk. His breath came in short, ragged gasps. Jane was bent over with her back to him, and as he approached her it dawned on him, for the first time, that the black-clad female fighting machine that had rescued him was—a pretty girl.

Almost pretty, anyway. Nice butt in tight jeans, nice legs when they weren't racing. She turned to face him and he saw eyes that were almost beautiful when they weren't bright with alarm or anger. Lips that might seem sensual when they weren't twisted into a grimace with fighting or fleeing. Nice hair. Nice tattoos. And under her leather vest, like a long-forgotten memory for Johnny, the alluring swell of—

"Jane," she said, and he realized it was an introduction.

"Johnny," he responded. He stuck out his hand but she was already turned around, bent over again, rummaging through a soggy heap of trash. She pulled a shoulder bag from the pile, checked its contents, and threw it over her shoulder.

Johnny was amazed. He was running for his life and

she was scavenging? "What the *fuck* are you doing?" he asked.

"My stash," Jane said, patting the purse. "I hid it here earlier." Then her eyes grew wide and she shouted:

"Look out!"

The eyes of the poster child above her on the wall also grew wide; as Johnny watched, they turned to gaping holes. Shreds of poster paper fell like confetti.

Blamblamblamblamblam!

Johnny wheeled and saw Pretty racing toward him in a crouch, a nine-inch switchblade gleaming in her hand. Behind her, Shinji was fumbling to reload the "broomhandle" automatic he had lifted from the Yakuza dispatched by Jane's throwing spike.

Jane pulled another identical spike from her shoulder bag—her stash, she had called it—and threw. It missed, ringing off the pavement, but it slowed Pretty, who flattened against the wall, ducking it.

"Shoot!" yelled Jane.

"I'm trying," said Johnny. The Tokarev 7.62 clicked ineffectively, once, twice, three times. Had it been unloaded all along? Disgusted, Johnny tossed it onto the trash heap.

Snack! Shinji snapped another clip into his gun and knelt to fire more effectively this time.

"Let's go!" shouted Jane, hauling Johnny around the corner just ahead of the shower of red dust raised by Shinji's bullets.

This is less complicated, anyway. The almost-pretty girl had transformed herself right before Johnny's eyes back into a lean, mean, fleeing machine and it was all he could do to keep up with her as she led him deeper and deeper into the maze of alleys and dead-end streets, under the looming canyon walls of darkened buildings. . . .

"Let's go, le'sgo, le'sgo!"

"Where?" Johnny managed to squeeze out from tortured lungs.

But if Jane heard him she didn't deign to answer. He had no choice but to follow, at least as long as his lungs held out.

"Up here!" she demanded.

"Through here!" she called back.

"You there?" she queried.

She seemed to know where they were going, as if she were negotiating familiar territory.

"I'm here," Johnny gasped.

"Where?"

"Right behind you." *So far.*

Left, right, right.

Left. Up a wall, down a passage. Through a fence, across an abandoned factory floor, machines standing unattended like ghosts.

And always behind them, sometimes closer, sometimes farther away, Johnny could hear footsteps—two sets of footsteps, as patient and enduring as four-footed hellhounds.

If Jane knows this territory, Johnny realized, *Pretty must know it just as well.* All the night muscle, Yakuza as well as free-lance, was recruited from the urban shadows, where generations of street kids grew like poisonous mushrooms into vicious fighters-for-hire.

It wasn't Johnny's scene; *mine or Shinji's, either,* Johnny thought. *We're the strangers here. We should be together; the girls should be chasing us.*

"Faster!" she whispered.

"I'm going as fast as I can!"

They ran past fires in oil drums, past shacks made of corrugated plastic and old tires, past rags on improvised clotheslines, past tents lit with bootleg TVs, past dogs barking from the shadows. But not a human soul was anywhere to be seen.

Where are the people? Johnny knew it was a foolish thought. This was the kind of world in which people were not seen unless they wanted to be; a lay-low world in which only the cruel and the cunning and the cautious survived.

"They're getting closer . . ." he gasped.

Jane could have easily outrun Pretty and Shinji. Johnny could have outrun them if it had been up to his feet. Even his lungs had found their second wind. The problem was his head. It seemed to hang on his neck like a melon, oversized, ripe and heavy with pain, throbbing, threatening with every step to pull him over and down. The pounding of his head, along with the pounding of his feet and the others' sounds on the gritty pavement, comprised a symphony of darkness and agony.

"This way!" Jane hissed.

Jane ran under a low arch, across booming plywood sheets laid over mud and rubble. She stopped at the edge, where the plywood ran out, and Johnny ran into her. In the dim light from a starless rectangle of sky high overhead, Johnny could make out what seemed to be stacks of lumber, poles, tiles, cinder blocks. He could smell the smoke of cooking fires and hear sporadic low murmurings. They were in an enclosed courtyard under sheer windowless walls that soared upward into darkness.

A dead end.

They were trapped. Behind, through the passageway, the footsteps were getting louder. Only now, there were more than two sets of feet. Lots more.

"I've got to get *out* of here!" Johnny cried.

Jane clapped her hand over his mouth. Her violet eyes gleamed in the half-light as she fished in her shoulder bag for more throwing spikes.

"No," she said. "We stand. I'll take 'em." She pulled Johnny with her. Back into the shadows.

* * *

A dead end. Shinji could smell victory. He had them.

He and Pretty led the way. Behind them came the two Yakuza who had joined the chase. One was carrying a Tek-9 full-auto, an old-fashioned noise-maker. The other carried the cryo-unit and the saber saw.

No surgical tools, no raincoats; nobody playing doctor anymore. They were ready to play straight-up butcher.

With a flick of his wrist, Shinji signalled the two to wait, so that he and Pretty could go ahead under the arch. It was better that way. Start and finish. A sort of symmetry. He wasn't going to be cheated out of this win.

The arch led into a cluttered, narrow courtyard. It was dark, but Shinji could sense people watching. He clicked off the safety on the Shansei .45. Pretty flicked out her blade. Together they made one sweet and deadly sound.

Flick/click.

Slick!

The plywood boomed as Shinji moved forward to the edge. Below and in front of him, a light clicked on. He saw eyes looking upward like a circle of owls.

The light was an old kerosene storm lantern. Around it a group of scavenging Loteks in ragged clothes sat sharing a pizza they had begged or stolen somewhere. Double cheese with mushrooms and pepperoni.

Shinji smiled and pointed his gun at the pizza.

Surprising him, the Loteks all smiled back. Shinji heard a chorus of clicks like summer crickets as their spring- and air-powered crossbows and dart guns came up as one.

Shinji's smile faded. The math was all wrong. The awesome power of the Shansei "broomhandle" would get most of them, but one, at least, would get him.

As if to confirm his fears, the red dot of a laser sight appeared on the lapel of his gray suit, like a tiny new heart.

Pretty was already backing away. She was replaced by the two Yakuza. The one that was armed didn't even bother to raise his Tek-9. The Yakuza had a principle about fair fights: They avoided them.

"We'll find you again, Mr. Smith," Shinji said into the darkness, over the heads of the grinning Loteks. "Count on it."

He followed his men out of the courtyard while the Loteks jeered.

While most of the Loteks were busy finishing the pizza, the one with the laser sight on his crossbow approached Johnny and Jane, who were just now stepping out of the shadows.

"J-Bone!" said Johnny, surprised.

"Said we were even before," J-Bone said. "Now you owe me one."

Jane looked at Johnny with a new interest. "You know these guys?"

One of the younger Loteks pointed at Jane's breasts. "Hey, Janey, when'd you grow these?"

His finger got a little too close and he suddenly found himself forced to his knees, howling, while Jane bent the offending finger backward.

"I didn't mean it!"

"Temper, sister," chided J-Bone.

"Temper my ass, J-Bone." But she let the kid go. "Now help us get out of here."

J-Bone picked up the lantern and led them to the far corner of the courtyard. He slid a sheet of paneling out of the way, exposing a dark hole. Johnny bent down and looked in. The hole led to a passageway that smelled like rats, urine and wet death.

"The subway?" Johnny asked.

"Our back door," said J-Bone.

With hardly a backward glance, Jane scrambled through the opening and started down. Johnny shrugged, held his breath, and followed.

J-Bone waited until he couldn't hear the sounds of their feet scratching in the darkness, then pointed to two of his lieutenant Loteks.

"You. And you. Follow them."

SEVEN

—■—

Here's the church and here's the steeple . . .

The building had once housed a movie theater, a Sony Super Twelveplex, with popcorn ground into the lobby carpets, espresso machines and automatically flushing urinals, pay phones and video machines, a relic of the salad days of celluloid cinema, a postmodern shrine to that epiphanous interface where commerce and entertainment combine into Art.

Then it had fallen into decline. It had become a flea market.

Then it had fallen still further.

It had become a church.

Above the marquee, a neon sign proudly announced CHURCH OF THE RETRANSFIGURATION in three colors, rippling steadily from left to right, from red to blue, a nonstop repetitive movement that suggested to some the miracle of stability in change, to others the impermanence of worldly things, and to still others the exaltation of credit over cash.

On the marquee, which jutted out over the street, providing on rainy evenings some shelter to the homeless, black letters proclaimed:

It was raining, and a small band of vagrants who had been "desecrating" the church by using its marquee as shelter from the elements were being hustled off with an electric cattle prod—especially effective in wet weather—by the church's single security guard, himself a homeless man, who had been ordered to keep the sanctuary entrance clear.

... *Open the door and see all the people* ...

Inside the double doors of the sanctuary, the urine- and Pepsi-stained seats were filled with men and women of all ages, but most of them old; of all classes, but most of them poor; of all colors, but most of them shades of brown. The people in the seats up front were shouting and clapping, swaying from side to side. Those in the seats in the middle were trying to doze and at the same time protect their precious few belongings, strapped into bedrolls or damp shopping bags. Those in the seats at the rear were shivering, still wet from the storm.

There was a movie screen at the front of the sanctuary. On it was projected an image of the crucifixion, inverted. The figure on the cross was a powerful, muscular man with long blond hair. His arms were held straight out and his back was to the audience. His head was pointed down and his feet up; his huge biceps, broad shoulders and massive thighs glistening with precious oils. He looked like a diver descending from heaven to Earth in a perfect swan dive.

Under the image on the screen, on the low, wide stage, a tall man with long white hair, wearing a burgundy robe, paced back and forth, clutching an inverted crucifix into which he chanted as if it were a microphone.

"Some teach that these are the final days! Others lose faith utterly, brothers and sisters. But let *us* not be numbered among them . . ."

Out front under the marquee, a gray limousine pulled up. The security guard caught sight of the small but conspicuous Yakuza emblem on the door, and raced over to open the back door.

The driver waved him away. The driver himself got out. He was carrying a cellular vidphone monitor in one hand and a small refrigerator-like box in the other.

On the side of the box it said *CryoCarryAll*.

"We have seen a new way, a new light!" ranted the preacher. "In this plague time, our goal is the image of the Retransfiguration!"

"Amen!" muttered the few in the crowd, mostly toward the front, who were paying attention.

"Amen," answered those in the back who were trying to fall asleep but who understood that participation was the price of a dry seat.

"To go forward, unflinching, into the transfiguring crucible of His technology!"

The preacher let his purple robe fall open. Under it he was naked except for silver-tipped cowboy boots and gold bikini briefs, and his massive torso was scarred with the marks of implant surgery.

"Amen!" responded the crowd; the flash of flesh seemed to awaken a new interest.

"I stand before you naked in the house of God, whole and strong . . ."

"Amen! Amen!"

"I who was as you are today. Cast-down, miserable, weak. I was taken up and made new. I was made—POSTHUMAN!"

"AMEN!" A collective shiver went through the crowd at the word "posthuman."

The preacher saw that he had awakened his congregation: It was thus time for the collection, no matter how pitiful it would be. Suddenly his eyes lit up. The collection wouldn't be necessary; a new opportunity was presenting itself.

A Yakuza operative was entering the back door carrying an unfamiliar box—and a familiar vidphone unit.

"But now—I sense a need for meditation, brothers and sisters," the preacher said. "Leave me now, the sermon is ended."

The preacher knelt before the screen image of the inverted Jesus, turning his back on the rows of now-eager worshippers.

There were groans of disappointment, which soon turned to curses as the preacher's security man prodded and poked the congregation. Reluctantly they gathered their pitiful belongings and filed back out into the rain from whence they had come.

The preacher remained kneeling in prayer as the Yakuza driver placed the CryoCarryAll and the vidphone on the floor beside him. The Yakuza bowed once to the preacher's back, a little insolently perhaps, and went out the front door to his limousine.

An image appeared on the vidphone screen.

It was Takahashi.

"Good evening, Karl. Hope I'm not interrupting anything, but I require your services on a rather urgent . . ."

"It was my *services* you interrupted," said the preacher, sulking. "We hold services nightly. You should join us."

"Perhaps, then, I should say it is your *talent* I require," said Takahashi.

The preacher rose and turned to face the vidphone. He seemed to glow with energy.

"You wish someone brought to Jesus?" he asked eagerly.

"Not exactly."

The preacher flicked a button on the inverted cross he wore around his neck. A blade *snick*ed out as it was transformed into a switchblade.

"You wish someone brought to *you,* then."

"Yes. But not entirely," said Takahashi.

The preacher frowned while Takahashi explained.

"The little box on the floor beside the vidphone is a cryo-unit. An organ freezer. I want his head brought to me in it. Intact. Undamaged."

The preacher smiled. "And who is this—lost soul? This sinner unrepentant?"

"A mnemonic courier. Carries bootleg data in his brain. Goes by the name of Johnny. Last seen at a club called the Drome."

"The Drome. I know it well. By reputation, of course. The very pit of Satan."

"I'm prepared to triple your usual fee, Karl, if you deliver his head to me within 24 hours."

The preacher looked at his watch, folded his knife, and fell to his knees again. "Perhaps you will join me in a little prayer, Mr. Takahashi . . . ?"

Takahashi smiled and shook his head. "Pray all you want. Just *do not fail me,* Karl."

The vidphone screen went black.

The preacher smiled and closed his eyes in what might have seemed to the uninitiated to be prayer.

Rats. Giant waterbugs. Wet, scurrying mice. Even a feral cat or two. Jane's light caught myriad scurrying shapes as she led the way through the abandoned subway tunnel. There were all sorts of life under the city. As he struggled to keep up with her, Johnny felt as if there were just as much life in his head. But while the life in the tunnel was agile, secretive and small, the life in his head was lumbering, huge, ponderous. It stomped through his brain like a herd of buffalo, trampling his synapses like grass.

"You okay?" Jane asked.

"Not really."

"What is it?"

"I have to get on-line. There must be somebody I can talk to, to square this, to get rid of this . . ."

Jane slowed, concerned, but kept moving, leading the way with her flashlight. Water dripped all around; it was like a rain forest in Hell. Not the kind of place that invited you to stop and rest.

"Fifty thou," Jane said.

"What?"

"Fifty thou. That's what you promised me."

"Oh, yeah. Right."

"Time I see the color, right?"

"You were terrific," Johnny said. "If you'll just point me the way out of here and give me an account number for the cash transfer . . ."

Jane shook the flashlight beam from side to side to indicate that her head was shaking. "No way. I'm on you like paint till you pay, mister. No mistake."

"Whatever . . ." mumbled Johnny.

"How come the Yakuza want to cut your head off anyway?" Jane asked. "I mean, usually they just kill people, you know."

"Long story."

"So? I'm not going anywhere till I get paid, remember?"

"I'm a courier," Johnny explained. "What they call a mnemonic courier."

"Like 'demonic'?"

91

"*Knee*-monic. Means memory. I can carry nearly eighty gigs of data in my head, one sixty if I use a doubler. Trouble is, somebody's stuck in a lot more than that and I don't know how to get it out."

"What's it for? Who stuck it in? Why do the Yakuza want it?"

"I don't ask those kinds of questions. Neither do the Yakuza. I suspect they're hired, just like me."

"I get it," Jane said. "You're a smuggler. Hey!"

She turned. Johnny was stumbling, wincing, clutching his head. He fell to his knees and, placing his palms together, began breathing deeply, performing the same meditational exercise he had used in the Beijing Ramada bathroom.

It worked: It cleared his head, at least temporarily, of the pain. Or at least turned it into something more manageable than pain.

"What're you doing, praying?"

Johnny stood and managed a small, quiet laugh. "You might say that. It's a breathing exercise. A guy in Bangkok taught it to me. Used to be a holy man, before he became a junkie."

He started walking and Jane dodged back in front of him with the flashlight.

"Bangkok? You from around there?"

Johnny didn't answer. Jane turned and saw that he was still stumbling. He tripped over the rail as if it were a waist-high fence and fell onto the wet cinders with a sickening crunch.

"Come on, man. Here . . ."

Jane picked him up and half-dragged, half-walked him to a ledge at the side of the tunnel. She pushed him up onto the ledge and sat him upright in the corner like a huge, limp doll.

"Gotta keep going," Johnny said.

Jane shone the flashlight onto his face.

His pupils were tiny; his eyes almost white. A thin trickle of blood ran from one nostril.

"Man!" she said, as much to herself as to him. "You are fucked up *severe!*"

"Gotta find . . ." Johnny tried to stand.

"No way," Jane said, pushing him back and clicking off the light. "Stay put, okay?"

EIGHT

—■—

Memory resides in everything. The memory of every sound ever made, even the death scream of the last dinosaur, is somewhere in the howl of the world-circling wind; the memory of every sight, the color of every flower, is wrapped in sunlight and stored in the far reaches of the universe. The memories are there; it is only the access codes that are missing.

Electronic memories aren't so far-traveling. They reside in the chips and the synapses, in the subaural hum of magnetic data and the digital whisper of silicon. Cold on their own, stored electronic memories can provide the access codes to warmer, more comforting memories; such were the digital holographic images, the memories of Mikiyo, that Takahashi used to access and awaken his emotions, to warm the cinder that was his heart.

But today was different. Today he was after a different sort of memory. A memory that disturbed instead of comforted him; that made him think instead of feel.

After telling his secretary he was not, under any

circumstances, to be disturbed, Takahashi closed the doors to his office and booted up the workstation on his desk, which was on the LAN with the Yakuza's security mainframe. With a "scouring" program he searched in the interstices of the system's residual memory for the image of the woman's face that had appeared to him, unbidden, the afternoon before.

Success. The face appeared on the screen, assembled pixel by pixel. While the woman's image was reconstituting, another program searched for her voice; but having never being bit-mapped, it was gone for good.

Takahashi backtraced the origin of the image, but it hadn't come through the lines. Nor was it cellular or satellite. The image had come from—nowhere. Or from the matrix itself.

Calling on the Yakuza's massive security database, Takahashi keyed a search, using the parameters for an "ivory" (99.44 percent) match. Hundreds of women's faces, most of them European, all of them middle-aged, some of them beautiful, fell across the screen like leaves, overlaying briefly atop the elusive face of the woman who had called to him personally from the screen only the day before.

Nothing. No match.

Memory. What was it? Did human minds remember the same way as machines, with endless repetition? Takahashi's mind wandered watching the monitor. He got up, looked out onto his carefully raked Zen garden, then walked to the bamboo and silk paper closet built into the wall of his office. Whenever he was bored, and always before an important meeting, Takahashi liked to change his shirt. He opened the closet door, revealing a stack of thirty dress shirts, all just alike: Egyptian cotton, French cuffs, single-needle tailoring, custom-made for him in New Hong Kong.

Takahashi looked behind him. The machine was still flipping through faces.

Memory.

He took off the shirt he was wearing and threw it into the corner. In the mirror he studied the intricate sequence of tattoos on his thickening but still powerful body. The memory that resided in tattoos was more accessible than the memory in machines. While the computer searched endlessly, and ineffectively, for the match to the mystery woman's face, Takahashi's mind immediately accessed and retrieved the memories brought back by the ceremonial tattoos, one for each stage of his secret samurai training.

Memory.

It resided also in swords. Putting on a fresh shirt, Takahashi reached up and touched the samurai sword that hung on the wall in its long, curved, beautifully engraved sheath. The sheath told an ancient story of honor and sacrifice. The sword and sheath had been a gift from his uncle, the only one in his family who had understood his need to be more than a businessman, to study a discipline instead of just a profession, to find a way of life that combined the nobility of the old with the unlimited power of the new.

He was buttoning his shirt when he heard something. At first he thought it was the computer telling him it had completed its search and found a match.

But when he looked behind him to the monitor on the desk, the images were still falling like leaves across the screen.

The noise came from beyond the door, from his outer reception room.

Takahashi tucked in his shirt and pulled the samurai sword from its sheath. The blade was also engraved, but it told a different story than the sheath. A story with a bloodier ending.

The door opened just as Takahashi was stepping out of his closet, sword in hand.

Shinji burst into the office, followed closely by two strange men. Behind them, red-faced, came Takahashi's private secretary, Mrs. Sutton.

"I'm telling you, sir, you can't just walk . . ."

Takahashi silenced her with a thin smile, and sent her away with a wave of his hand. She shut the door carefully behind her.

The two men with Shinji were not Yakuza. Both were Americans. Guns bulged under their cheap suits. They wore the wrong shoes.

One of them, an Anglo, spit out the door into the sand garden. The other, a Latino, started looking through the items on Takahashi's desk. He picked up the gold-framed holo of Mikiyo and set it back down.

"Yo, check it out," he said to the Anglo. "Three-fucking-D!"

Takahashi ignored them both. He ignored Shinji's tiny, insolent bow.

He spoke in Japanese: "Who are these creatures?"

Shinji answered in Japanese: "They are my *kobuns.*"

The Anglo had just reached the desk and was starting to pick up the holo when Takahashi killed him with a single expert thrust up under the ribs into the heart, where the bleeding would be mostly internal. The Latino made more of a mess. He was reaching under his synthetic fiber sport coat for his gun when Takahashi sliced him from his neck downward, at an angle, severing both his spine and his jugular with one stroke.

He fell, pumping blood, which pooled under the desk and began to lap against the rug.

"I gave you no permission to have *kobuns,*" Takahashi said, still in Japanese.

Shinji didn't answer. He stood and watched, unmoving. His face was frozen somewhere in that vast empty country between terror and rage, where fighters dwell.

Takahashi bent down and tore a piece off the Latino's 50-50 dress shirt and used it to wipe the blade of his sword. The rip in the shirt revealed an intricate series of tattoos on the dead man's back.

Takahashi pointed with the tip of the sword at one of the designs and asked in Japanese: "What does this mean?"

Shinji had regained some, but not all, of his insolence. He answered in English. "It's Japanese. Sir."

Takahashi answered, also in English: "It's misspelled."

Shinji said nothing. His eyes glowed with hatred.

Takahashi rolled the Anglo's body over with his foot. He spoke this time in Japanese: "They should be honored to have been dispatched with such a fine instrument."

He inserted the sword back into its sheath on the closet wall and looked for the first time directly at Shinji. He spoke in Japanese:

"Twice you have attempted to capture the mnemonic courier in my territory. Twice you have failed. In neither instance was I informed. That must not happen again."

Shinji waited as long as possible before answering. "Yes, sir."

"Locate him. Inform me. Then I will supervise his capture. Understood?"

"Yes, sir."

"I want it done now. I intend to have his head before morning. Is that clear?"

"Yes, sir." Shinji gave a slight, cold bow and left, leaving his dead *kobuns* behind.

Takahashi rang his secretary. "Mrs. Sutton, call housekeeping for a cleanup." Then he sat down at his desk, careful to keep his tasseled loafers out of the pooling blood, and went back to scanning the search images, still fluttering across the mystery woman's face on the monitor, like leaves or the ghosts of falling leaves. . . .

Like memory.

Johnny was having a dream. He could tell it was a dream because it had a faded, grainy look, like an ancient home video. Real life is high-res.

In the dream Johnny was only a few feet tall.

In the dream walking was hard and involved a lot of stumbling.

In the dream Johnny was crossing a huge room, as big as a field, and on the other side of the room there was a desk, and it was a big desk, and at the desk there was a woman, and she was very pretty, even though she was looking down at some papers. He knew it was his mother because he couldn't see her face, but maybe if he got close enough she would look up and . . .

"Hey! What's the matter?"

There was a face. A woman's face. But a different kind of woman's face. White skin, red lips, black eye-shadow, spooky but almost beautiful in the spill-over from the fading flashlight. Johnny studied the face of the woman sitting beside him in the darkness.

"You looked so sweet," Jane said. "Then you looked sort of sad. Then you woke up, all suddenly."

"I was having a dream," Johnny said, still groggy. He looked around at the damp, dripping tunnel, leading off into the damp, dripping darkness. Then he sat up with a sudden cry. "I can't believe it! You let me sleep!?"

His anger took Jane by surprise. She lurched backward off the ledge, dropping her flashlight, knocking over her shoulder bag. Everything tumbled out.

"Damn!" she said. The flashlight picked out a weird array of weaponry, trash and gaudy junk strewn across the grimy concrete ledge: makeup, gum, `Ninja

99

throwing spikes, sunglasses—three pairs—credit cards under several names, nail files, a pearl-handled knife, a key chain.

Johnny picked up the key chain. There were no keys on it. It held only a miniature hand grenade and stainless-steel can opener.

"What's this?"

Jane grabbed the key chain and threw it, with everything else, back into the bag. "Some kind of antique, called a 'church key.' Where do you come off yelling at me, anyway?"

Johnny wiped his nose and studied the back of his hand. A smear of blood. "I *told* you," he said. "I'm in a hurry. I'm a dead man, and soon, if I don't get this stuff out of my head."

He slid off the ledge and onto his feet. He tried walking. It was barely possible. Jane shouldered her bag and fell in beside him. They trudged along the track, stepping onto the rails over the puddles, trying not to notice the shrill squeals and scurryings underfoot.

"How come you knew those—guys?" Johnny asked. "That helped us out."

"The Loteks?" said Jane. "I used to hang out with them. Before."

"Before what?"

"Just before. Besides, I might ask you the same. You seemed to know J-Bone."

"He's fucking world famous," Johnny said, as if that explained anything.

"As if that explained anything," Jane said. They walked on in silence, neither completely trusting the other, yet both wanting to trust someone, just once. Just for a while.

The tunnel curved on ahead, seemingly endless. *Wonder what we do when the light burns out*, Johnny wondered. He didn't ask. Didn't want to think about it. Too many small creatures underfoot.

"Ever sneak a look?" Jane asked.

"At what?"

"At the data you're carrying."

Johnny shook his head. "Usually there's a download code, like a lock, on it."

"When there isn't?"

"Wouldn't mean anything to me, anyway. Just data. Safer not to know anyway. Safer for me and safer for the client."

"How did they get it into your head?"

Johnny took her hand with the flashlight and pointed it toward the small jack behind his ear. "Implant."

Jane nodded. "Wetwired." She didn't have one herself but she had seen plenty of them.

"I had to dump a lot of long-term memory to become a courier," Johnny said, almost conversationally.

"Like what?"

"My childhood."

"All of it?" For the first time, Jane looked a little shocked.

"All of it."

"You can't even remember . . . your parents?"

Johnny shook his head. "There might be some residual stuff in there. Every once in a while I get a flash, or a dream."

"That's seriously fucking weird."

Johnny shrugged. "Maybe I didn't lose anything I wanted to keep. I needed the space for the job."

"But—no parents?"

"*You* got parents?"

"Sure," Jane said, a little too quickly. "One, anyway. Used to run a little greenhouse. Haven't seen him in years."

Johnny looked at her triumphantly, as if he had proven his point. Then compassionately, as if he wished he hadn't.

"Yeah. . . . Anyway," he said. "Anyway, I don't think about it."

Jane steadied the flashlight on the steel rail curving off into the darkness. "So what do you think about? When you're alone?"

"Right now," said Johnny, speeding up the pace, "I think about where I can go to log onto the Net."

"The Net? What for? You can dump the data that way?"

"No. But I can use the Net to find out where they faxed the download codes. I have one image, the Yakuza have one, maybe two. Maybe all three got faxed through and I can get hold of them somehow. It's a long shot but it's better than no shot—so let's get moving!"

One of the unofficial perks of Hooky's job as bartender at the Drome was the rent from the little back room. He rented it by the hour to the regulars who needed it—for sex or solitude, for intimidation or meditation, for blackmail or blackjack or whatever.

Hooky didn't care. It was none of Hooky's concern what people did with the room as long as they paid him, up front. He didn't even mind cleaning up after them. When the room was used by lovers the cleanup usually involved only a condom and maybe a roach and a Kleenex. When the crime orgs used it for what they called persuasion, the cleanup might involve a little blood, or even a severed finger or ear.

Hooky didn't mind that, either. He was a man of the world and he'd seen a thing or two in his time.

But this was going too far.

The Yakuza had hauled off their dead "muscle" with the spike in his forehead, but they had left Ralfi for Hooky.

The talent agent who had once used the half-round booth near the bar for his office was now in three pieces. His handsome little face still had a worried look on it. Too bad, Hooky thought; he'd been a good tipper. He swept and squeegeed the body parts into three plastic bags, dragged them out back, and dropped them into three separate Dumpsters.

No sense involving the cops; that just created paperwork, and if there's one thing bartenders hate, it's paperwork.

The blood on the floor came off with a mixture of Lysol, Murphy's Oil Soap and turpentine. The blood on the walls was more of a problem. The big smears toward the baseboards came off okay, but drops and gobbets were spattered almost all the way to the ceiling, and many of these had already dried.

Hooky was studying the problem, trying to decide whether it would be easier to scrub or to paint, when he heard the outside door to the bar open.

"Hey, we're closed," Hooky called out. He put down his mop and looked out. Crossing the now-empty dance floor was the man known locally as Street Preacher. He was carrying a little case with a door on it, like a small refrigerator.

"The priest and the prophet have erred through strong drink," said Street Preacher. "They err in vision, they stumble in judgment."

"Whatever," said Hooky. "I thought I locked up. How'd you get in here?"

Street Preacher set the little case on a table. On the side it said *CryoCarryAll*. He sat down beside it and continued declaiming:

"For all the tables are full of vomit and filthiness, so that there is no place clean . . ."

"You can say that again," said Hooky. He sat down at the table with Street Preacher and lit a cigarette. Street Preacher was a nut, but that was okay. Hooky was a bartender and bartenders are comfortable with nuts.

"Name?" asked Street Preacher.

"You know my name. Hooky."

The preacher leaned over and snagged a finger through Hooky's gold loop earring. "Are you saved, Hooky?"

Hooky gently, patiently removed the finger. "Not so's you'd notice it."

"Let me save you then. . . ." Street Preacher opened the door of the CryoCarryAll, and a cold, small fog rolled out onto the table. He grabbed Hooky's elbow and guided his stainless-steel prosthesis into the open door of the cryo-unit.

"Hey!" Hooky tried to pull away, but Street Preacher was strong. Incredibly strong.

Then Street Preacher pulled Hooky's prosthesis out of the cryo-unit and closed the door. He let go of Hooky's arm and asked, again: "Name?"

Hooky looked at his hook curiously; the prosthesis was white with frost, but unharmed. Did this nut think the cold would hurt him or something?

"You know my name, dammit!" He was beginning to regret sitting down with him.

"The girl," Street Preacher said.

"Huh?"

"The girl who took Ralfi's boy out of the back room." Street Preacher's voice had lost its dreamy tone. He took the inverted cross from around his neck and hefted it like a little hammer. "Who is she?"

"You think I keep track of half the lowlifes who come in here?"

Street Preacher smashed the cross down on Hooky's prosthesis. The supercold steel shattered like brittle glass.

"Man . . . !" Hooky jumped to his feet, staring unbelievingly at his ruined hook, in shards on the table. And looking at Street Preacher with a newfound fear.

This guy was serious.

As if to confirm Hooky's revelation, Street Preacher flicked the cross open, into a vicious nine-inch bowie.

He reached up and extended the blade eagerly, almost tenderly, along the top of Hooky's ear.

Hooky sat back down.

"Who's the girl?" Street Preacher asked again.

"Some wannabe. In here hustling for work."

"Name?"

"Jane."

"More."

"One of Spider's jobs."

"Spider?"

"Flesh mechanic. Implants and stuff. Cranked up her nervous system a little, you know. They say he was like a legit doctor before, had a license and everything."

"Where?"

"To find him. How should I know . . . I . . ."

Street Preacher put a little more pressure on the knife.

J-Bone had long eyes.

At the "receive" end, in the Passaic bridge hideout known as Heaven, he sat sprawled in a comfortable padded chair liberated from a long-forgotten prime-time news anchor, linked to the "send" end via a cellular nanovideo unit in a pair of binoculars, which were scanning the streets of Newark from a steel beam projecting from an abandoned building, part of the inextricable tangle of depreciated architecture that loomed over the Drome.

The nanovideo binoculars were wielded by two Loteks taking turns. Tibbs, a Lotek with braided hair and a belt festooned with knives, reluctantly gave up the binocs and lay back on the beam to light a cigarette and relax. His turn was over. Stump, too young to be missing a leg, but too old to waste time regretting it, eagerly picked them up—and struck paydirt.

Stump was as eager as Tibbs to please his leader, so he felt a thrill of excitement as the man they had been staking out emerged—finally!—from the darkened nightclub, carrying a small, square cooler with a door like a refrigerator.

"Whoa, Street Preacher's out," Stump said. "J-Bone, you copying?"

J-Bone was indeed copying. He was studying the scene on a bank of monitors, watching the long-haired man with the cryo-unit swing down the empty street.

Two young Loteks stood beside J-Bone, one on either side of his chair.

"Look at that son of a bitch," J-Bone said, as much to himself as to them. "Doesn't have a natural bone left in his body. So jacked up he oughta squeal when he walks. Takes that collection plate money and has himself shot up with Brazilian fetal tissue . . ."

"He really a preacher, J-Bone?" asked one of the Loteks.

J-Bone shrugged, as if to say that was the wrong question. "Motherfucker's got God and technology ass-backward. Kills people for money to keep that steeple over his head."

"Want us to follow him?" Tibbs asked, from the "send" end.

"Yeah, but be careful. Keep the fuck away from him. Crazy's okay but that dude's a little *too* crazy. . . ."

NINE

———■———

Darkness.

That's good.

One tiny red light blinking, high on the wall just inside the door.

That's good.

Johnny slipped his lock-picking tools into his pocket and stepped inside the door, with Jane right behind him. He reached up toward the blinking light and ran his fingers around the alarm box until he identified the make and model. Hohner-Daewoo.

Piece of cake. He counted four wires down from the top and pulled, just enough to break the connection without snapping the sheathing interlock.

The red light stopped blinking.

"You can turn the flashlight on," he said.

Jane did. "Slick," she said. "Where'd you learn that?"

"Summer job," said Johnny.

"Summer job doing what?"

"Breaking and entering." His eyes followed Jane's

107

flashlight beam around the room. They were in a computer repair shop. The shelves were jammed with boxes, spare parts, circuit boards, tangles of wires and chips, mixed with a few new boxes and cartons.

Johnny nodded, satisfied. "For starters, find me a SinoLogic 16," he said as he cleared a place on the workbench.

"A sign of *what?*"

"Never mind. I'll do it myself. Give me the light."

He began pulling parts off the shelves, muttering to himself: "Thomson eyephones . . . Sogo Seven data-gloves . . . GPL stealth module; good, they've got the upgrade. Burdine intelligent translator . . ."

Jane sat back in the darkness and watched as he pulled together the parts and assembled them on the bench. The SinoLogic 16 looked like an antique laptop, as big as a notebook and almost an inch thick. Johnny plugged the gloves into one of the serial ports, the goggles into another. That left one port.

He unraveled a length of phone cable and plugged one end into the third port—and the other into the wetware jack on the side of his head.

He seemed to have forgotten Jane was here. That suited her just fine. She felt almost happy as she watched him boot the machine, then pull the gloves on and the goggles down over his eyes.

Whatever happened now, it was all up to him.

The headache went away in cyberspace. Once he had opened the program and jacked in, Johnny felt a cool rush of virtual air; he knew it was all illusion but it felt good. It was like entering an air-conditioned theater on a hot summer day.

Amazing how much better he liked this universe. Cooler. Cleaner. A blue grid in a pearl gray space that curved away in a curve that wasn't a curve in every direction . . .

It was like flying. The grid rolled away under him as

he swung through it, "arms" extended just for the thrill of it. *Too bad you had to have a body,* Johnny thought. *Be great to just stay here all the time, where there's no pain, no want, no hungers.*

But forget all that: There was work to do. Shapes appeared ahead in the near distance, and Johnny swooped between them—triangles, heloids, octagrams, cerulean and magenta; followed by shapes less euclidean and colors from far out of the spectrum. Nothing looked familiar but he cruised on ahead, looking for landmarks; that was easier and quicker than cruising over into Helpspace, which was slower and often crowded these days.

There. The inverted Y of the Yakuza West Coast database loomed ahead. Johnny pushed on, bound for virtual north. He was tempted to soar unassisted between the East Coast and the PR net, but he felt wobbly and didn't know how good he would be after so long out of cyberspace. Plus he didn't know how long it would take in real time, and who knew what the girl was doing, sitting all alone in a dark, burglarized computer shop?

He flew past the Mill Valley Yakuza archive—ugly fucking thing!—and gatewayed into virtual north, toward the Puget Cluster, an entertainment and insurance diversicon. Instead of soaring, he slowed, and gophered through a series of small LANs and servers, business and edu modules, trying to read the numbers and shapes that elmed by, trying to guess which one might be connected across the Pacific.

There: Chinese characters! Johnny circled back in a long veronica and saw a half-round icon that could have been a tree stump or a fuel pellet, but what the hell did he care? He opened it with a touch and it unfolded like a flower, becoming an entire universe, with another universe inside it, and another nest-egged inside that one. *Straight hierarchy: a good sign.* He entered them all—open, open, open—a triangle, then a bell-shape, each becoming a universe, each unfolding to infinity all around him, as if glad to become a universe at last!

And then each gone—one after the other.

"What're you doing?" asked Jane. Her voice came from nowhere and yet everywhere, and Johnny answered as he binaried down into another expanding structure.

"Trying to get to China." *Straight through the Earth.* Flying straight through cyberspace's long curve. It was slow but not as slow as navigating straight across the sectored grid.

Aha. A small pyramid with an eye, a marker for one of the restricted access nodes of Pacific Rim Bell. Johnny laughed as he flew past, and turned it over, and zipped through the little window at the top. Expanding like space itself, rolling under him.

"What are you doing?" asked Jane. Or was it the same question, looped?

"Looking for a phone number." *Ahhhh* . . .

A hotel icon with Chinese characters flew by and Johnny slowed, turned and trailed after it, looped back in a slow veronica.

Inside was a scroll of numbers. Arabic, thank God. But they meant nothing as they flew off into infinity while Johnny watched.

"Fax charges," Johnny said aloud, his voice booming through the heavens.

"What?" asked Jane.

"Nothing," Johnny said. She was part of another universe. Johnny was good at living in two at once.

"Room 2727. 15 January, 2021."

A new line of data scrolled by. Still in Chinese.

"On-line translation," Johnny said, impatiently, his voice shaking the heavens again. *The program should have extrapolated that!* Should have picked that up. Then . . .

"Shit."

"What?" Jane's huge voice.

"Shit!"

"Shit what?" asked Jane.

Johnny was sitting at the desk, wired to the SinoLogic through the wetwire jack on the side of his head, as were his goggles and the oversized silver gloves he wore. His gloved hands—which had at first been extended outward as if soaring, or cybersoaring, and had then been held in front of him on the desk manipulating invisible objects—had suddenly stopped.

"It's a fucking all-night copy shop," he said.

"What are you talking about?"

"They were sending the fax to an all-night copy shop. In Newark."

"What fax?" Jane asked. But Johnny was gone again, his head turning from side to side, his hands opening and closing tiny invisible boxes.

Jane lit a cigarette and tried to think of something else. But she couldn't take her eyes off those silvergloved hands. It was spooky.

And sexy, in a way.

Johnny executed a neat little unloop escape, backing out of the Pacific Rim's net, closing one window after another as he soared backward through them until he glimpsed, like a curving LAN-scored shell, the grid of the matrix itself. Cyberspace was open here, except for a few faraway blocks of data, glowing with the heat of ghosting anodes as he soared past. He was getting his bearings again, finding the instinctual sense of direction that had made him one of the best of the "cowboys" when he had made this kind of run two, even three, times a month. He runiqued past a low-lying maze of glowing lines, veronica'ed back, and gatewayed in, watching the lines spread out before him like an accommodating lover, one blossom continuously opening. It was the airline reservations grid; through it he made the trans from "east" to "west" in microseconds. It spit him out high above the Seaboard, the giant half-lit jumble of icons that was the web of the Sprawl.

Newark was in there somewhere, in hundreds of different forms. Question: Which one did he want?

There was no time to experiment; he was looking for something familiar. He keyed onto the immense ICE-protected octaplex that was Seaboard Consolidated and dove straight in, trusting it to open before him, hoping that the shell he had booted was updated on its access charges.

Seaboard opened, folding him into another and then another universe. The web was gone, and he could hardly see for the blizzard of unorganized data falling around him. The Seaboard system had been up for sale for months and it looked like no one had bought it yet. The US grid had been falling apart when Johnny was a cowboy; he could see that things had gotten even worse since he had quit the game.

He pushed on, almost blind. The "snow" made stuff harder to find and easier to lose. In the past, when he had been in the business of deliberately losing data, that had been cool. Now it was a problem.

He runiqued past a few lighted edu LANs, too insignificant to fool with. He flew too low, using them to navigate, since he knew they would be aligned in the general direction of Jersey Bell.

He felt the slight *ping* of a whois ID check. *Odd.*

He flew on.

He didn't notice that one of the LANs was connected, by a glowing ribbon of virtual light, to an inverted pyramid on the horizon, the icon of the Yakuza intelligence database.

* * *

Some twelve miles away in "real" space, in the basement center of Yakuza intelligence, a goggled operator lifted his eyepiece, checked to see that no supervisor was scoping him, and dialed the number Shinji had given him, scrawled on a $100 bill.

"Found him," the operator said in a whisper. "A computer store, Eastgate Gridworks. 5326 Passaic Plaza, Sublevel Three."

Some ten miles from there, on the dark, rubble-strewn surface streets of Newark, a cruising limo with a discreet Y on the door hung a quick U and sped off in the opposite direction.

Toward Passaic Plaza.

He was play-gliding again. Jane found that the spookiest—when Johnny looked like a kid playing airplane, gloved hands outstretched, goggles straight ahead.

"Stop . . . !" Jane wanted to say. But didn't.

Johnny cruised along the edges of the phone net, WAISing through the feeders for an easy access in. Now that the chase was on he felt fulfilled, feral, finer than fine. All faculties engaged. It was like the old days when he had been a full-time "cowboy," the best on the Net.

There in the distance was the blue, ICE-protected cube of the Pentagon, smaller systems clustered around it in drab blues and grays. Johnny soared between the steepled icons of the university edu-banks, wimpled where they were connected bottom-to-bottom to the low-stacked boxes of the multinationals. The power company grid peeled off into the distance, but Johnny ignored it, doing a slow runique down through the nodes. He was looking for something much more homely; a small icon, almost LAN-sized.

There.

There it was. Looked promising. A small icon, document shaped, like the kind a proprietary sat-link might use.

With a touch he opened it and sailed inside. The universe opened like a flower with a little window at the center, and he veronica'ed down and touched it. It was like dancing!

He had stopped play-gliding. Now he sat up straight with his hands over the desk, palms facing together, like a potter shaping an invisible vessel. Now together, now apart, as if he were taking things apart and piecing them back together. As he worked, the graceful dance of his hands was offset by the awkwardness of his head, as the goggles pulled it now up, now down, now left, now right.

The peculiar combination of grace and awkwardness, ugliness and beauty, the jerky motions of the head and the smooth dance of the hands reminded Jane of something. . . . But of what?

She couldn't quite put her finger on it.

The old videos in music class, when she had been forced to attend school.

The teacher droning on about the greats from the past, so-called musical geniuses, mostly just noise to the kids.

Then the one she had genuinely loved, the one that had captured her soul, watching him play. One of the classical greats. Beethoven, Mozart, Charles . . .

That was it! Ray Charles.

Johnny in cyberspace reminded her of Ray Charles.

Beyond the first window was another window.

Johnny slipped in, stroking the menu as he went. Accounts, numbers, IDs, machine-terminal IDs.

That was it! The termination codes . . . all the machines had buffers.

They opened before him.

"Got it . . ."

Numbers scrolled down from heaven, across the sky. . . .

With a virtual nod Johnny transformed the ascii codes to letters. As they rippled into their new form, the scrolling slowed, but that was all right; he was getting closer. *Let's just hope the buffer was big enough.*

"Got it!"

Jane knew better than to answer this time; Johnny was talking to himself. He was playing what she thought of as the shell game again. Opening tiny, invisible boxes.

"The addresses are in the buffer, all the users . . . alphabetical . . .

"Now by date . . .

"Time . . .

"Length of document—three images; *that* has to be it . . .

"No!"

In spite of herself, seeing the anguish on his face, Jane answered: "What is it, Johnny?" He was so immersed in cyberspace that he didn't notice her hand on his shoulder.

"It's a fucking will-call. For a Dr. Allcome." *Sounds like a phony name!*

Johnny's hands closed in two fists, then extended outward again as if he were a gull about to take off.

At the end of the block, a limo rounded the corner. Slowly.

Its headlights were off. A small spotlight from the driver's side played across the building numbers. 5312, 5320, 5322.

* * *

115

Johnny unlooped the windows all at once and they propelled him backward, breathless, flinging him back out into the Net.

High high high. . . .

"Let's go, okay?" Jane's voice booming, filling the matrix like a new color, a little panicked. "This place is spookin' me."

"Gotta try one other thing," said Johnny.

"Thing?"

"Guy called Strike."

Johnny dropped, searching; idling up the Seaboard between the utilities grids, looking for the larger pyramid of the Sprint communications megatrust that linked Toronto and Detroit with the Sprawl. "Runs a BBS somewhere in this sector. Toronto, I think."

Boards were usually fanciful icons, not hard to find, but scattered, disorganized, no hierarchy. Anarchy. . . .

Johnny could have flown down and accessed in through one of the Sprint gateways, but that was too slow, involving him in myriad directories and protocol trees. Instead he trusted to instinct, runiquing down the ICE-encrusted pyramid of the Sprawl net until he saw a light that looked familiar.

He veronica'ed around it once, then took a chance and dove.

Just like Strike. A keyhole. Johnny gophered in. He was in a room with a raven sitting on a box.

"Who's there?"

Johnny felt a whois ID *ping*.

"Johnny! Get off my board, man. You're too hot. You're a hit waitin' to happen!"

Johnny moved the raven and opened the box and he was in a tower, looking out at a sunrise. The sun that came over the horizon was a smiley face. Grandiose nerd humor but Johnny was used to it. He wondered how he appeared to Strike. Probably just a generic "visitor" icon, a bird or a fish.

"You owe me, Strike," he said.

"I don't owe you that much!"

"I can crash you from here, Strike," Johnny bluffed. "I'm logged in through the New Jersey Bell satellite. If I flop without logging off clean I'll wipe your whole board . . ."

"You wouldn't do that . . . ?" Strike sounded unsure. Just enough.

"What's the word on the Net, Strike?"

"Find out for yourself, Johnny."

"Don't have time! What am I holding and why's the Yakuza after it?"

"Seriously, Johnny, I don't know. All I know is you've got a head full of Pharmakom data and the Yakuza want you bad."

Pharmakom?

Strike's smiley-sun image was about to answer when suddenly it began to morph. *What's this new trick?* Johnny wondered. But Strike's smiley face was frowning as it morphed . . . Must be the Loteks, thought Johnny, expecting J-Bone's wry visage to appear. But the resolution was too high for the Loteks. Strike's smiley face morphed into the face of a woman, a woman who was strange and yet, somehow, totally familiar. . . .

Johnny was sitting still for the first time. That was even spookier than waving his arms. And there was something about the silence outside that Jane didn't like.

It was quieter than quiet.

Then she realized what it was. The cats had stopped howling. Didn't sound right: Newark at night without the cats howling.

Jane got up and left Johnny at the desk, his hands still, his eyes in the goggles staring into cyberspace.

She walked to the front display window of the shop and looked out.

Nothing. Not even a cat.

The window extended a foot or so into the street. She rummaged around in her shoulder bag until she found a makeup mirror, wiped it clean, and used it to look around the corner and up the street.

Nothing there.

Down the street. And there it was. A Yakuza limo, moving slowly, too slowly. Headlights off.

It nosed into a parking space between two burned-out hulks of cars. It stopped.

Two men got out.

Men in long, black coats.

The woman was in her fifties, well-dressed, European, with *yin* and *yang* earrings. She wasn't Strike's doing, Johnny knew; he was strictly a cartoon dude. She wasn't Lotek, either. The resolution was too high. Something about her felt real, too real. Johnny found the keyhole and exited back, out of Strike's tower.

"Johnny . . . ?"

He stopped. "How do you know my name?"

She morphed into a full figure and extended what resolved itself into a hand. Johnny, against his better judgment, obeying some hidden yearning that came to him unbidden, moved toward her, back through the keyhole.

"How do you know my name?" he asked again.

But instead of answering, she disappeared; the universe disappeared.

"Move!"

Jane ripped the goggles off Johnny and threw them across the room. She pulled the jack out of the SinoLogic 16, leaving the cord dangling from Johnny's head.

Johnny sat watching her, dazed.

"Come on!" Jane said, in a loud whisper.

There was the sound of breaking glass. Johnny turned and saw the front door shatter inward. A hand reached in, turned the knob.

"How? Who . . . ?" Johnny tore off his gloves, still dazed.

"Yakuza," Jane said. She grabbed his collar and yanked him out of his seat, and he wondered, still dazed, *How could such a little girl be so strong?* She pushed him toward the back door with one hand, as she reached into her bag with the other.

The first man through the door was Shinji.

At the bottom of her bag Jane found the key chain with the grenade on it.

She pulled it loose and threw it.

Johnny fell against the back door where Jane had pushed him. Trouble has a way of waking you up, and he was no longer dazed. As a matter of fact, he felt clearer than he had felt in days.

He unbolted the door and was about to step out into the alley when he saw a carton on the shelf over his head.

INFOBAHN 3000. A handy hacker's tool.

"Jesus!" Jane said.

"Just this one item," Johnny pleaded as he grabbed the box and pulled it down just as Jane flew past him into the alley.

He followed, spinning around just in time to see Shinji catch the grenade Jane had tossed him.

With cold Yakuza presence of mind, Shinji tossed it out the front door to the man behind him, and hit the floor. His men were expendable; he wasn't.

Johnny flew around the corner, following Jane's footsteps, as the front blew off the store.

TEN

■

You can judge the health of a city by its malls.

Newark's were dark, dim, dingy, poorly ventilated, underutilized, crime-ridden, trash-encrusted, rat-infested, littered with paper and papered with litter, smelly, stygian, odoriferous, ominous, orwellian, dank, dangerous, echoing with unsavory elevator rock and buzzing with going-bad neon. In a word, dying.

The perfect place for two people on the run.

From the half-asleep, spike-haired surly teen at the Java & Pizza kiosk, Jane picked up two poly cups and carried them over to the picnic table where Johnny was sitting.

She set them down carefully; the table had one short leg and it rocked.

"Great! Now I'm a waitress," she said.

Johnny wasn't listening. He was taking the INFOBAHN 3000 out of its carton. He set it on the table in front of him. It had a small numerical keypad and a screen, and a short curly cord with a clip on the end for a phone card.

"What does it do?" Jane asked.

"What I tell it to do."

"Which is?"

"Breaking and entering," Johnny said.

He dumped the contents of his billfold onto the table. He straightened and shuffled the small stack of phone, bank and med cards. He dealt them out one by one, reading them like a tarot deck.

A disappointing tarot deck.

"I can't use any of these," he said, shaking his head. "The Yakuza found me by scanning the Net. They'll still be watching, looking for the first transaction."

"Your coffee's getting cold," Jane said.

Johnny seemed to notice her for the first time. But it was her shoulder bag he was noticing. He turned it over, dumping its contents on the table.

"Hey!"

Johnny pulled a phone card out of the pile. "Mind if I use this?"

Jane shrugged. He slipped the card into the clip on the INFOBAHN.

"Man owes me fifty thou and he's scamming my phone card," Jane said.

Johnny grinned. He got up and headed for the pay phone on the wall nearby. "And it's still our first date," he said.

Jane followed him, bringing both coffees.

"What do you mean, 'breaking and entering'?" she asked.

"Watch."

Johnny turned on the INFOBAHN 3000. An hourglass appeared in the small screen while it booted. He then inserted the clipped card into the pay phone. The dial tone came through a speaker on the INFOBAHN.

Johnny dialed 411. A graphic ideogram of a question mark holding a phone came up on the vidscreen of the pay phone.

"Information," came through the speaker.

"Could I have the number for Pharmakom Industries?" Johnny asked. "Their Newark branch."

"Please hold for the number," said the voice over the speaker. The question mark on the pay phone's vidscreen was replaced by a cartoon smile. "That number is 609-4253-6528."

Jane was scornful. "You don't need a little computer to get information," she said. "Or is the whole point to make it a speakerphone?"

"I said *watch,*" said Johnny. "I didn't say listen."

He pointed at the small screen on the INFOBAHN, then dialed 609-4253-6528 on the pay phone.

The number appeared on the screen of the INFOBAHN.

RINGING said the screen.

Then CONNECT.

A corporate logo came up on the screen.

"You have reached the offices of Pharmakom Incorporated," said the voicemail recording over the speaker. "A subsidiary of Pharmakombinat International. If you know the number of the section to which . . ."

Johnny pointed at the INFOBAHN screen while the voicemail droned on. A diagram of a phone tree appeared. Johnny scrolled through it. It was clearly an internal document. At least a third of the numbers were marked R. Several were marked RR. One was marked RR!!

Johnny punched the RR!! number into the keypad.

The voicemail quit and a live voice answered on the first ring. The face came up on the pay-phone screen. A young black man in a gray suit.

"That you already, Ben?" he asked.

"Pharmakom Security, I presume," said Johnny, into the phone.

The eyes on the screen grew wide even as the voice grew cool. "You have reached a double-restricted number. It is a federal offense for an unauthorized . . ."

"That's why I'm calling, pal."

"Who the hell is this?"

"Don't like surprises?"

"No. Not at all. What do you want?"

"Question is," said Johnny, "what *you* want. I happen to be holding 320 gigabytes of Pharmakom data."

The security man sat up straight. He glanced to one side as if alerting a partner.

"Don't bother sending somebody after me," Johnny said. "I'll be out of here in twenty seconds. I'll have to come to you."

"What is it you want?" the security man asked.

"I want your data out of my head. I've got one image of the download code. Can you get the other two?"

The security man looked offscreen again and then nodded, a little too eagerly. "Sure. No problem. Where can we meet?"

"I'll come to you," Johnny said.

"Okay. My office is at . . ."

"I have it right here," said Johnny, tapping the INFOBAHN screen. "Sit tight. Forty minutes. I'll be there."

"You're crazy!" said Jane. She was following Johnny up a long-dead escalator, toward the dusty solarium of the almost-deserted mall. "They're lying through their teeth. Pharmakom can't get the codes. They'll chop your head off!"

Johnny climbed faster. He didn't need to hear this. He was trying to convince himself.

"Maybe they're not lying," he said. "Maybe they intercepted the fax or something. They're professionals. They're corporate. They're not going to kill me."

123

"Corporate!" Jane spat. "So's the Yakuza *corporate.*"

They reached the top. The lower levels had been empty, but there were people here in the dusty upper atrium of the mall: the homeless and some late-shift workers getting off.

Johnny joined the thin stream of foot traffic. Jane followed, two steps behind.

"Listen, if you don't want to come with me, fine," Johnny said over his shoulder. "It's a business meeting. Not your kind of scene. If it works out, I'll get you the fifty thou I owe you. If it doesn't work out . . ."

"If it doesn't work out, you're dead," Jane finished for him.

Johnny stopped and turned on her. "I'm dead anyway if I don't get this shit out of my head!" he shouted. The sparse crowd parted and made room for them. Johnny's voice boomed, echoing down from the roof, awakening a flock of starlings who flew in crazy circles looking for a way to escape.

Jane stepped back, startled by Johnny's vehemence.

He turned on his heel and walked off. She raised a trembling hand and called out after him:

"H-hey. Listen! This guy, Spider? H-he used to be, like, a doctor, you know? He could, like, fix you, maybe, your h-head . . . ?"

Johnny stopped. There was something about the sound of her voice. It was almost frail. He turned.

Jane was leaning over, her knees knocking, as if she had lost control of her legs.

"Hey. What's with you?"

"I'm all right. I just—"

She pitched forward. He was already running toward her and he managed to catch her before she hit the ground.

The late-night crowd parted around them, as if they were a rock in a stream.

124

"Jesus," Johnny said. "You're sick! You strung out or what?"

Jane shook her head, too violently, trying to pull herself together by sheer force of will. "I'm not, no . . ."

"You've got NAS," Johnny said, his voice almost a whisper. Involuntarily, he let go of her, then caught her again before her head hit the floor.

Jane's eyes rolled back in her head. "Spider. . . . He's got a drug that helps me . . ."

"No, goddam it. I've got a *meet!*"

"Place not far from here, dead end of . . ."

"I can't deal with this. Not now. Understand?"

Jane nodded, clenching her teeth.

"Whatever it is, you're sidelined till after I make this meeting. Right? *Comprendo? Capiche?*"

No answer. Johnny looked at his watch, then looked up as if pleading at the passersby. None of them looked down.

"Hey, can you hear me?" he asked.

Jane's eyes were closed. She was starting to tremble, faster and faster, more and more violently.

"Shit!" Johnny said, picking her up in his arms and starting for the door.

Cities are like arctic tundra molds, spreading out and drawing back, expanding and contracting with the seasons, except the seasons that affect them are not the solar light cycles of biological growth and decay, but the deeper, longer sequences, the generations-long rhythms of war, riot, prosperity, uncertainty, celebration and demolition.

It may be that these cycles are as diurnal as the seasons, but depend on some greater, more mysterious orbits, the great wheel of the galaxy or of the universe itself, not just the sun.

Newark, in one of its earlier expansions, had littered a tidal meadow with taverns and factories, plank roads and slums, then pulled back and left them all to bleach like shells in the sun. Decades later the city had come back with landfills and toxic dumps, rerouting the riverine marshes with low ranges of mountains made of orange peels, scrap paper and the colorful hard-shell corpses of cars. Then it had pulled back once more.

The road to Spider's garage had been patched together out of driveways, parking lots and entrance and exit ramps for primordial parkways. It wound through a concrete reef of shattered condos (decorated with a few lights as people had moved back in, fleeing the receding glacier that was central Newark); across the lot of a stadium that had been blown up by terrorists for a long-forgotten cause; switchbacked along the base of a contoured mountain of generations of compacted garbage.

The road was gravel, then plank, then concrete, then asphalt, then mud. Then gone.

Dead end. "This is the place?" Johnny asked.

No answer. Jane, who had given the instructions to the cabbie, lay sleeping, with her head on Johnny's shoulder; but it was not a peaceful sleep. Her teeth chattered and she shivered as if in the grip of a storm only she could see and feel.

"You promised a hundred bucks," said a voice from the front of the cab.

"Yeah, yeah." Johnny dug a piece of gum— probably left by an angry fare—out of the slot in the pay console and swiped his card through.

"That's it? That's fucking *it?*"

"The hundred includes the tip, pal."

Johnny got out and pulled Jane after him. She woke and tried to stand but her knees were knocking; her legs were trying to fold up under her.

Johnny reached behind him to shut the door of the cab, but it was already rolling, almost taking his hand with it. It made a U-turn and roared off into the night, the acceleration slamming the door.

"Well, here we are, Jane," Johnny said. "I hope."

There was only one building, down at the end of the street. It was a rough, single-story shed apparently constructed from scraps of billboards ("Drive One Today"), fiberglass sheets, and mysterious, official white-lettered on green signs facing in every direction:

NEXT RIGHT
REST AREA
14C
HOLLAND TUNNEL

Johnny half-carried, half-walked Jane to what appeared to be the front of the building. It was, in its own squat way, formidable: a low, rectangular fortress with no apparent door, no windows. Light was leaking out through the seams, and Johnny could hear machinery inside. But where was the entrance?

He banged on a green metal sign; it boomed like summer thunder.

He stopped. He heard a whining sound above him.

Johnny looked up and saw a crude video/intercom unit wedged under the roof and secured with duct tape. The video camera whined as it scanned jerkily from side to side.

A voice came through the intercom:

"If you aren't expected, you aren't invited. So fuck off, okay?"

Johnny backed up, pulling Jane with him; he held her in his arms, waiting for the videocam to come back around.

It stopped on her.

"She says you know her," Johnny called out.

"Janey?" said the voice on the intercom.

"Get down here, man! Open the fucking door. She's sick!"

127

Jane opened her eyes and looked around. "H-hey . . . Spider, babe . . . I . . ."

She started to thrash. Johnny set her down, let her stand alone. It was hideous. She started walking in a circle around one leg. "Spider, I think I . . ."

She tried to raise her arms but they seemed pinned. She fell to her knees.

An engine groaned somewhere inside the crude fortress, and a sign that read LAST EXIT BEFORE TOLL began to rise slowly straight up. Without waiting for it, a tall man in a filthy lab coat ducked under and knelt beside Jane.

"Spider . . ." rasped Jane. She began to choke.

Spider looked up at Johnny as if seeing him for the first time.

"Your wallet, man!"

Johnny backed up, disappointed but not surprised: This dude was a regular doctor, demanding an insurance card or payment up front, just like the rest.

"Your wallet!" Spider shouted. "Get your wallet in her mouth, before she bites her tongue off!"

Johnny whipped out his wallet, spraying credit cards all over the muddy ground. He handed it to Spider, who wedged it between Jane's chattering teeth.

She bit down hard; it seemed to relax her.

Her eyes rolled back in her head.

Spider picked her up and slung her over his back in a fireman's carry and started through the door, hitting a button as he passed.

The LAST EXIT BEFORE TOLL door started creaking back down.

Johnny scrambled to pick up as many of his credit cards as possible, then hit the dirt and rolled under the door just before it closed.

"Janey!" Spider was crooning. It sounded like a wail for the dead.

ELEVEN

The first thing Johnny noticed was the gloom. It was everywhere, like a substance: It covered the floor, it was stacked in the corners, it layered the air, it dripped off the walls like cheap paint. The room was filled with it, as if Spider were a collector of glooms and this was his precious stash.

The room seemed as stuffed with gloom as Johnny's head was stuffed with the painful data that was surely, and not so slowly, killing him. . . . *What am I doing here?*

"Look, man, I gotta run," Johnny said, eyeing the now-closed door behind him.

"Shut up and help me get her on the table."

As his eyes adjusted to the gloom, Johnny saw that the shed was a garage with a dirt floor. A stepvan with a spider image painted on its side was parked against the far wall. At the center of the garage was a table set up on concrete blocks.

Johnny helped Spider lay Jane on the table, as gently as possible. Spider reached overhead and switched on a light.

It was as bright as a sun—an operating room light.

The table was stainless steel—an operating room table.

On rollaways and trays to either side of the table were tools, some shiny, some dark with what could be either oil or blood. Or dirt. They were a strange mixture of automotive and surgical tools. To Johnny the whole place looked like a cross between an abortion clinic and a transmission shop.

Spider moved fast. He had already peeled off Jane's sleeveless leather jacket and was cutting up the front of her black tank top with a pair of blunt emergency room scissors. She lay face up, under the glaring three-lensed light, still shaking uncontrollably.

"Look, man," said Johnny. "I'm late for a very important appointment, and . . ."

"Shut up and give me the muscle relaxant," Spider said. "Behind you. The red one."

Johnny turned and rummaged through a jumble of wrenches and scalpels, vacuum testers, syringes, bearing pullers and catheters until he found a pistol-like plastic injector. It was red. It looked vaguely medical.

He handed it to Spider, who took it with one hand while with the other he finished cutting off Jane's tank top. He pulled it out from under her, wadded it up, and tossed it into the darkness with one swift motion.

Johnny was surprised, somehow, to see that Jane had a rose tattooed just under her left nipple. It didn't seem to fit her tough-guy image. Her breasts were small, and perfect, and somehow alarming. Johnny found himself staring. Jane seemed at once very naked and very unashamed. It was as if, even unconscious, she were telling him, "I'm a woman. Got a problem with that?"

I don't have a problem with that, he answered, in his head.

But Jane wasn't entirely unconscious. "Where's

Johnny, is he . . . ?" Jane tried to sit up, eyes wide open but unseeing.

"Johnny? Hold on, girl." Spider pushed her back down, pressed the nozzle of the injector against the skin between her breasts, and pulled the trigger. Jane closed her eyes as the muscle relaxant hit. She stretched her arms up over her head, almost like a cat. She didn't shave under her arms. She yawned, her tongue as pink as her nipples, which Johnny had noticed were very, very pink.

Looking up and finding Spider's black eyes, behind huge horn-rims, trained on him, Johnny blushed. For himself or for Jane, he didn't know.

"It's NAS, right?" he asked. To change the subject.

"Yeah," said Spider. "Nerve Attenuation Syndrome. The black shakes. Like half the people walking around this goddam town."

He put the instrument away, in a drawer this time, in the top of a red *Snap-on* cabinet. Then he turned back to Johnny, his eyes narrowing with suspicion and jealousy.

"And who are you, anyway? *Johnny?* You a client or a boyfriend?"

Johnny shrugged but didn't answer. It was too complicated; he didn't know what to say.

"Name's Johnny."

"Johnny who-the-hell?"

"Just Johnny."

"Understand one thing, 'Just Johnny,' okay?"

"What's that?"

"It wasn't my work that got Jane fucked up this way," Spider said. "I do augmentations and amplifications, and my work is *clean*. Besides, you don't get NAS from aug and amp jobs. That's just a myth."

"So what does cause it?"

Spider smiled wryly. "Causes it? The world causes it."

131

He walked from the operating table across the room to a cluttered workbench, and gestured toward a floppy drive, a gutted answering machine, a dusty fax, a telephone.

"*This* causes it . . . *this* causes it . . . *this* causes it. . . ."

He stalked around the garage, picking up odd items of clutter and setting them down, while Johnny watched, amazed and more than a little wary.

"*This* causes it . . . and *this* causes it . . ." Spider raged on, picking up a circuit board, a shielded cable, then tossing them into the shadows.

He grabbed Johnny by the shoulders:

"*You* cause it. *I* cause it. NAS is about information *overload*, man! All the electronics around you, poisoning the airwaves. Technological fucking civilization!"

Spider let go of Johnny. He looked around as if trying to remember where he was. He looked at Jane, dozing like a bare-breasted Sleeping Beauty under the light, and his voice dropped. "But we still have all this shit because we can't live without it. Now let me do my work. . . ."

He picked up a wicked-looking electric drill.

"Your work?"

"Don't worry, man! I'm not going to turn her into a boy. I'm putting a tapedeck in my stepvan."

It was still early, hardly midnight. Johnny was only an hour late for his appointment.

Maybe they're still waiting for me, he thought. *Maybe if I call . . .*

Jane had said Spider had no phone. But there were ways to get around that.

Johnny looked around the garage. The whine of a drill came from the stepvan against the far wall. Jane lay on the table, sleeping peacefully. *Whatever that relaxant is, it works,* Johnny thought. Taking one last, lingering look at Jane's breasts—a look almost as intimate as a touch—Johnny turned off the light and left her sleeping peacefully, cloaked in the gathering folds of Spider's collector gloom.

Quietly, careful not to alert Spider, Johnny rummaged through the junk on the workbench until he found a phone, or half a phone. He clipped it to a comm board pulled from a gutted fax, then plugged it into the back of the computer that ran the intercom, and plugged that into the SCSI port of his INFOBAHN 3000.

A dial tone. Success! Spider wasn't on the phone lines, but he was wired into the Net by cellular satellite.

Johnny dialed Pharmakom's main number. That would put him on the tree, where the INFOBAHN would automatically hack him through to security.

The now-familiar logo came up on the intercom screen.

"You have reached the offices of Pharmakom Incorporated," said the voicemail recording. "A subsidiary of Pharmakombinat International. If you know the number of the section to which . . ."

The logo was becoming wavy. At first Johnny thought his world-class headache was worsening, and he grabbed his temples.

But the problem wasn't in his head. It was on the screen. The wavering Pharmakom logo was morphing into another image.

A woman.

Somehow familiar.

The same well-dressed, middle-aged woman with *yin* and *yang* earrings who had morphed onto Strike's BBS.

"Johnny," she said.

She knows my name?

"I need to talk to you."

133

Johnny grabbed his head. It had to be in his head. This was the synapse leakage, the overload, finally getting him. It *had* to be. . . .

"I'm losing it," he moaned.

"Losing! Yes!" the woman said. "We have all lost so much!"

"I'm fucking seeing things. I've got to get this dataload out of my head!"

"Yes, Johnny, *seeing* things. That's good. Remembering things. Try to remember it all, how it all felt. How each thing smelled and tasted. When we stayed at the Plaza, you used to like to put your tongue against the iron railing and look across the park, Johnny. You told me it made a taste in your mouth like blood."

Johnny backed away from the intercom monitor, almost tripping over a box of transmission parts on the floor. "Who are you?" he demanded. "Where are you getting this from?"

"Let me take you home, Johnny. . . ."

"What the *fuck* do you think you're doing?" Spider's angry voice broke through Johnny's concentration like a pistol shot. Spider stood in the doorway to the stepvan, holding the drill like a pistol.

"Nothing."

The intercom monitor was black. The woman was gone. A dial tone hummed over the speaker.

Johnny hung up the INFOBAHN and the dial tone cut off. "Just looking," he said.

"Don't touch anything!" said Spider. "I have my reasons for staying off the Net, okay?"

"Okay, okay!" Johnny sat down, his head in his hands. It was too late anyway. He was screwed. A new wave of pain crested, broke, receded.

"Hey?"

Johnny looked up.

Spider was standing over him, still holding the drill. Looking at him intently. "You got it too, huh?"

134

"Me? NAS? No," said Johnny. "Something else."

"You've had brain work, right?"

"You might say that. Silicon implants. Neural overlays. Memory augmentation."

"All that here in Newark, Just Johnny? Kinda upscale for us, you know."

"Got mine in Singapore."

"And it's gone bad? What's the deal, Just Johnny?"

Johnny looked Spider up and down, a look somewhere between the look one gives a god and a demon.

A last-hope look.

"I got this problem," said Johnny. "Up here. Maybe you *can* help me."

One good thing about erasing all your childhood memories, Johnny thought wryly, *is that you also erase your childhood terror of dentist's chairs.*

He was sitting in a dentist's chair in Spider's fortress-shed. Spider, wearing a filthy white lab coat over even filthier jeans, rotated the chair by hand as he did the brain-scan. It was set on a wet corner of the floor, and the chair rocked slightly as it turned, making sucking sounds in the muck.

In the center of the room, behind them, Jane still slept peacefully on the operating table, facing up into the darkness.

Spider whistled as the first image came up on his brain-scan monitor. "Man, they did some serious shoehorning to get that stuff in," he said, adjusting the resolution with one hand while he raised the chair slightly with the other.

"Let's skip the technical critique, okay?" Johnny said. "I just need a little help here."

"A little help? You don't know the half of it, Just Johnny." Spider turned the chair so that Johnny could see the X-ray image of his head on the monitor.

There was the outline of his skull; there was the wetwire socket and the familiar hardwire implant crouched inside the gray shadow of his brain like a fetal stowaway. And all around it were dark streaks, spreading tendrils penetrating deeper and deeper into the gray. *Looks like the site of an oil spill,* Johnny thought.

"Must hurt like hell," Spider said.

"Think I need you to tell me that? I got 320 gigs in there."

"320 gigs!" Spider looked at the monitor and then at Johnny, suddenly very interested. "320, you say? What is it exactly? What kind of data?"

"Haven't got a clue. And don't give a damn. Just want it out of there before it kills me."

Spider continued turning the chair, which rocked and sucked at the soft mud.

Outside, in the night, there was another sucking sound.

Boots in the mud.

Pointy-toed cowboy boots, with a silver cross on each toe.

Street Preacher looked at the instructions Hooky had given him just before Hooky had died.

Died such a terrible death.

Good thing there was life everlasting. Forgiveness of sins and all that. Hate to think of a world without mercy, Street Preacher thought.

There were no street numbers. The ugly little building up ahead was the last building on the street.

There were no windows. No doors. It looked like the scrap pile of a sign shop.

PEPSI'S THE ONE
NEXT RIGHT
LAST EXIT BEFORE TOLL

Could this be the place?

Street Preacher saw something gleaming in the half-light from the mercury-vapor lamp.

He bent down to pick it up.

It was a credit card.

He rubbed the mud off and read the name.

A common name, but wasn't sin common?

Wasn't death common?

Steel teeth gleamed.

Street Preacher smiled as he walked on toward the ugly little building, as slowly and as inexorably as destiny itself.

"You guys . . . doin' okay?"

Jane was standing at the edge of the circle of light. Wrapped in a sheet, she looked angelic and impish all at once.

"We're doing fine," Spider said, before Johnny could speak. "Good girl, Janey. You brought him to the right place."

"You can fix him?"

"I don't know." Spider reached up and adjusted the monitor again while he held Johnny's head steady with his other big, long-fingered, spidery hand. "With this kind of seepage, even if I *can* work a download, I'm not sure the product will be coherent."

"Fuck the product," Johnny said. "I just want it *out.*"

"Hold still! I wish it were that simple."

"Allcome," Johnny said. "That's who was going to pick up the download code. Dr. Allcome. Ever hear of a Dr. Allcome?"

"Uh . . . Holcomb?" Spider said, a little too nervously. Johnny felt the hand on his head tense.

Johnny looked up and watched Spider's face and repeated, "Allcome. Like ALL COME."

Spider shrugged. "Maybe."

Johnny jumped out of the chair. "You *know* who it is, don't you? Where is he? Who is he?"

Spider had regained his composure. "I said 'maybe.' Why do you want to see him, anyway?"

"What're you talking about? It's fucking life and death!" Johnny shouted.

"C'mon, Spider," Jane said.

Spider looked from Jane to Johnny, then put his arm around Jane. Protectively, and perhaps a little more. . . .

"Don't worry, Janey," he said. "I'll see that Just Johnny gets to see who he needs to see. Meanwhile, you need some rest. Some downtime. Here."

Janey pulled away from him and stood beside Johnny. "No way! He's my client."

"Just tell me where to go," Johnny said.

Spider looked at the two of them, with something like longing in his eyes. Then it was gone. He looked past them both to the stepvan against the far wall of the garage.

"Better than that," he said. "I'll drive you."

Street Preacher heard voices.

He approached the ugly little building and leaned against the front wall.

Listening.

A man . . . two men.

A woman.

He smiled.

As patient as Job, as relentless as God, he circled the building, looking for a door.

Or at least a window.

Johnny hung onto the door frame of the stepvan and stared out into the gloom of the garage as Spider turned the key and the ancient starter wheezed.

Curr-ankh—

Curr-ankh—

Curr-ankh—

Jane dropped her sheet and modestly turned her back to slip on her sleeveless leather jacket, retrieved from the operating table. Johnny's eyes met hers as she turned back around, and he reached out. She caught his hand and pulled herself up into the stepvan.

Curr-ankh—
Curr-ankh—
Curr-ankh—

. . . Faster and faster . . .

Johnny heard a hissing. He leaned out and looked up. The bag on the top of the stepvan was inflating.

Curr-ankh—
Curr-ankh—
Vvvrrroooom!

The engine started, backfired, stopped.

Curr-ankh—
Vvvrrroooom!

It caught again. No backfires this time.

It slowed to a rough, loping idle, like a steeply cammed street 'rod.

Spider jumped out and unhooked the hose from the now-bulging bag on top of the stepvan, and hung it onto a hook on the wall. A foul, familiar odor filled the garage.

Jane frowned. "Who farted?"

"What do you run this thing on, anyway?" Johnny asked.

"Methane," said Spider, sliding back into the driver's seat. "I pipe it in direct from the landfill. Beats waitin' on Exxon."

He hit a button on the wall and a motor whined overhead.

The wall in front of the van began to rise upward in short jerks.

Street Preacher heard a grinding noise.
Then a popping.
He frowned.

He heard the sound of an engine, starting, racing, idling.

Then a whine, and the creak of a door opening, around on the other side of the shed.

Street Preacher's steel teeth gleamed. He was smiling.

He flicked open his silver-inlaid, custom-made crucifix-switchblade bowie.

Still smiling, he began to run.

Slowly, careful not to hang the gas bag on the raised door, Spider maneuvered the stepvan out into the night.

He hit the remote and the door began to close behind him.

He dropped the stepvan into drive and turned onto the street, just as—

"Shit!"

A large figure under a gleaming shock of white hair, with silver toes on muddy boots and gleaming knife in hand, came hurtling around the corner of the shed.

"Shut the door!" said Spider, flooring the accelerator.

"There is no door!" said Johnny.

"Shit! I forgot," said Spider. "Well, hang on!"

Jane fell back into Johnny's arms as the stepvan spun its wheels and then charged forward.

The figure Spider had recognized as Street Preacher angled across the muddy lot, seeking to cut off the stepvan before it started down the hill.

Spider fishtailed. The engine screamed.

Street Preacher leaped for the open side door, his knife in his teeth.

Spider ducked—then saw the windshield shatter as Street Preacher hit it with his chin.

Crrracckk!

Street Preacher bounced off the shattered glass and rolled into the mud as Spider's rear wheels found stone, then asphalt. The stepvan, careening like a runaway stagecoach, sped down the hill.

Johnny leaned out and looked back. A body lay in the street. It was already getting up.

"What the fuck was that?" Johnny asked.

Spider drove with one hand and hung on with the other, leaning out so that he could see around the spiderwebbed windshield.

"You don't want to know," Spider said.

Street Preacher got up.

He found his knife, closed it and hung it, inverted, back around his neck.

He wiped the blood off his face with his hands, then wiped his hands in his hair.

He started down the street at an easy lope, following the stepvan.

His steel teeth gleamed red in the taillights.

He was still smiling.

TWELVE

A match.

FIRST MATCH.

He had found her.

Takahashi sat alone in his dark office. The moonlight filled the Zen garden outside, but his attention was on the monitor on his desk in front of him.

On it was a woman's face.

CONTINUE SEARCH FOR SECOND MATCH?

An attractive, middle-aged woman wearing *yin-yang* earrings; not a live transmission but a still picture, a file photo.

He pressed NO.

He had found her.

Using a selective, semivalent, cross-platform multi-table query, a relational sorting of the 5.8 billion-strong portion of the earth's elusive, evanescent humanity that was listed, finger- and voice-printed, photo-ID'ed, DNA-scanned, accessed and integrated; after mixing, matching, sorting, sifting, measuring and cross-checking face after face with Yakuza's dedicated security 34ii25-based, double-integrated relational database—he had found her.

And now he knew why the search had been so difficult; why it had taken so long to come up with a positive identification of the woman who had been appearing sporadically on his phone and computer monitors, attempting to communicate with him.

He had mistakenly, foolishly, naively instructed the program to search among the living.

Anna Kalman, the voiceover read. *Late CEO of the multinational . . .*

"Late!" Takahashi said, shaking his head in wonderment.

. . . Pharmakombinat Industrie, Zurich. Born 1 August 1965. Died 3 September 2015.

"Died. Six years ago!"

She was scanned in and imprinted to Pharmakom's neural net installation in Zurich prior to the onset of morbidity.

"Imprinted!"

Her neural net persona has Swiss citizenship under the Artificial Intelligence Law of 2006. She advises the current board from—

Takahashi turned away from the monitor and looked toward the garden, the source of all his peace. What little peace he had been able to find lately.

"A ghost!" he said to himself. "She's a ghost."

Newark's Union Station was once considered one of the architectural wonders of the Northeast, a four-story art-deco masterpiece celebrating the alliance between the great houses of commerce and culture, the stormy and fecund but regrettably short-lived marriage of transportation and art. The station's great arched windows faced a small park once filled with sycamore and plane trees in the European style, which had all long ago been cut down and burned for firewood, also in the European style.

The long, curved driveway once used for cabs and limousines was now empty, except for an ambulance or two. Until Spider's stepvan pulled in and screeched to a halt in front of the station's big revolving door.

"What are we doing here?" Johnny asked, but he got no answer.

Spider seemed preoccupied. He shut off the engine and pocketed the keys. The gas bag on top of the truck began to slowly sag, now that the engine's modified flywheel was no longer pumping ambient air to pressurize the methane.

Spider searched in his pocket and pulled out a crumpled dollar. He tossed it into the crowd of urchins that had gathered around the stepvan to beg, and called out:

"Watch my wheels! I don't want nobody slitting the gas bag for kicks."

Jane and Johnny followed Spider into the revolving door.

It spun them into a scene from Dante.

The first thing Johnny noticed was the noise. The inside of the station was filled with sound, just as Spider's garage had been filled with gloom. The sounds were sounds of pain and death: moans and screams, dying wails and death rattles, cries and pleas, oaths and sobs. The sounds all issued from people, most of whom were prone. They lay on old wooden waiting-room benches, on stretchers on the floor, on beds against the cold marble walls. Some were with their families, others were alone. A few sat propped up, gathered around dim TVs, jerking spasmodically. Others lay back and stared up at the darkness that gathered toward the high ceiling like smoke, waiting for death to come and rescue them. The few erect, moving figures were nurses and orderlies in stained, ragged uniforms, stooped with fatigue, who wove their way between the ranks of patients, pulling carts of medications, pushing IVs and oxygen tanks, hurrying from one hopeless scene to the next.

Johnny stopped just inside the door, overcome first by the noise, then by the smell, then by the sight. He had never seen such suffering; or if he had, he had avoided looking closely at it.

He felt something brush his hand; it was Jane's hand. He took her hand and held it, and together they stared into the chaos, neither wanting to speak or look at the other.

Meanwhile, Spider was busy. He took a filthy white smock off a hook and put it on over his coveralls.

"Spider, thank God you're here," said a young black nurse, shoving a clipboard into his hand. Her white dress was almost clean, and she might have been beautiful if she hadn't looked so exhausted.

Spider studied the clipboard and shook his head. "This many, just since last night?"

The nurse nodded.

"What's going on here?" Johnny asked.

"NAS," Spider said. "We're the only treatment center around. Since the government gave up."

He pointed around the room at the nurses and orderlies hurrying around; judging by their jerky movements, some of them seemed to be suffering from the disease themselves.

"Did you know about this?" Johnny asked Jane in a whisper. She shook her head.

"All volunteers," said Spider.

"Like you?" asked Jane.

"Like me," said Spider. Then he was gone, threading his way through the mattresses and stretchers, stopping here and there to look at a patient, or just to share a word. Johnny followed, amazed at the outlaw doctor's transformation from mad scientist to a sort of urban Albert Schweitzer.

"Is this where we find Dr. Allcome?" Johnny asked.

145

Spider laughed wryly, talking back over his shoulder as he continued his rounds. "'Dr. Allcome' is the name we page in hospitals if we've got a major problem and don't want to spook the civilians."

"Huh?"

Spider stopped, turning to face Johnny and Jane, dropping his voice into a simulation of an announcement:

"'Dr. Allcome to Ward Seven.' That sort of thing. We all drop everything and haul ass to Ward Seven or wherever. Usually it means we got a crazy, somebody violent. It means we need all the help we can get, fast."

"But I saw it on the fax buffer," Johnny said. "It was the pickup for the download code."

"I know," said Spider.

He ducked under a flap, into a shed partitioned off with plywood and canvas from the main area of the terminal. Johnny followed, with Jane right behind him.

"What do you mean, 'you know'?" demanded Johnny.

Spider switched on a light. The shed was an improvised operating room, in which Spider's inventive hand was evident: Homemade and jerry-rigged contraptions were hung on one wall, along with antique medical equipment—and more modern apparatus, which appeared to be borrowed or stolen.

Spider closed the flap behind them, and turned to face Johnny and Jane as if making a formal announcement.

"I know because that fax was for us," he said.

"What?" Johnny exclaimed. "Who's *us*?"

"The NAS underground. People who try to keep this place going. People like me. Get on the table here."

Johnny backed up a step; he bumped into Jane. "Why?"

Spider was throwing switches on an electronic console. A light gleamed on a monitor set against a wall. "Come on, Just Johnny. Don't be a bigger asshole than you have to be, okay? Lie down."

"I don't know . . ."

"You want that stuff out, right?"

Johnny lay down.

Spider pulled a video scanner on a segmented extension down from the wall. He placed the helmet-shaped scanner over the top of Johnny's head.

The monitor showed concentric circles. All the circles were closed, and none of them connected. A dark stain spread over them, and it seemed to be moving.

Jesus! No wonder my head hurts, Johnny thought.

Spider shook his head. "No access code."

"Except for one image out of the three," Johnny said. "I have it right here in my pocket."

He started to sit up but Spider stopped him with a touch on the shoulder. "It won't help. What did they use, random images?"

"Yeah. From the TV."

"Shit." Spider fished through a drawer until he found a CD-ROM disk. He loaded it into the console and hit the keyboard.

"I have a library of decryption programs here. Shareware, but who knows? We could run them, see if we get anything."

"You can break the code, right, Spider?" Jane asked. She perched up on the table and sat beside Johnny. She sat on her hands to keep them from shaking.

"If I get lucky," Spider said. *"Real* lucky." Touching her forehead gently, he tilted her face up and looked into her eyes. "But Janey, honey, you need some rest. Big time. You really should lie down."

Jane lay down beside Johnny.

147

"Not here, goddam it!"

She sat up, surprised at his anger. Then she recognized it as jealousy. "Sorry . . ." she began.

But Spider had already turned away. He was watching the monitor as each of the shareware decryption programs circled, searched for a way through the code barrier. Each was turned back with the same message:

UNABLE TO READ.

UNABLE TO READ.

UNABLE TO READ.

"Shit."

Johnny sat up on one elbow. "No dice?"

Spider pushed away the video scanner angrily. It hit the wall with a soft *clunk*. "No dice."

"What does that mean?"

"It means zip, zero, zilch, *nunca, nada . . .*"

"Does that mean you can't get the data out?"

"I can get it out." Spider was washing his hands with green soap. Surgical soap.

Johnny didn't like the look of it. He sat up. "How?"

Spider dried his hands on a bloody towel. "With a general anesthetic, a cranial drill, and a pair of forceps."

Johnny swung his feet off the table. "You're joking, right?"

Spider shook his head. "No joke."

"He'll *die!*" Jane protested.

"It's going to kill him anyway, and soon," Spider said to her. Then he turned to Johnny. "I take it out and you'll survive. You'll lose some fine-motor skills, you might not be able to remember anything for longer than three minutes, but you'll survive."

"Fuck that," said Johnny. "And fuck you."

He stood up, but Spider pushed him back onto the operating table.

"Let me tell you something, Just Johnny," Spider said. "Let's start with what you got inside there."

148

He tapped Johnny's head and Johnny winced. "Let's start with what it's worth to the world."

Spider paused, looking at Jane and then back to Johnny. Then he said, "What you're carrying is the cure for NAS."

Johnny studied Spider's face, looking for signs he was being bullshitted.

He didn't find any.

"You're telling me that what's in my head is . . . ?"

"Pharmakom's complete R&D on their cure for Nerve Attenuation Syndrome. Plus the records of the field trials to prove it works. *And it works like a motherfucker!*"

Jane's fluttering hand rose and touched her cheek in surprise and hope. "You mean . . . like a real cure?"

"A real cure," Spider said. "They could have you straightened out in three weeks, Janey."

Spider pulled back the flap to reveal the shadowy terminal floor littered with the dead, the dying, the past-hope and the still-hopeful. "You and everybody else."

"But wait a minute!" Johnny protested. "How could that be? The Yakuza are trying to cut *off* my fucking head?"

"They're working for Pharmakom. They want your head so they can take it back to Saigon and run it under a quantum interference detector and reconstruct the data. Don't you get it?"

"I'm just a courier!" Johnny said. "I try *not* to get it."

"Well, you better start understanding," said Spider. He sat down beside Johnny, impatiently, as if he were with a stubborn child. "The data was stolen by the men who hired you, the two Vietnamese. They had been Pharmakom scientists but I guess they had an attack of conscience. They saw how important the cure was, and they wanted to share it with the world.

149

Pharmakom wants to get it back so they can *hold* it back; so they can piece it out, sell it off: slowly, expensively—make all this suffering pay off for them . . ."

Spider put his hand on Johnny's arm. "The cure can save millions of lives."

Johnny shook his arm free. "What does it matter to me, if I'm dead?" He tried not to look at Jane. "Why should I give a damn?"

"You're dead anyway if we don't get it out. If you leave it in your head, the cure is lost. Already the seepage is corrupting the data. If we don't act soon . . ."

"Why should I trust you?" Johnny said. He turned to Jane. "Why should I trust either of you?"

As if in answer to his question, a wheeled gurney suddenly burst through the canvas flap into the shed. The young black nurse Johnny had seen before lay on the gurney. She was wearing a bright red apron over her whites, her mouth wide open.

At first Johnny thought it was some kind of horseplay—tasteless, considering the surroundings. Then, as the gurney hit the operating table and the nurse rolled onto the floor, he saw that her mouth was open in a silent scream, and that her "red apron" was bright, new blood.

Her throat had been cut.

"Praise the Lord!"

Street Preacher came through the flap right behind her, his hands outstretched, as if he wanted to embrace the entire world. "Praise be. The cure is Love. Behold your Savior!"

Jane reached into her shoulder bag and stepped in front of Johnny. Spider saw what she was doing, and stepped between her and Street Preacher.

"Run for it!" Spider shouted.

Street Preacher reached out and picked Spider up

by the neck, tossing him aside as easily as if he were a rag doll.

Johnny rolled off the table backwards and grabbed a scalpel from a tray against the wall. He threw it at Street Preacher, who ducked.

Jane pulled two throwing spikes from her shoulder bag.

The first one missed.

The second one went into Street Preacher's shoulder.

Deep.

Street Preacher looked down, surprised, and plucked it from his shoulder. Grinning, he aimed it at her and pulled back to throw.

Spider tackled him from the side. "Run, dammit!" he shouted again.

Johnny didn't wait to be asked a third time. He pulled Jane toward him, across the operating table. There was a crack in the plywood wall behind him, large enough for them to squeeze through one at a time . . .

"Jones, Janey!" Spider yelled. "Get him to Jones!" He reached into his pants pocket and grabbed something and threw it.

It jingled when Jane caught it.

It was the keys to the stepvan.

Street Preacher pulled his leg free from Spider just as Jane and Johnny slipped through the crack in the plywood and began to run across the floor of the terminal toward the door.

He started to pull the wall apart, so he could go after them; but he felt a restraining hand on his foot. Again! He looked down and saw Spider clutching at one of his expensive cowboy boots.

Profaning it with his filthy hands.

He dragged Spider one step, two . . . then he paused.

There was an easier way to do things.

Also more fun.

He picked Spider up and slammed him against the wall of the shed with one hand.

Glass and instruments fell crashing to the floor.

"Let him go!" A few nurses and orderlies hesitated at the entrance to the shed.

Street Preacher turned toward them and snarled.

They fled.

Street Preacher turned back to Spider. "Who is Jones?" he asked.

"Nobody . . ." Spider groaned. Blood was coming out of his mouth and ears.

Street Preacher tightened his grip and lifted Spider higher, so that his feet were kicking ineffectually against the wall.

"Who is Jones?" he asked again.

"Just a dealer. Hot wetware, in Cleveland."

Street Preacher reached behind him and rummaged blindly through the medical instruments on the tray.

Forceps. Saw. Hemostats.

"You can't lie to me, sinner. *Jesus is my co-pilot . . .*"

"F-fuck you!"

Scalpel.

Street Preacher drove the scalpel through the palm of Spider's outstretched hand, pinning it to the wall.

Spider screamed.

"Now. Tell me where they have *gone . . .*"

He reached back, searching for another scalpel . . .

Jane heard what Johnny hadn't wanted her to hear, what she herself didn't want to hear: Spider's scream.

The scream was entangled at first, rooted in the swamp of cries, moans and whispers from the NAS-afflicted multitude that overflowed the emergency hospital. Then, as Johnny and Jane fled through the revolving doors into the waiting night, the scream rose in pitch and intensity: It soared through the night, taking wing as they climbed into the waiting stepvan. A scream like nothing either of them had ever heard before.

"Spider . . . !"

Higher and higher, the lead solo in a symphony of loss and terror and pain.

"Don't listen," Johnny said, as he helped Jane put the key into the ignition. She was fumbling. He thought it was tremors from the NAS, until he saw her cheeks in the streetlight, splashed with tears.

"But Spider . . . he's sacrificing himself. . . ."

"Then let's make sure it wasn't wasted," Johnny said.

The scream rose into a new crescendo as Jane turned the key and the starter whined, the air pumps groaned.

"We can't just . . ."

"It's over," said Johnny.

And suddenly, it was.

"Let's get the hell out of here." The engine roared to life. The kids scattered into the shadows. Johnny checked the digital taped to the dash: 3:44 A.M.

Do you know where your children are?

"Who's this Jones?" Johnny asked, as they roared off through the deserted streets of what had once been Newark's downtown.

Jane seemed evasive. "Friend of J-Bone's. Hangs with the Loteks. Sort of."

"That where we're going?"

She nodded. "Heaven. Out in the Ratlands."

"Is there a vidphone in this rig?" he asked.

She nodded again. "Try the glove compartment. And under the seat. There's a little more up there under the sunvisor."

As he assembled the various mismatched pieces of Spider's improvised cellular vidphone—a dusty circuit board, a few jacks, a grungy handset, a cracked liquid crystal screen—Johnny found himself admiring the outlaw doctor's wizardry, the amazing virtuosity that created the simulacrum of modern technology from the detritus of civilization. Once he had put the vidphone together, he plugged in the INFOBAHN 3000 and called up the special RR!! routing he had coded into the memory the first time he had hacked through to Pharmakom Central Security.

Johnny was a little surprised to see a different security man pick up the vidphone, a white guy with a ponytail and a thin moustache. "Who the hell are you?" he asked.

"Don't worry about that," said the security man. "I know who you are. That's what counts. What happened?"

"Couldn't make the meeting," said Johnny. "Unavoidable system errors. But I'm still up for it. Are you?"

"Certainly."

"This time the place is the Lotek hideout called Heaven. A Passaic bridge somewhere out in—"

"I know where it is," the security man said. "The Ratlands."

"Good. I have one piece of the code. You can still get the rest, right?"

"I'll be there. I'll bring it."

Johnny switched off the vidphone before the call could be ID'ed. As he did so, Jane turned to him, her eyes blazing.

"Are you crazy?" she spat. "Spider sacrificed himself to save you, and now you are betraying him! Betraying all of us! Not if I can . . ."

"Chill," said Johnny. "In the first place it wasn't me

he died to save. It was the data. And you." He watched her reaction from the corner of his eye. She drove on, her jaw set in anger.

"And in the second place," he lied, "I have a plan."

From another monitor, in another part of Newark, the ponytailed security man stared straight ahead as if brain-dead. Indeed, he was brain-dead. His eyes were blank, his mouth sagged, his jaw stretched, his forehead bulged grotesquely as Takahashi scratched his own jaw thoughtfully with the video-puppet glove.

He wants the rest of the code, he thought to himself.

The video puppet Takahashi used to simulate Pharmakom Security disappeared from the screen as he took off the glove and placed it on his desk beside the monitor. The blank screen was filled with an antique cartoon screen-saver.

"He has one image," Takahashi said to himself. "If he gets hold of the other two, he can download the data on his own. Then his head will be worthless. Like my honor . . ."

A cold horror fell over Takahashi at the thought. He turned toward his Zen garden, as he always did when he wanted to settle his thoughts, but something caught his eye.

Something strange.

On the monitor, Takahashi's antique screen-saver was wavering. The toasters were morphing into faces, into a woman's face.

One familiar face. With *yin* and *yang* earrings.

She was back.

"Listen to me, Takahashi," Anna Kalman said. "Before it is too late."

Now that he knew who she was, Takahashi was prepared to listen. She was a ghost, and he had been brought up to respect and even fear ghosts. Even electronic ghosts.

"You are a man with a sense of right and wrong," Anna said. "Your daughter is gone and you feel that is a great wrong. But I offer you a chance to right a greater wrong."

"Leave my daughter out of this," Takahashi said. He reached over to switch off the monitor, but she stopped him with a look.

"I've learned so many things since my death, Takahashi. I fled into the Net, and there I saw everything. I saw that they—"

They? Was she suggesting he betray his employer?

"No!"

Click.

She was gone.

He stared at the screen, then at the Zen garden in the moonlight. They both seemed equally empty— empty of honor, empty of meaning.

Empty of hope.

When it was first built, in the first half of the previous century, the Passaic Bridge had spanned a muddy tidal arm of the river, completing an access highway to the tunnels to New York. It was a draw-bridge, raised to allow shipping to pass under it, through the winding narrow passages of that great marsh known as the Meadowlands.

First the shipping had gone, lured south by container cargo wharves in Baltimore and Norfolk, toward the southern reaches of that East Coast megalopolis that later became known as the Sprawl.

Then the tunnels to New York City had gone, all three of them, destroyed by plastique within twenty minutes of one another during one muggy summer while they were choked with Fourth of July weekend traffic; irritated families dragging themselves home after fireworks and barbecues, only to find themselves the fireworks, themselves the barbecue.

Then the truck and auto traffic had gone, diverted

156

first into the decaying expressways and then, with the end of cheap oil, into the terminal junkyards that would preserve their colorful bones and shells for future scholars. The bridge's approach ramps went as the rotten, subspec concrete (Mafia contracted, under a Jersey construction bond) collapsed, and the roads that led to them were chopped up and boiled to extract the precious oil that saturated the asphalt.

By then the Meadowlands themselves had gone, the riverine marshes filled in with layers of garbage, paper, rubble, detritus and debris. The otters and the eels were only a memory but other life flourished, giving the Meadowlands its new name. The Ratlands.

Then the river itself had gone, reasserting itself a few hundred yards to the east in a new channel, leaving the bridge totally stranded over dry landfill—a flaking, rusting, cantilevered iron monster almost a quarter of a mile long, lying across its hundred-foot-high concrete abutments like the horizontal framework of a dismantled skyscraper.

Then the Loteks came.

They claimed the structure for their own, seeing it as a natural fortress: dependable, defendable, delightfully dramatic, with an unobstructed view of the Ratlands for miles around. The long-forgotten drawbridge engines were tapped into the underground cable, enabling the Loteks to "liberate" electricity undetected. The bridge's iron frame served as a signal tower for the pirate signals they bounced off satellites and sent around the world.

With world-class ingenuity the Loteks stole, borrowed, scrounged, lifted, boosted and heisted electronic equipment, furniture, bedding, weaponry, clothing, tools and miscellaneous machinery, constructing their own city in and around the bridge girders, along the bottom edge of the sky.

And called it Heaven.

From below, Heaven looked like a hornets' nest, an organic and natural accretion, with cargo containers, subway cars, small boats, salvaged aircraft, and mobile homes lashed and pinned to the girders of the bridge; connected by dizzying walkways of rope and plank, all swaying and creaking in the breezes that still blew across the half-remembered marsh.

In the jumble the Loteks created, one could find apartments, bunkrooms, playrooms, storage spaces, TV studios, weapons caches and bunkers. Heaven was a combination outlaw city and fortress, a modern-day faux castle moated by thin air, and ruled by one man who was, himself, only a few years away from being a boy.

J-Bone.

At the moment, J-Bone was hard at work in the #2 broadcast studio, a hijacked Channel 5 News van that hung, wheelless, from a high girder at the northern end of the bridge. With one of his hackers working the boards, he was breaking into TV shows around the world, spreading the Loteks' message of freedom, insouciance, *audaz* and autonomy.

While J-Bone rapped, sentries at either end of the bridge scanned the fill prairies of the Ratlands, making sure that no one unexpected approached.

At the southern end of the bridge, this job was undertaken by two men. Or rather, by a man and a boy.

The man, Buddy, was almost twenty-one, one of the Lotek veterans. The boy, known as Stick, was only sixteen, a newcomer to the loose-knit gang. He had shown up and asked to join only a few months earlier, after walking across the Ratlands from downtown Newark, where both his parents had died of NAS.

It was the graveyard shift, four to seven A.M. All the two had to do was watch the dirt road winding through the rubble piles and deserted factories. They weren't expecting trouble, and while they sat on the high beams, Buddy was trying as conscientiously as possible to fulfill his other assignment. He had been asked by J-Bone to "fill the kid in" on the history and principles of the Loteks.

"Information should be free," Buddy told Stick. "It should be used to liberate, not oppress. So J-Bone and the other Founding Brothers and Sisters liberated a bunch of computers and stuff, and patched it together into the most sophisticated communications system on the planet."

"That's great!" said Stick.

"Wrong," corrected Buddy. "What it meant was that we had every law enforcement agency, every insurance company, every multinational, and every communications cop on the planet after us."

"Bummer!" said Stick, who was getting turned on to the adventure.

"Wrong," corrected Buddy, who thought that the only way to teach the young was to correct them on everything. "It was the best thing that ever happened to us. It meant that we had to go underground, hacking into the systems from satellites, scrambling our signals so that we couldn't be blocked or traced."

"Awesome!" said Stick.

"Wrong," corrected Buddy. "Going underground meant making contact with organized crime, and some of us were tempted to use our skills for commercial purposes—sell time on pirate frequencies, break into shows with bootleg commercials, do our thing for *profit.*"

"Bad scene, right?" said Stick, who was becoming a little less sure of himself and his perceptions.

"No, it was good," corrected Buddy. "It meant we had to finally tighten up the organization, separate the sheep from the goats. That's when we chose J-Bone leader, to help us sift out the real Loteks from the wannabes."

159

Stick nodded. "That must have been a good thing, right?"

"Are you kidding? It meant all of a sudden there were ex-Loteks all over the place, ready to sell us out. A bunch even joined with our arch-enemies, the Aryan Dreads, over in Secaucus."

"That was . . . bad?" ventured Stick.

"On the whole, it was good," corrected Buddy. "We pulled back a little and holed up here, did a lot of construction work. That's when Heaven was really created."

"Then I guess that was good."

"No way!" corrected Buddy. "The Dreads found out about it and decided they had to have the place, so here they came with all sorts of machinery and weaponry, trying to starve us out."

"Bad scene, huh?" Stick tried.

"That shows how little you know," said Buddy. "There's nothing like a siege to bring a community together. We were able to get rid of the Dreads for good with a little invention of J-Bone's called the beetle-bomber."

"Then that was good, right?"

"Not for them it wasn't. Dig!"

Buddy led Stick to the end of the bridge, where a steep ramp was tilted over the end of the road below. On the ramp were three VW beetles, lined up single file. They were held in place by a spring-loaded gate. Each beetle was packed with glass Mason jars of watery gasoline, used naphtha, and other flammables too filthy to burn for fuel.

"This lever here is the joystick," said Buddy. "Each time you pull it, one of the beetles rolls off the end of the ramp. As soon as the car starts rolling, it hits a bump on the ramp, which knocks over an open jar of gasoline on the dash. Then the car rolls past a hook that pulls loose the battery cable under the seat, causing a spark that ignites the whole goddam thing from the inside. It's burning when it rolls off the end of the ramp, and then . . ."

Stick touched the lever gently, grinned, and said, "Bad!"

"Right," said Buddy. "Now you're catching on!"

"Good!"

Buddy held up his hand.

"What's the matter?" Stick asked. "Did I say something wrong?"

Buddy shook his head. "Hear that?"

"What?"

"A motor. Sounds like a Chevy. A stepvan. There, I can see it, heading this way."

THIRTEEN

—————■—————

When he had first seen it from a distance, Heaven had looked to Johnny like a castle of iron. From closer, perhaps because he was forced to look up, it suggested flight, not defense. Flight and age. Flight through time. From below, the Loteks' high steel redoubt looked less like a fortress than like a spaceship just settling back to Earth; a generational starship returning from a long voyage, a Magellanic wandering that had battered and beaten it almost beyond recognition. The planet it was returning to was equally scarred, scoured and scratched, so that the reunion of starship and home planet was less an occasion for joy than relief, and was greeted not with cries of exaltation but with weary sighs of relief.

Or maybe the sighs were coming from the stepvan: it seemed to be running out of methane. It was slowing, missing, the engine stuttering with foul-smelling gasps as Jane drove across the last few hundred yards of Ratlands fill to the riverbank. *I'm running out of gas, too,* Johnny thought. *And out of time.*

The pain in his head had settled down to a dull ache, but he noticed that every time he wiped his nose there was a trace of blood. There seemed to be some kind of leakage around the wetwire jack above his left temple. He touched it gingerly but resisted the urge to examine it in the rearview mirror. It was best not to look at such things too closely.

How much time do I have left? he wondered.

Synaptic leakage. There was some kind of leakage over the low ridge of the Palisades to the east. It was the future leaking back into the present, just beginning to color the sky. Dawn couldn't be too far away.

He consulted the clock on the dash: 4:21. He thought of Spider's sacrifice as Jane dropped all the way down into first gear, weaving the stepvan through the soft dirt where the bones of ancient enterprises stuck through: a wire, a bed frame, a gleam of glass in the ash-colored dry soil. Johnny wondered what he would do if a similar sacrifice were asked of him.

He hoped he wasn't about to find out.

The south approach to Heaven had been sheared off in some long-forgotten war, shattered into shards of concrete and twisted strands of steel, and Jane wove the stepvan between these, up under the towering south-bank bridge abutment. Above, ends of beams and dangling cables stuck out like a bad haircut. Beyond, on the still-intact main span, a few lights gleamed in the twisted warren of cars, cargo containers, wheelless buses, shanties and shacks that the Loteks called home.

There seemed to be everything but a ladder.

"Is there a doorbell?" Johnny asked.

In answer, Jane honked the horn. Like everything else in Spider's private creation, the stepvan's horn had been modified. It made a plaintive, haunting cry like nothing Johnny had ever heard before.

"What was that?"

"Wild goose," said Jane.

Johnny laughed. "How the hell would you know what a wild goose sounds like?"

Jane shrugged. "Spider said." She honked again. There was no sign of life from above.

Johnny stepped out onto the dirt and cupped his hands and hollered up: "Yo! Hey! Wake up, dammit! We need some help!"

Still nothing. The engine to the stepvan died and there was a slow sigh, followed by a foul smell.

"Out of gas," said Jane. "Hey, Johnny, you okay?"

"Looks like it's wearing a hat," said Stick.

"Don't lean out so far," said Buddy.

"Smells like a fart," said Stick.

"Don't lean out so far," said Buddy.

"A fart wearing a hat," said Stick.

"It's Spider's stepvan," said Buddy, forcing himself to lean out far enough to look down at the vehicle that had just pulled up under the south bridge approach. Buddy couldn't let the younger Lotek know that he was afraid of heights. "That bag on top is for the fuel. Runs on methane."

"Who's Spider?"

"One of the Founding Brothers. He and J-Bone— But where's Spider?"

"That's not him?"

"Naw. That suit? That's some other guy. Spider must be inside. There's Jane, though."

Stick leaned over to see. "Where? A girl?"

"Of course a girl! Jane's the coolest . . ."

"Let me see!"

Stick leaned out and looked down. Unlike Buddy, he liked the dizzy feeling.

"I don't see no girl."

"Well, she's there," said Buddy. "They want to come up. Let's go lower the cage."

"I see her!" said Stick. He leaned out further. "I—"

He slipped and grabbed at the beam, but missed; grabbed at a cable, but missed. Then he caught an upright lever. It gave, then held.

"Oh, shit," said Buddy.

"I'm okay," said Stick.

"Oh, shit," repeated Buddy.

"No big deal," said Stick. He couldn't understand why Buddy looked so horrified.

Then he heard the rumbling.

He turned and saw the first of the three VWs rolling down the beetle bomber ramp, just getting under way.

"Oh, shit!" said Stick.

"You okay?" Jane asked again. Johnny was leaning against the side of the stepvan, shaking his head from side to side in pain.

She called up again: "Hey, anybody home?"

"I'm okay," said Johnny. "Just this . . . headache. Gotta get this stuff out." He reached out for her hand, which was fluttering slightly in spite of her efforts to control it. In his own hand it felt soft and warm.

"Besides," he said, "you're in worse shape than I am."

"Am not."

"Are so."

Jane pulled away and looked up: "Hey, you fucking layabouts! Lower the cage!"

Watching her, Johnny realized, suddenly, that if he did have the cure for NAS in his head, he would make a sacrifice to get it out intact. Not *any* sacrifice, but *some* sacrifice. And not for humanity—what the hell did he, Johnny, care about humanity?

For this nervous, skinny, violent, almost beautiful girl.

"Tell me about this Jones dude," Johnny said. "This guy Spider said was our only chance. He's up there?"

"Yeah," said Jane. "He's not exactly a dude. He's, uh, hard to explain."

"What do you mean, hard to explain?"

"He was in the Navy. In the war. They put a lot of stuff in his head. Like you."

"Hardwired stuff? Memory augments?"

"Yeah." Jane shrugged. "You'll see. Jones is, is— he's real fucking different."

She heard a rumbling high above. "Finally! Here they come."

It was just like Buddy had said.

The VW beetles had no tires; and when the first one began to roll, rumbling on the rough concrete slab, the motion tipped over the Mason jar of gasoline that had been balanced on the dash.

The gasoline was still soaking into the seat and sloshing around on the floorboards when the hook tied to the bridge frame ripped loose the battery cable under the front seat.

The arc from the positive terminal ignited the gasoline with a *whoosh,* so that the VW looked as if someone had turned on its interior lights as it rolled off the end of the ramp and dove, nose first, the 110 feet toward the ground.

At first, when he looked up, Johnny flashed back to an ancient circus trick he had once seen in a video: a mule diving off a hundred-foot-high ladder into a plastic wading pool.

But there was no wading pool.

And that was no mule.

The little car tucked under in a slow flip, filling the air with gasoline and naphtha vapor, and then exploded in a *WHOOSH* in midair, illuminating the bottom of the bridge and the ground beneath it like a little sun, stopping time, so that Johnny saw it all in one long, agonized instant:

Two faces peering down from the high steel . . .

Jane, one hand on the stepvan, looking up, more astonished than scared . . .

Himself, half-running, half-diving toward her. . . .

"Look out!" Johnny said as he hit her, hard, and they both went down and then went rolling, rolling, through the soft dust littered with the debris of discarded civilizations, toward the high swamp grass at the river's edge, away from the dusty parking area under the bridge.

Away from the light. Away from the little sun.

They rolled. Johnny looked back with each roll so that he saw the beetle crash into Spider's stepvan, and a few seconds later heard the crunch of glass and steel and plastic; he saw the flare, then heard the greedy flames howling for air; he saw the mushroom cloud, then heard the glass popping as the fire settled down to feast on what was left of Spider's van.

He stopped rolling.

The light was softer here at the edge of the clearing, under the tall reeds. The fire fifty feet away sounded almost peaceful.

Jane's eyes were closed. Johnny lay on top of her, suddenly aware of the softness of her body under him, her breasts heaving as she fought for breath. Her lips red in the firelight.

She was bleeding a little, where she had cut her lip, and without thinking Johnny kissed it away.

Jane opened her eyes, that astonishing, astonished violet.

Then closed them again as she kissed him back, long and slow and deep.

Then Johnny pulled away, suddenly, savagely, and stood up, brushing off his knees. "What the *fuck* was that?" he demanded.

"A kiss?"

"Not that—*that!*" He angrily pointed toward the

inferno that was lighting up the night. The VW and the stepvan were locked in a final embrace, indistinguishable. "I thought these assholes were your friends!"

"I thought so too," said Jane, standing up and brushing off.

"Here I thought I was doing you a fucking favor, and your friends try to kill us."

Jane shrugged. "Chill," she said.

Johnny held his head; waves of pain, frustration, and a new emotion he didn't recognize—or care to identify—were washing over him, each indistinguishable from the other. "I should have known better!" he said.

"Known better than what?"

"Known better than to try to help. All my life I've been careful to stay in my own corner, looking out for number one. No complications. Now suddenly, according to Spider, I'm responsible for the entire fucking *world,* plus everybody and his mother is trying to *kill* me, which is totally unnecessary since my head is going to blow up first!"

Jane found that she was angry, too. "Maybe it's not just about you!" she said, turning on him angrily. "Did you ever think that other people might have problems, too?"

Her hand was starting to flutter again: Spider's muscle relaxant was wearing off. Jane stopped the fluttering by putting both hands in her back pockets. She was looking up toward the creaking noise that came from the bridge above. Something was coming down.

Johnny followed her eyes and groaned. "What fresh hell is this?"

"What *idiot . . . !*"

J-Bone saw the two VW beetles, still on the ramp,

and the flames, roiling below. The two Loteks on guard, the older and the younger, both looked sheepish.

"It was an accident!" Stick wailed.

J-Bone looked at the kid and then at Buddy, for confirmation. Buddy shrugged.

J-Bone peered over the edge. "Is that . . . ?"

Buddy nodded. "Spider's van, J-Bone."

"Jesus! We better get down there!"

"I already started lowering the bucket for them to come up."

J-Bone saw the winch, ratcheting the free-swinging cage elevator down. Without waiting, he tore two rags off Stick's head.

"Hey, does that mean . . . ?" Stripped of his colors, Stick tried to hold back his tears.

"Quit your whining," Buddy said. "Just means he's in a hurry." Squinting against the glare from below, he watched as J-Bone wrapped the rags around his hands and slid down the cable, so that he and the cage reached the ground at the same time.

"J-Bone," said Jane.

J-Bone climbed down off the cage top, unwrapping his hands while holding them up to shield his face from the heat of the blazing stepvan and beetle.

"Janey. What are you doing here?"

"We have to see Jones, J-Bone! Spider sent us."

"Spider. . . ." J-Bone walked as close as he could to the inferno, then stepped back. "Spider," he repeated slowly, as if trying to memorialize the name of his old friend.

"He's dead," Jane said softly.

"That fucking kid! I'll . . ."

"Not in that," said Johnny. "Not here. Earlier."

"Street Preacher killed him," said Jane. "Trying to get to Johnny here. Seems that . . ."

"Take us up, okay?" Johnny cried. "We got to get to

this Jones guy!" He grabbed his head and bent over in sudden pain.

"Jones *guy?*" J-Bone eyed Johnny suspiciously, then looked at Jane. "Well, if Spider sent you . . ."

He opened the door to the cage, and Jane helped Johnny in.

"What's the matter with him?" J-Bone asked, as he closed the creaking door behind them. He pulled a cord and the cage started up.

"Mnemonic stuff," Jane said. "He's some kind of hardwired courier dude. Got all this data in his head. And what he's got is—"

"Here we are," said J-Bone.

The cage rattled to a stop. They stepped out into a circle of Loteks—all armed to the teeth with crossbows, zip guns and knives.

Takahashi's private executive secretary had, as far as Takahashi knew, no life. There are multinationals in crime as well as commerce—indeed, the line between the two is less than fixed—and executive secretaries for multinationals of both sorts are accustomed to keeping irregular hours, and being constantly on call.

Mrs. Sutton kept a studio apartment in the Yakuza complex, only an elevator ride away from her boss's office. So when he intercepted the call from the mnemonic courier, it was a simple enough matter for him to ring her to make the arrangements for his sudden departure. Even at four in the morning.

She was at his office in five minutes, letting herself in with her own key.

Takahashi was at his large closet, changing his shirt for the fourth time that day.

"Order me a helicopter," he said, as he buttoned the white Egyptian cotton shirt. "And get me a cryo-unit. One of the portable ones. What are they called?"

"CryoCarryAll."

Mrs. Sutton made the calls on the vidphone, one to Transportation and one to Specialties, both of which were, much like herself, open twenty-four hours a day.

Meanwhile, Takahashi was admiring the samurai sword in its sheath on the closet wall. He smiled, remembering the embarrassment he had caused Shinji by killing his vulgar henchmen.

Served him right. The man had no business going out of channels. Perhaps he had learned his lesson.

Takahashi left the sword in its elaborately carved scabbard. It was too obvious, too obtrusive. From the bottom of his shirt drawer he chose a shorter sword, one he could conceal inside his suit jacket.

He chose a tie, a silk foulard, and knotted it.

The doorbell rang and Mrs. Sutton answered it. It was a messenger from Specialties with a box, smoking with cold.

"Your cryo-unit is here," she said, shutting the door and tipping the messenger.

"Good." Takahashi slipped on his jacket. He crossed to his desk, opened a drawer and took out an antique but formidable projectile gun—a .357 magnum. He put it into his briefcase.

"Is my helicopter ready?"

Mrs. Sutton nodded toward the roof, where a distinct *whump whump whump* could be heard.

"Good. I should be back by nine o'clock or so."

"Very good, sir."

Takahashi left. The door clicked shut behind him. Mrs. Sutton waited a moment.

Then two; then three.

She straightened a pen set on the massive oak desk. She looked outside, to where the Zen garden was lightening with the first faint promise of dawn. Or was that her imagination? It was still early.

She heard the *whump whump whump* of the helicopter increase, then fade as it left. She punched a number into the vidphone on the desk and a face came up on the monitor.

It was Shinji. "Yes?"

"He's on his way."

Once the gasoline and naphtha had burned away, the flames settled down to feed on more sedate fare, such as the upholstery, rubber, cardboard and plastic trim of the two entangled vehicles.

The fire no longer roared, it crackled.

It was almost homey.

Two derelicts staggered out of the night, drawn by the promise of warmth, of comfort, the ancient promise fire has held out to mankind for millennia.

The bottle they passed between them held another promise, one only slightly less ancient.

Other denizens of the night were drawn to the scene. On their way in and out of the pylons of the bridge, fluttering dark shapes flew closer and closer to the flames, as if to see how close they could get without singeing their wings.

"Bats," allowed derelict #1, passing the bottle to the other.

"Starlings," contradicted derelict #2.

They had been roaming the Ratlands together for the past six years, drinking from the same bottle, eating from the same plate, sharing bedroll and blanket. One black and one white, one tall and one short, one fat and one skinny, chained together by poverty, alcoholism and bad luck as surely as by the steel links of a chain-gang shackle. And they had never once, in all that time, agreed on anything.

"Have some more sherry," said derelict #1.

"It's port," said derelict #2. "But I don't mind if I do."

Another figure joined them and they moved over to

make space by the fire, even though there was plenty of room.

This man seemed the sort for which one moved over.

He was half again as tall as the derelicts, with massive shoulders and an unruly shock of white hair that gleamed in the night like a bank of dirty snow. He wore an inverted cross around his neck and silver crosses on the toes of his cowboy boots. He carried a little box in one hand, about the size of a case for a bowling ball. The box was steaming, but the steam was cold.

Derelict #1 screwed the top onto the wine bottle and tossed it to the stranger. Most politely. "Howdy," he said.

The stranger caught the bottle, held it up to the light, then tossed it into the flames.

Then smiled. "Cast you away the ways of sin," the stranger said.

"What the hell!" Derelict #2 picked up a two-by-four and was about to issue a formal protest over this treatment, when the stranger turned from the fire to face him. Or rather, look down at him, with grinning steel teeth and wild eyes reflecting the glare of the firelight . . .

Derelict #2 stepped back.

Derelict #1 was about to take the stranger from behind, when he got a good look at those massive shoulders, that short bull neck.

Derelict #1 stepped back.

The stranger was paying no attention. He was looking up, toward heaven.

"Repent, sinners!" he said.

He slung the box over his back on a long cord. He reached up and grabbed hold of a beam of the bridge, and swung himself up. "You can run, but you can't hide!"

173

While derelict #2 watched in amazement, the man began to haul himself upward, hand over hand, slowly but steadily into the night.

Meanwhile, derelict #1 had retrieved the wine bottle with a stick. It was warm, like mulled wine, but it still tasted pretty good.

"Good fucking riddance," said derelict #2, pointing upward with a rheumy eye and a raised eyelid.

"Agreed," said derelict #1.

They drank to that, and why not? It was the first time they had agreed on anything in six years.

Johnny was having a dream. He knew it was a dream because his mother was in it, and his mother was no longer in his memories, only in his dreams. He knew it was his mother because she sat at a desk and he couldn't see her face, just as he couldn't remember his mother's face.

In the dream he was a child again. He was walking toward his mother, feeling strangely peaceful. He liked the fact that it was a dream, that he was a child again. He liked being here in a world without pain, without sorrow, without either memory or forgetfulness.

His mother was getting up from the desk. Instead of coming toward him, bending down to pick him up, however, she was turning away, turning away, turning away. . . .

"Hey! You okay?"

Johnny woke up. His mother was gone. He was lying in the softest bed imaginable, looking up at soft violet eyes, violet as Morning Glory (not the flower, which Johnny had never seen; the shampoo).

It was Jane. He was lying with his head in her lap.

Her hand touched his forehead and she was looking down at him with an expression he couldn't quite recognize, an expression he had never seen before, a soft, wondering . . .

"Hey, man," she said, "you looked so sad, like you were about to cry."

"I was having a dream."

"What about?"

"I—I don't remember. Why are you smiling like that?"

"Don't know. Can't help it. I guess I'm kinda glad you're okay, you looked real bad back there."

"It was the head thing. It comes and goes."

Johnny was suddenly conscious of her hand on his forehead. He reached up and touched her cheek, then put his hand up behind her head and drew her down to him. She had a cool, sweet smell, like summer rain . . . and a warm, sweet taste like . . .

"You feeling better?" she asked.

"Infinite," he said.

He didn't know what to do with his other hand but she did. Her breasts through the T-shirt were small but perfect, shy but unembarrassed. Assertive, like the girl herself.

They kissed again, stretching out together, his fingertips suddenly knowledgeable, easily finding their way under her loose T-shirt.

"Hey, guys."

It was J-Bone. He stood in the door of the room, a faint smile on his face. Stick, apparently back in favor, stood behind him, his rag bandanna back on his head.

"We got special rooms for that," J-Bone said. "But it's time, you dig?"

"Time? What time is it?" asked Johnny, suddenly remembering his head, and the danger and the promise he carried in it.

"Time to meet Jones," J-Bone said.

In the Ratlands, the rats are bold.

Derelict #1 heard an engine approaching in the distance, and nudged his partner.

"Car."

175

"Car," derelict #2 agreed. This mutual agreeing was getting to be a habit.

As the car approached, they stayed by the fire, passing the bottle back and forth. They saw no reason to retreat to the shadows. They were creatures of the night, and there was nothing in the night they feared.

Or so they thought.

The car approached, neither slow nor fast. It was a limousine, long and black.

Derelict #1 nodded and passed the wine bottle to derelict #2. The night was getting interesting.

The limousine stopped on the other side of the low-burning fire that had once been Spider's stepvan. The firelight revealed the emblem on the front door—a tasteful, small gold Y, discreetly guaranteeing certain traffic and parking privileges.

And the derelicts were gone, both of them, #1 and #2, slipping away in such a hurry that they left their wine bottle behind.

In the Ratlands, the rats are bold.

But not *that* bold.

Three people got out of the rear of the limousine. Three got out of the front. All six wore black jumpsuits, Italian rock-climbing shoes, and web belts hung with matte-black, null-reflectant climbing gear: carabiners, snap links, pitons, twisters, jammers and coils of lightweight black nylon rope.

Two of the six were women.

One of the four men was Shinji.

One of the Yakuza opened the trunk of the limousine; three black nylon carryalls clinked softly as they were set down on the ground.

Meanwhile, Shinji scanned the dark piers and beams above with an infrared monocular.

The largest member of the Yakuza assault team, a bald African-American with a short, neatly trimmed beard, opened one of the carryalls and lifted out the forward section of a Russian-made Thermidor shoulder-mounted heat-seeking anti-aircraft recoilless missile launcher.

A Scandinavian woman whose short blond hair was blackened with grease lifted the rear section of the same launcher out of her bag.

The two Yakuza faced off and came together like fighters in a clinch, with a loud *snap*. When they parted, the woman held the assembled missile launcher, four and a half feet long.

She hefted it admiringly. "Sweet baby, come to Mama," she said; then rested it in the crook of her arm and waited, with the others, for orders.

Shinji lowered his monocular and turned to the bald man and the blond woman. "You two stay here," he said. "Cover the car and cover us from below." He looked pointedly at the Thermidor missile launcher that the woman cradled in her arms like a baby. "That thing gets used only if we require a diversion. Or if you come under attack."

"Who's in command?" asked the bald man.

"You are."

The bald man smiled and held out his hands toward the missile launcher. "Then I get first turn. Come to Papa."

FOURTEEN

—■—

There are no handrails in heaven. The Loteks had webbed their hiding and huddling places to the bridge's rusting iron structure with twists of rope and tangles of cable and gobs of epoxy; they walked and ran on rods and beams, then slept in high-slung hammocks or dreamed on steel mesh balconies as frail as Delancey Street fire escapes. Their territory was so attenuated that in places it consisted of little more than holds for hands and holes for feet, sawed or burnt into the ancient steel beams.

J-Bone led Johnny and Jane from level to level, post to beam, up concrete stairs and down steel ladders with perforated rungs, in hooped ladderways and out through meshed shafts, under collapsed walkways and over narrow plankways rattling above a dizzying abyss of thin, dark air.

Johnny was glad it was still dark and that he couldn't see what lay below them. Even the spectacle of Spider's burning van was out of sight, obscured by the southernmost abutment of the bridge almost a quarter of a mile away.

But what was holding up the dawn? The sky over the low ridge of the Palisades to the east was barely pink.

J-Bone's flashlight beam led the way, with J-Bone behind it, a swaggering but, Johnny felt, utterly trustworthy figure, hung with self-awarded medals and decorated with beads and small silver oddments. Lotek fashion ran to scars and tattoos, and J-Bone was liberally garnished with both.

An old schoolbus hung from a rusted winch like a giant trophy catfish, barely swinging in the pre-dawn breeze so that they had to time their jumps through the open door.

Inside was a schoolroom, judging from the way the windshield had been replaced with a blackboard, and the windows with maps, most of them already out of date. Out the other door, beyond and above the bus, was a greenhouse, fashioned from the plastic dome of some long-abandoned airline terminal. Inside, even though it was past four in the morning, a Lotek was quietly tying up beans while he hummed softly to himself and ignored their passage, except for a slight nod to J-Bone.

Another gangway, this one a shallow arch of illegal plastic milk cartons held together by particle physics and phone cord. Far below, through a million diamond iron-mesh holes, Johnny could see the gleam of oily water. He reached for the nonexistent handrail with one hand, for Jane's hand with the other. That part felt just right: her hand in his. The rightness of it alarmed him, and he wondered, *When did this happen?*

"Through here," J-Bone said. Ahead, up a short ladder, was a deck leading to a larger-than-usual space: the gutted fuselage of a C-144, still blackened from a long-ago fire, winched against the bottom of the bridge with cables, wedged solid with old tires. Through a tiny row of windows under the words AIR

NATIONAL GUARD Johnny could see the familiar blue light of TV monitors, blue and rose, the colors of cyberspace—or at least of those windows in this world that peer into it.

This door, alone of all the doors through which they had passed, was locked.

J-Bone rapped on it with the heel of his hand; or, rather, with the stud of the leather and metal bracelet that wrapped his wrist. A complicated Latin rhythm: *da da dadada da da! dadadad . . . da da daadadad da!*

A face appeared at the window, distorted against the glass; then it pulled back, and the door opened.

"Come on in," J-Bone urged.

He didn't have to insist. Johnny almost floated into the room, Jane right behind him. With the cool colors, the soft electronic buzz, Johnny felt almost as if he were heading home.

Wherever the hell that was.

"We call this Times Square," said J-Bone. "Spider's people, they give us information and we out it . . ."

"*Out* it?"

"Wide-band. Global. Give it away. Jones hacks for us, breaks us into all the comsat nets, fiber-optic webs, sneaky-like, so nobody can flame us or keep us out." J-Bone grinned. "You've seen."

Johnny nodded, remembering the wall of monitors repeating J-Bone's face in the hotel lobby in Beijing. And the white dolphin, the fish symbol: What did that mean? Were they nothing but Jesus freaks after all?

"Hey, Janey!" a Lotek called down from an office chair strapped with ski line and speaker wire onto a hydraulic boom marked "CBS Sports."

The Lotek was adjusting a bank of monitors, none of them matching, that faced into the room from the wall behind Johnny. Under the monitors, two men and a woman in Lotek gear worried over a sound-board, sliding the knobs up and down according to

180

signals they were apparently getting through their earphones.

All this was pretty much what Johnny had expected; it matched the Lotek spirit and style. What he hadn't expected—what surprised him—was the twelve-foot-diameter blue plastic swimming pool, four and a half feet deep, a freestanding backyard model set against the far wall. Cables led into the pool from the main control console, from the bank of monitors, from the power terminals on the floor and from the dish antenna above the ceiling on the roof; beside the pool, on segmented hydraulic stalks, were two arrays of cone-shaped scanners stamped US NAVY.

There was a clear glass panel in the front of the pool, and the glow through the water showed that there were instruments under the water, as well as a bank of brightly lighted buttons, and—

And there was something else in the pool.

Something moving.

Something big.

Shinji never asked his people to do anything he wouldn't do. That's why he was always the first in the door or the first out of the door.

Shinji put away his infrared monocular, reached into one of the nylon carryalls, and pulled out an oversized gas-powered pistol that resembled a flare gun.

From the hollow grip of the pistol he pulled a dart that looked like a crossbow bolt with an expandable head. He unhooked a coiled climbing rope from his belt. He clipped one end of the rope to the dart, and laid the rest of the coil on the ground at his feet.

He loaded the dart into the muzzle of the gun.

He aimed up into the darkness. And fired.

Six sets of eyes followed the line as it disappeared into the shadows of the bridge, the rope coils on the ground by Shinji's feet growing smaller and smaller.

The dart hit something high above with a distant *clang!*

Shinji pulled on the rope. It held.

Three more lines were fired up into the darkness. Three more were tested and held.

Shinji took a small, battery-powered electrical device about the size and shape of a hardcover book, and clipped it over the rope. It was a 4.5 hp Victorinix electrical line climber.

Behind him, more line climbers were clipped onto three more ropes.

Shinji shaped his web belt into a hanging seat and clipped his carabiner onto the line climber.

Three more Yakuza did the same.

He pulled a black mask with two eye slits down over his face. Three others did the same.

Only the bald man and the blond woman, standing guard by the fire, left their faces uncovered.

"They teach you all this at Ninja school, boss?" the bald man asked.

Shinji nodded. He turned to the three masked figures. "Remember," he said. "If Takahashi makes it here, he is mine."

Three masked heads nodded. Four motors hummed and four professional killers ascended into the darkness, like four spiders converging on a single fly.

Four eyes watched, peering up until the spiders were lost in the web. Then they turned to look into the fire.

"Let me hold it awhile," the blond woman said. She looked at the missile launcher hungrily.

The bald man shook his head.

"Shinji said take turns," the woman said.

"I'm in command," the bald man said with a smile. He hugged the missile launcher closer to his massive chest. "I'll tell you when it's your turn."

* * *

"A fish?"

"Watch that!" said J-Bone. "Jones is a friend of mine."

"He's not a fish," said Jane. "I learned it in school. He's a mammal. Like a whale, or a mushroom."

"He's hardwired like you, Johnny," said J-Bone.

More than wired, Johnny saw, as the dolphin surfaced sluggishly, his grace nearly lost under the crusted ferroplastic articulated armor gleaming dully along his side. Faded stencils read US NAVY. Twin bulges on either side of the dolphin's skull gave him the clumsy look of an AWACS spyplane.

"Jones is a cyborg, surplus from the last war," J-Bone explained.

"And *this* was Spider's best bet?" Johnny said—amazed, then dismayed, then finally, angry.

"One thing Spider wasn't," J-Bone said, "was a fool. Jones is our main hacker here. He's connected to the satellite dish up top; logs us into the comsats, juggles the frequencies. Makes it all work. Might say he's the Loteks' CPU, and he's a multi-tasking motherfucker, let me tell you."

"Yeah, but . . . ?"

"But hacking's just a sideline for Jones. Spider knew that Jones is really designed to work with SQUIDs, sucking the codes out of enemy subs."

"Squids?" Johnny looked deeper into the pool for things with arms. Jones was on the surface, thrashing, making chirping sounds.

"Superconducting Quantum Interference Detectors," J-Bone explained. "See those bulging implants where his eyebrows oughta be? He's hardwired to suss out software, capture the codes out of enemy subs. Jones is a code breaker, Johnny. Infrasound scans right through the hull."

"You're saying he can read this chip of mine? Figure out the download code?"

J-Bone shrugged. "Even the primitive SQUIDs could measure a magnetic field a millionth the strength of geomantic force. It's like pulling a whisper out of a cheering stadium. And according to Spider, Jones is late-model."

Jones was still thrashing, and the cheeps and chirps were getting louder, almost forming an approximation of intelligent sound. In fact, J-Bone seemed to understand them.

"Okay, sailor," he said. "Jane, can you take care of Jones?"

"Sure." Jane opened a drawer and rummaged through it until she found a syringe. Holding it in her fist, she leaned over the pool.

Jones surfaced, heaving half his armored bulk over the edge of the pool. Instinctively Johnny jumped back in alarm, afraid the cheap blue plastic pool would crack.

Jane stabbed Jones overhand with the syringe, striking between two of its armor plates.

Johnny could have sworn Jones was smiling as he slid back into the water. "What the hell was that?"

Jane handed Johnny the empty syringe. "What do you think?"

Johnny held it up to the light. "Heroin?"

J-Bone nodded. "He's a junkie. We keep him supplied with smack."

"But—how does a cybernetic dolphin get hooked on smack?"

"The war," J-Bone said, shrugging. He seemed surprised at Johnny's naïveté. "The Navy had them all hooked. How else do you get 'em working for you?"

In the darkness under the bridge, the ropes hung down like thick tendrils, heavy with black, poisonous fruit.

Motoring up, Shinji and his Yakuza assault team were black shapes barely distinguishable from the night.

They moved like death itself, injected into hanging veins.

Nearby, deeper in the girders of the bridge, moving more slowly but even more inexorably, like a force of nature, was another shape. Its shock of white hair and the mist off the cryo-unit slung across its back would have given it away, were it not resting, hidden behind a girder as the Yakuza Ninjas rose higher.

Street Preacher watched.

He loved competition.

He smiled. Steel teeth gleamed.

He continued on his way.

The Loteks brought a chair out of a closet. It was wired with jacks, cables, fiber optics. On the back it said CNN. They rolled the chair to the center of the floor right in front of the pool.

They positioned it on top of a yellow triangle painted on the floor.

"You've done this before?" Johnny asked, looking at the chair suspiciously.

The Loteks were too busy to answer, plugging in wires, checking gain, aiming the cone-shaped ultra-sound scanners.

Jones was relaxing, rolling on his back. *Blissed out*, thought Johnny. He didn't know whether to be envious or concerned. On a schematic world map high on the wall, lights came on and off as the dolphin accessed and logged out of different parts of the international satellite net, surfing along the matrix that connected the world's communications systems.

Johnny had forgotten about Jane—until she appeared from the closet with a pair of earphones in one hand and a VR helmet in the other.

"What's this?" asked Johnny. *"Earphones? And a helmet?"*

"The earphones are for *him,"* J-Bone said, pointing to Jones, who lay happily on his back in the pool. "Jones doesn't dig visuals. His is a sound thing. So to speak. The helmet is for us, so we can follow the scan on the monitor. Now get in the chair if you want us to unlock these codes. Then we can dig this crap out of your head."

Johnny got into the chair.

"Has Jones done this before? Have you?"

J-Bone laughed. "Are you kidding? I'm not even sure it's fucking possible."

Johnny started to get out of the chair but J-Bone held him back with a hand and a laugh.

"Just chill, okay? He's gotta triangulate the infrasound in your implant. It all makes noise, did you know that? The electrons rushing along the wires, the capacitors discharging, the chips loading up, the memory cells groaning with overloads. The snap and the crackle and the pop. It's not a big noise but it's real. Jones has told me all about it. 'Course, it could be just the heroin talking to him. Smack makes a singing . . ."

"This is bullshit!" Johnny started to get up but Jane held him back this time.

"Try, Johnny," she said. "What choice do you have? What choice do any of us have?"

He looked into her eyes; for the first time, she looked scared. He leaned back as another Lotek fitted the earphones over his ears and set the gain.

"Hold still, okay?" J-Bone said with a laugh. "Don't want him microwaving your frontal lobe . . ."

"Fuck you," said Johnny. "Fuck the whole bunch of you."

As if in answer, Jane took his hand.

"Now give me what you've got off the download code," J-Bone said.

Johnny reached into his pocket and pulled out the torn paper and handed it to J-Bone.

It was the Japanese cartoon character.

"Far out," said J-Bone. "Captain Kitano! Okay, roll 'em, boys!"

FIFTEEN

—◼—

Buddy had always been afraid of heights, even as a kid back in the South Bronx; when his mother sent him out on the fire escape to bring in the laundry, he cried like a child and she did it herself.

He had hooked up with the Loteks four years ago, at eighteen. He was just out of Rikers after eleven months awaiting trial on a drug rap, a phony one—though he was guilty of enough for which he had never been caught; he was a street kid, after all—and when the charges were eventually dismissed, instead of trekking back home to the South Bronx, where a Jesus-freak uncle and a gameshow-addicted Mom were waiting in front of the 27-inch color set he had boosted for them, he had slept for a week on the faux-oak benches in Penn Station, picking up a few bucks watching over commuters' shoulders at the pay phones and spying out their calling-card numbers, wholesaling them to a phone-freaquer who retailed them to a man who brokered them to a man who job-lotted them to a man who turned out to be a man called Spider.

Spider was and wasn't a Lotek, a doctor/genius/freak/hacker who was also a fierce loner, and Buddy had drifted into the orbit of his colleague-in-crime and in many ways opposite, J-Bone, who was also a genius but far less of a loner, the kind of guy other guys follow because he has a fire burning in him that makes him sort of a beacon. A light on a hill. Or a bridge.

J-Bone's fire was for freedom, freedom of everything—free love, free drugs, free information; and mainly, free people. He called himself an anarchist. And he wanted only followers who followed of their own free will.

Which suited Buddy fine. He was, like most people, better at following than leading; and he was, also like most people, looking for something or someone to believe in. And the Loteks had *style*. As J-Bone used to joke, the Loteks had lots of 'tude—*atti*tude and *alti*tude. It was the second of the 'tudes that bothered Buddy. He didn't mind acting cool or getting cooled, the beefs or the fights; he didn't mind prowling like an alleycat through deserted neighborhoods, boosting weaponry and "liberating" electronics hardware; he didn't mind dealing with the crime orgs on one hand and the cops on the other, the intricate protocols of underworld life; he didn't mind the sleepless nights, the long dull days of waiting for this or that delivery, the surveillance or the boredom that went with the membership in a quasi-military organization—even one based on anarchist principles.

The only thing he minded was being "at home." The only thing he minded was Heaven. Up on the bridge, Buddy remembered—his genes, his nerves, his marrow and his myelin remembered—that he was afraid of high places. Most of the Loteks weren't, maybe because their eyes weren't any good, or maybe because they lacked some gene left over from prehistoric life in the trees.

Buddy had read about genes and jungles in the three-month science and social history course that J-Bone made all the Loteks take, insisting that there was nothing more dangerous than ignorance. "Knowledge is freedom," J-Bone maintained. "That's why we fucking give it away."

Buddy kept his fear of heights hidden, concealing it carefully from J-Bone, pushing himself to follow the other Loteks along the narrow walkways, forcing himself to sleep like them in a web hammock over a yawning abyss. He had never really conquered the fear but he had mastered it, whipping it back to a dark corner of his brain where it waited, like a pit bull, snarling, ready to spring on him if he ever lost his concentration.

Which is why he carefully controlled his breathing as he made his way along the narrow bridge beam, back toward the south platform, where he had been sent to resume his watch after J-Bone had taken Jane and the suit called Johnny to meet Jones.

Something was different below. Something had seriously changed while he had been gone. There was a car in the circle below, and two people stood by the still-blazing fire that had once been Spider's van.

Steeling himself to keep the pit bull of fear at bay, Buddy leaned out and looked down to see who they were; and it was at precisely this instant, when his nerves were thus engaged, that a black-hooded figure crept up behind him and with one swift, silent stroke—a motion almost beautiful in its practiced easy grace—cut his throat from ear to ear.

Buddy fell.

He found that he couldn't scream without a throat, but that was all right, he didn't need to.

Buddy fell.

It was almost a relief to finally let the pit bull loose and find that it was just a puppy, an eager, joyful little being, all soft edges, that leaped and barked happily around him as he spun, spun, spun down into the night, toward the guttering fire.

Shinji never asked his Yakuza to do what he wouldn't undertake to do for himself.

He cleaned his knife and inserted it back into his ankle holster, even as the body of the creature he had just killed was crashing into the dust 110 feet below, between the two Yakuza standing by the fire.

The bald Yakuza walked over to the body, rolled it over with his foot, noting the clean precision of the wound. "The boss himself," he said admiringly.

The woman with him nodded but didn't answer.

She wasn't speaking.

He went back to watching the fire.

She went back to watching the firelight gleam off the Thermidor missile launcher in his arms.

Above, Shinji started off along the narrow beam, leaving the rope behind, walking on the balls of his feet, moving now less like a spider and more like a cat.

Toward the glow at the center of the bridge that was the Lotek electronic command center, Times Square.

Three soft pairs of cat feet followed.

"I thought you said Jones was all about *sound,*" said Johnny. He was watching one of the Loteks feed the image of the Japanimation superhero into a scanner.

"He is," said J-Bone. "But visual or aural, it's all information. It'll be up on the monitors so we can see. Jones sees in his own way. Here it comes . . ."

The superhero image appeared on one of the monitors over the control console. The two others at either side were undifferentiated snow.

"Now if Jones can retrieve the other two images, we'll have the code," J-Bone said.

Jane reached over and squeezed Johnny's hand.

"Let's go, then," said Johnny. "Let's *do* it."

"Not yet," said J-Bone. "First you and I got to make a deal."

Johnny looked over warily. "Now what?"

"I know what's in your head," said J-Bone. "Jane told me. We all know. And if Jones gets it out, the world knows."

"What do you mean?"

"The cure for NAS. We broadcast it. Put it on the Net, right across the planet. Free. *We give it away.*"

Johnny considered this concept. He realized he had never *given* anything away before; he lived in a world in which everything, including his very memory, had always been for sale.

A slow grin spread across his face. "Listen, if you can get it out . . ."

"Yeah?"

"Be my guest. Knock yourself out. Give it away."

Jane grinned and squeezed Johnny's hand again.

J-Bone turned to the waiting Loteks, all business: "Let's get Jones's ultrasound antennae up and running. Get ready to broadcast on the external bands; lock us onto a satellite. Everybody clear of the ultrasound area!"

A switch was thrown, a lever pulled: A motor whined and the two cone-shaped arrays on each side of Jones's pool began rotating slowly—until they each pointed toward the chair.

"Move, Janey!" J-Bone grabbed her and pulled her away from Johnny, out of the yellow triangle.

Shit! Johnny closed his eyes.

Whump . . .
Whump . . .
Whump . . .

The Daihatsu 444 beat its way over the Ratlands, the staccato whine of its alcohol-powered Wankel engine swallowed by the beat of its rotor blades. On the side of the sleek fuselage, just behind the clear plexi cockpit, a tasteful gold Y glinted in the scattered light from below.

In the cockpit, the pilot watched for abandoned communications towers, dangling powerlines, unmarked pylons and towers. He didn't like flying so low; he definitely didn't like flying at night without lights; and he didn't like flying over this area, which was off the standard routes, and all but off the map.

And he didn't like the man sitting next to him. His passenger was one of the Yakuza big boys, polite but cold, like somebody visiting from another age. One of those Shogun dudes from central headquarters.

The passenger was dressed as if for a board meeting: dark blue, expensively tailored suit; crisp new white shirt; silk tie. Tasseled oxblood loafers.

The river below gleamed like a ribbon of mercury, a man-made (or mis-made) substance thicker than water, so viscous that the wind from the whirling rotor blades barely ruffled its surface.

The pilot felt a hand on his arm. The passenger was pointing up ahead, to where a former drawbridge, a dark and deconstructed pile of rubble, refuse, remnants and rubbish rose from the Ratlands into the night sky.

"There," the passenger said.

On the riverbank, two faces looked up from the reeds where they had been hiding as the helicopter passed over.

Whump . . .

Whump . . .

Whump . . .

"Cops," said derelict #1, upending the wine bottle as the dark shape passed over.

"Robbers," said derelict #2, taking the last drops of wine from the bottle.

They were back to their disagreeing. Or thought they were.

The thing is, they were both right.

The sound started as dolphin-speak and grew even higher, even weirder, even squeakier.

Jane watched as Johnny grew rigid, leaning back in the chair, his teeth and fists clenched.

In the pool, Jones was trembling. The water was dimpled with tiny waves.

The sound grew higher, modulating into a painful squeal—and then was suddenly gone. An eerie silence fell over the room.

"The ultrasound suppresses all the normal over-tones," J-Bone said. "Notice how my voice sounds weird?"

"Like you're far away and close at the same time," Jane said.

"Whatever." J-Bone led her to the control console, where they watched the monitors over the Lotek techs who were working the board.

"Those three screens at the top will show the *code,* if Jones can get to it," J-Bone said. He pointed to the bank of three CBS Sports monitors. The center screen displayed the Japanese cartoon figure; the two on either side were still blank with snow.

"And those on the bottom show the progress of the code *breaker,* the SQUID."

The lower bank of Eyewitness News monitors all displayed the same image: an X-ray of a skull, complete with a tiny implant curled up like a baby. Only this time, in addition to the data oozing out like an oil spill, the image showed wavering tendrils trying to get *in.*

"That's Johnny?" Jane asked.

"Well that's the head part of him," said J-Bone. "And that's the SQUID, those fingery things."

"They're beautiful," said Jane.

J-Bone stared at her. "Beautiful?"

Jane shrugged. How could she explain that they reminded her of the plants her father had grown in his nursery in Brooklyn? He had once shown her a time-compressed video of tree roots searching for water, trying to break through concrete and steel, and eventually succeeding.

"The city makes trees stronger," her father had said. "The search for water makes water taste sweeter." She remembered the hug he had given her. "It's like love."

"Hey, Janey!" J-Bone was still staring at her. "Where'd you go, girl?"

"Nowhere. Just thinking." Brought back to reality, Jane looked back at Johnny. He lay back in his chair, tensed, rigid; a curious reversal, the mirror image of a man at rest.

In the pool, Jones seemed perfectly still. Only the tiny waves roughening the surface of the water showed that he, too, was rigid with—what? Effort? Fear?

There was no way to know.

"Outta sight!" said Stick.

He could hardly believe his luck.

Instead of punishing him for his accident, J-Bone had placed him in charge of the beetle-bomber. Which was good. It meant he no longer had to listen to Buddy's lessons.

Buddy was a nice guy but bothersome. Jesus! He always had to be, like, correcting you all the time.

Stick only had to be corrected once. Once he figured out a thing, he had it.

He made mistakes, like anybody, but he made them once, and that was it.

J-Bone understood that, and Stick loved him for it.

Maybe if Spider had been in the stepvan, it would have been different; but once J-Bone had found out that his friend was already dead, and that it hadn't been Stick's fault, he had cooled out. Maybe he'd decided Stick was ready for some responsibility.

Maybe J-Bone had even wanted to make it up for how he had gone off on him.

Whatever. Anyway, it was done with, and here he was. Stick felt like a real Lotek now, on duty in charge of the Loteks' heavy weapons system, the beetle-bomber.

The improvised siege warfare device was not usually manned, but tonight there was a half-alert, since J-Bone had taken Jane and her new client, the suit, into Times Square to see Jones.

There was all sorts of stuff going on.

Even a strange limo, down below.

Buddy had been the first to see it, over on the far pier. He had told Stick to just watch the car, stand fast, and wait for his next all-clear. As the south pier sentry leader, Buddy gave the all-clear every fifteen minutes, tapping on a beam three times.

It had been fifteen minutes, for sure. He would signal anytime soon.

Stick would be ready. Stick was disciplined, patient, alert, a real Lotek now.

Cool. Standing to one side of the release lever, in full control of the two gasoline-filled VWs left on the ramp.

Proud. A true Lotek.

Which was his last thought when the bolt penetrated the right side of his heart, severing the main artery even as it collapsed the ventricle in one last spasm.

The good thing about a crossbow bolt is that it kills quickly and quietly.

The bad thing is that it hits so hard it knocks the victim down.

Which was a problem, Shinji saw, as soon as he had fired.

Instead of sinking to his knees, as he might have with a poison dart, or falling in two pieces, as he would have if sliced by the filament, the Lotek sentry fell straight back into a structural upright, some kind of piece of railing.

At least Shinji thought it was a piece of railing. But when the kid hit it, it went down too easily, almost like a lever.

Shinji heard the rumbling to his left. He looked over just in time to see the VW start rolling slowly down the ramp, picking up speed as it sailed off the end, already glowing with the flames just starting to lick at the gasoline-soaked seats.

"That's disgusting," said the female Yakuza.

"What's dis*what?*" said the male.

"What you're doing."

What he was doing was going through Buddy's pockets.

"He almost fell on me," the bald man said. "I figure I'm entitled. He owes me something."

"Grave-robbing," the woman said. "Child robbing."

"This guy is no child. Look at this." The man held up a pair of brass knuckles from Buddy's pocket. "Is this a toy?"

The Yakuza turned Buddy over; his head lolled back, almost severed by the cut that had taken his life.

"Help me drag him into the fire."

"Do it your fucking self."

"Damn it, woman. Are you forgetting who's in charge here? Hold this." He handed her the Thermidor heat-seeking missile launcher and bent down to pick up the body.

It was limp and hard to lift, and what if the head came off? That would be unpleasant as all hell. He was carrying it to toss it into the fire, but . . .

"Look out!"

197

But when he looked up he saw that he needn't bother. Tossing the body into the fire, that is. The flaming car heading down was only 1.4 seconds away from incinerating them both.

"Damn!" said the blond woman, rolling out of the way.

She scrambled to her feet, beating out the gasoline and naphtha flames that had splashed onto her jump-suit.

She peered into the pyre where the other Yakuza had been. She could hardly suppress a grin. She was in charge now.

She shouldered the Thermidor. There was no sense waiting for Shinji's orders. If this wasn't a case of *under attack,* what the hell was? Hardly pausing to aim, she fired the missile up into the darkness.

Whump . . .
Whump . . .
Whump . . .
"Closer."
Whump . . .
Whump . . .
Whump . . .
"That's good. Thanks."

And fuck you, too, the pilot said silently as he held the Daihatsu 444 steady at eighteen inches from the upper tower of the bridge—twelve inches closer than he liked to get to anything more solid than a radio wave.

The passenger got out, carrying a cryo-unit in one hand like a small, square suitcase. For such a large man, he was very agile. He seemed to have no fear of heights. He stood on the top of the bridge pier and shouted through the open door:

"Pull off a hundred yards or so and wait. Pick me up here in twenty minutes. Sharp."

The pilot nodded. *Jesus!* These execs treated helicopters as if they were rowboats, as if they could just sit in the air and float. Whereas actually it was more work to hover than to fly.

The door slammed and the pilot pulled off as the passenger—ex-passenger—started climbing down the pier on a steel ladder, the cryo-unit slung over his back.

The pilot pulled off a hundred yards. He searched for a cigarette and found one in his shirt pocket.

Whump . . .

Whump . . .

Whump . . .

He searched for a match. It was against the rules to smoke while flying but what fun is life without its little secrets?

No matches. *Shit!* he thought. Then he saw a tiny light, looking almost like the tip of a cigarette, as if someone had read his mind and was passing him a light.

Except that it was so far away.

And approaching so very fast.

It lived!

Its short but magnificent life was ruled by one passion, one desire.

Heat.

Not the heat of the engine that propelled it from the shoulder-mounted tube, or the pyre of the burning VW beside it. It was programmed to ignore heat behind and below its arc. That was not in its nature.

And not the dim organic heat of creatures scurrying through the cold steel and concrete of the bridge, for that heat was too dim to awaken its passion. That was not in its nature either.

No, it sprung, it leapt to life, and immediately drew—as we draw breath—a bead on the beautiful, inviting electronic aura of the Loteks' electronic command center, Times Square, with its clusters of chips and wires and circuit boards emitting flirtatious waves of erotic warmth.

But constancy was not in its nature, either.

It was approaching Times Square, when over its event horizon appeared an even more voluptuous, more tantalizing source of heat: the contained explosions of two fiery chambers, 11,500 degrees in the Daihatsu's Wankel, a heat source so throbbing with negentropic sexuality, so pulsating, so deliriously desirable that it changed course immediately and rose to blossom and unite with its beloved in a fiery ecstasy of perfect love.

The explosion rocked the entire bridge.

The debris raining down from the fireball where the helicopter had once hovered clattered off the roof of the C-144 fuselage that housed Times Square.

"Stations!" J-Bone shouted. "You all know the drill!"

"What's happening?" Jane asked.

"Somebody's idea of payback," J-Bone said. "An attack! Come on! We need you!"

Jane looked at Johnny, still rigid in the chair; at Jones, quivering in the pool; at the CBS monitors, where images were struggling to form through the snow; at the Eyewitness News monitors, where the tendrils were still caressing the image of Johnny's brain, trying to get in.

Love seeks a way, her father had always said.

"No way," Jane said, pulling free from J-Bone's grip. "I'm staying here!"

Johnny was having a dream. He knew it was a dream and not a memory, because there was his mother again, and he had erased her from his memory.

So she was not his real mother but his dream

mother. Or was a dream mother a real mother? Wasn't a dream you cherished more real than a memory you had erased?

Johnny was walking toward her. She was at the desk, turned away.

But wait. This time there were shimmers of light breaking into the room. Johnny noticed it was a strange light, wavery and soft, as if he were underwater: But how did a kid know what it was like to be underwater?

He was walking toward the desk, where his mother sat. He knew she was his mother because she was turned away.

Mother: turned away.

But something was different. This time. In the light. She was turning toward him.

"Eat this!" the blond Yakuza said. She raised the missile launcher and fired again. Up into the night. The neat thing about the Thermidor was that you didn't have to aim.

It aimed itself.

And she didn't have to worry about hitting her people. Her people were all cool.

It was heat the missile sought.

"Come on!" J-Bone said. "Jones will either get it or he won't. He doesn't need you. But we do!"

"Look," Jane said.

On the Eyewitness News monitors, the tendrils exploring the image of Johnny's head had found an opening.

In the pool, Jones was trembling as well as vibrating. The waves were getting higher. Water was splashing over the rim of the pool, onto the scuffed linoleum floor.

In the chair Johnny was almost smiling. Or was that a look of terror on his face?

On the leftmost of the CBS Sports monitors, to one side of the Japanese cartoon superhero, a face was appearing, as of someone approaching through a thick snowstorm.

It lived!

Its short but magnificent life was ruled by one passion, one desire.

Heat.

Not the heat of the engine that propelled it or the pyre of the burning car beside it; not the dim, organic heat of creatures scurrying through the cold steel and concrete of the bridge—these were not in its nature.

Nor was it tempted, as its predecessor had been, by the voluptuous heat of a twin Wankel, for the helicopter was gone, leaving only a warm spot in the sky.

No, it sprang to life, and locked its bead on Times Square, and left it there: focusing the passionate intensity of its lust on the beautiful clusters of chips and wires and circuit boards emitting flirtatious waves of erotic warmth.

It rose through the air, ecstatic, toward the beckoning electronic bonfire contained in the hulk of the old C-144, and burst through the steel and plastic floor in a display of romantic ardor that was seen for miles. Is there anything more explosive than the orgasmic consummation of a lifetime of devoted love? For a lifetime is a lifetime, no matter how short.

The explosion knocked Johnny out of his chair.

Jane rolled over on the floor, unthinkingly, to cover him; he seemed somehow as defenseless as a child.

Jones's pool rocked with the blast, sending waves over the rim and onto the floor. Jones himself began to scream, terrified squeals breaking through the air as the frequency dropped. He began to swim in small circles, like a convict pacing his cell.

One of the ultrasound scanner towers collapsed

slowly, folding hydraulically, like a flower at night. The other scanner ratcheted and wheeled, searching for its target lock as the program that controlled it repeated in a mindless loop.

"Jane."

It was Johnny. His eyes were open. He was bleeding again from his mouth and one ear. He seemed somehow stronger, though, than before. He got up and pulled Jane to her feet.

"How's Jones?" he asked. Jones seemed all right. He was still swimming in circles, but at least the water wasn't bloody.

Johnny and Jane limped toward the smoking console, where J-Bone and another Lotek were frantically throwing switches.

"Did he get it?" Johnny asked. "Did he get the code?"

"See for yourself," J-Bone spat.

Up on the CBS Sports monitors, the center screen still showed the cartoon superhero. The other two, including the one on which Jane thought she had almost seen the faint outline of a woman's face, were white with snow again.

"Shit!" said Johnny.

"We almost had it," said J-Bone. "But now . . ." With a sweeping gesture he took in the broken scanners, the water sloshed out of the pool. "We're in damage-control mode here. Can somebody give Jones a fix? And somebody check with security. . . ."

"J-Bone." A Lotek directed his gaze to one of the smaller security surveillance monitors, a black and white unit over the door. This one was supposed to show the central span sentry team.

It showed a Lotek screaming silently, nailed to an improvised wooden cross.

"Sweet Jesus!" J-Bone ran out the door, slipping a bolt into his air gun, followed by the rest of the Loteks.

Johnny sat down with his head in his hands. Jane sat beside him.

"Jones was almost there!" she said. "He almost had the image for the code."

"I know," said Johnny.

"How could you tell? What do you remember?"

"Nothing. I don't remember anything. Just a feeling. I could feel everything in me starting to break up, like ice cracking. And the funny thing is, Jane, it was a good feeling." He took her hand. "The funny thing is . . ."

Suddenly, a strangely formal voice penetrated the gloom.

"Mr. Smith?"

SIXTEEN

---◼---

Spider had known his business. The lessons he had learned from working with patients whose nerves had been damaged by NAS had been used to modify the nerves of healthy people: to tweak and twang and soup up the synapses of those who were still normal—or better than normal; bunching and rerouting the neural pathways that had been cobbled together, by a million years of chance and evolution, into logical systems and streamlined pathways; adding silicon-chip switching nodes and intradermal relays to supplement and speed up the comparatively slow myelin-sheathed biologicals, so that in most cases the body was responding long before the message had reached or even been routed to the brain.

It was a modification for athletes. Or fighters.

Jane was his final masterpiece. Even now, with NAS beginning to ravage her system, she had faster reflexes than most "normal" people . . . which was why she had thrown herself down behind Johnny's chair and rolled under the fallen control console even before her brain "heard" the smooth, formal voice from the shadows, and long before she saw the dark-suited man step out into the cool electronic half-light, his arms held stiffly down at his sides.

Johnny was still in his chair, still in a stupor from the ultrascan, almost a dream state. He didn't even notice Jane was gone. He saw the man in the corner and asked, his voice slurred as if he were a little drunk, "Pharmakom?"

"Afraid not."

"Aren't you the security guy? With the codes?"

"Afraid not."

Jane made her move. But now that she was acting by design and not instinct, she lost most of the speed routed into her by Spider's neural modifications.

Plus, the man was fast.

BLAM!

He raised and fired the .357 toward her in one easy movement, and she hit the floor and rolled over— running on pure reflex again—as the bullet whipped past her temple with a soft, malicious whisper. She crawled back into the shadows under the control console with a new respect for her adversary. Middle-aged, overweight, but fast, and light on his feet—like a boxer or a sumo wrestler.

To Johnny it all still seemed dreamlike. Who was this dude in the dark suit with the immaculate white shirt? "Whoever you are, I know what you want. The data. That means you can't shoot me."

"Not in the head," Takahashi said. As if to emphasize his point, he lowered the .357 so that it pointed toward Johnny's gut.

Johnny closed his eyes. *Maybe it won't be so bad, after all; finally end all this shit. . . .*

But instead of firing, Takahashi bent over to set down the cryo-unit he was carrying in his left hand. As he straightened, Jane was preparing to leap; but she

206

was afraid he would fire as she hit him, and this time, with the gun trained on Johnny's midsection . . .

Then she saw Takahashi shift the gun to his left hand. With his right, he reached behind his back, under his suit coat, as if reaching for his wallet. But instead of a billfold he pulled out a short sword that gleamed in the cool electronic light from the banks of monitors that provided the only illumination in the room.

Jane moved forward, coiled to leap. She would have to take her chances.

The light on the sword flickered, and she thought for a moment that he was already swinging it.

But it was the monitors. They were flickering, all in strange unison, faster and faster: the Sonys, the Samsungs, the CBS and Eyewitness loot, even the little nine-inch black and white Zenith security monitors over the door. Dusted with static and snow, flickering faster and faster—

Then, suddenly, they all carried the same image: a middle-aged woman with short, dark brown hair. Conservative, well-groomed; *yin* and *yang* earrings. Her voice through the missile-damaged speakers was hoarse, like a whisper:

"Takahashi!"

Takahashi froze, sword in one hand and pistol in the other.

Johnny turned in his chair and looked up, toward the monitors. He felt a new wave of confusion. Why did the face look familiar? Was he still awake, or had he slipped back into his dream?

Jane dropped back down into the shadows, her heart pounding. She would use the diversion to creep up a little closer.

"You!" said Takahashi to the face on the monitors. He stood rigid, as if at attention, his own face a mask. "Are you everywhere?"

207

The woman didn't deign to answer his question. Instead she asked one of her own: "You don't even know what he is carrying in his head, do you?"

"I neither know nor care," said Takahashi. "I am a Yakuza, a professional. I know that what he is carrying must be worth billions, for we are being paid millions to recover it. And I know that honor demands that . . ."

"You fool." The woman's voice was scornful. "You are weak, Takahashi. Your honor is a mask. You are blind. You have no idea what you are returning to Pharmakom."

"Enough!" said Takahashi. He approached another foot toward Johnny, raising the sword.

Under the table, Jane tensed, ready to leap.

"He carries the cure to Nerve Attenuation Syndrome," the woman on the monitors said.

"You lie!"

Takahashi raised the .357 and fired three times. Three nineteen-inch screens exploded; three images of the woman disappeared.

"You are a ghost! You are madness! You *lie!*"

The woman's face on the other monitors softened with what might almost have been pity. "They had the cure a year ago, Takahashi. It was not necessary for your daughter to die."

Takahashi winced as if he had been struck by a bullet. He raised the pistol to fire again, but even as he did, the face on the monitors that were left morphed into a familiar image: a little girl at play with her dolls.

"Mikiyo . . . !"

But she was gone, and the woman's face was back.

"Pharmakom is keeping the cure off the market for the sake of the sell-through," she said, her voice steely hard again. "Treating the disease is far more profitable than curing it. That's why the scientists stole it. Their consciences demanded . . ."

"NOOOOOoooo!" Takahashi's face twisted with rage, then composed itself again into the emotionless mask of pride, of honor—only this time there was a lunatic edge to his features as he methodically fired his three remaining shots into three of the remaining monitors.

But still, the woman looked on from the monitors that were left, against the ceiling, over the doorway . . .

Takahashi threw down the .357. As it clattered across the floor, he raised his sword with both hands and brought it down onto the twisted strands of cables leading into the central control console.

Jane and Johnny both ducked as the room flashed bright with a shower of sparks, then grew dim again as all the monitors went blank with static and snow.

Takahashi raised the sword for the second strike, poised over Johnny who lay in the chair, staring up, wide-eyed, as if into the eye of eternity itself.

"Don't," Johnny said. It struck him as foolish even as he said it, and he was irritated with himself that he had wasted his last words. He closed his eyes, as if in prayer.

There was a whisper, and he opened his eyes again. He saw Takahashi, wide-eyed, open his mouth as if to speak.

Then fall to his knees.

The sword rang like a bell as it hit the floor.

"Hello, Johnny."

As he spoke, Shinji was holstering his pneumatic pistol inside his black nylon jumpsuit. He peeled his mask off his head. Behind him, a second Yakuza, still masked, scanned the room with an air gun poised.

Shinji unscrewed the tip from his thumb and shook

out the filament, a bright wrinkle in the dim space-time of the room.

"Didn't think we would meet again, did you?"

With a twist of his thumb, coupled with a short arc of his arm, Shinji swung—Johnny ducked—and the filament sliced an ellipse from the back of the chair where Johnny's head had just been.

Jane slipped closer, and this time the Yakuza behind Shinji saw her, turned, and fired. Her reflexes were faster than her vision, though, and she had already ducked under the console by the time he got his shots off. The gun made a fierce whispering noise, like a long curse, and darts rattled off the console, the floor, and the wall.

Johnny backed away, reaching behind him on the ground, searching in arcs for the .357. Instead, he found Takahashi's sword. He almost smiled as he held it up in front of him, and stood—

And his smile disappeared as Shinji swung again. The bright loop of almost-nothingness sang through the air—and the sword Johnny held became a stump with an elaborate ivory handle.

Johnny dropped it and backed up against the wall.

There was nowhere else to go.

"Mama's sweet baby," said the blond Yakuza, cooing to the Thermidor missile launcher cradled in her arms. She caressed its cute little trigger lovingly. . . .

Jane uncoiled across the floor like a snake, striking out with her arms and pulling the second Yakuza off his feet. She was already beside him as he hit the floor, and her fist found the mark, striking him square in the throat. There was a crunch, like a cabbage snapping off its stalk.

And no cry at all.

* * *

"Raise your chin," said Shinji. "Let's make this clean."

It lived.

J-Bone loved problems. One of the more interesting ones he had faced was in the construction of Heaven's largest single space, the electronic command center, Times Square. The salvaged Air National Guard C-144 had been too large to lift into place with the crane that the Loteks had liberated for their construction work, so J-Bone had split the fuselage into two equal parts, hoisted them up separately, and then stitched them back together with duct tape, fiberglass rods and steel cables. It not only held, it was flexible enough to allow for the inevitable expansion along the joints in winter, and for the sway of the bridge when it "sang" (the choir of heaven, J-Bone called it) in the fierce winds that swept across the Jersey Ratlands every spring.

The seam itself was invisible, but divisible. Thus, when the third Thermidor missile, seeking the residual heat stored in the capacitors and turned-off monitors, struck the seam, it passed through instead of exploding, separating the space into two almost equal parts, leaving one half of the room still secured to the bridge frame, and the other barely balanced, ripped open, rocking, tipping down toward the river 110 feet below.

When Johnny heard the hissing of the missile as it passed, he thought it was Shinji's killer filament zipping through his neck. He felt his head spinning, falling; and, opening his eyes for one last look at the universe that had never been too kind to him, was surprised to find that his head, though indeed falling, was still attached to his body.

He was falling sideways across the floor. Which

seemed odd until he realized that the floor was tilted thirty, now forty, now fifty degrees from the horizontal.

Something brushed his hand and he caught it. It slid through his fingers, burning, and he loved the burning because the floor was gone and the burning was the only thing slowing him down; he grabbed tighter and yanked to a stop.

It was a cable.

He held a twisted bunch of fibers, cracked insulation and fourteen-gauge wire, like vines; and there was nothing under his feet but pure empty night, and he was swinging, out, over the darkness . . .

. . . And back.

"Hold on!"

Johnny looked up, toward the blown-open end of the steeply tilted fuselage that had been Times Square. Shinji, a worried look on his face, was crawling down the littered slope, hanging onto a steel beam that was wedged into the rubble, extending his hand toward Johnny.

"Hold on, I'm coming!" he said.

Johnny suddenly laughed.

"If I fall you don't get the head," he said. "If I fall you're fucked, right?"

"Just hold on . . ."

Johnny let go with one hand and kicked, so that he swung out into the night, and back, Tarzan-like.

"Hold on. . . ."

Johnny laughed. His assassin wanted to save him! He howled with laughter, swinging out into the night on his electronic jungle vine.

He had the distinct feeling that his life was almost over, but what the hell. At least the universe had a sense of humor.

She was alive. He was dead.

Her split-second inventory completed, Jane rolled

off the corpse of the second Yakuza. His shattered windpipe had ceased its gurgling.

But what was that new sound? A wild laugh, almost a howl of triumph?

Jane got to her feet unsteadily on the buckled floor. The missile had struck and passed through the Loteks' command center, splitting it in two. The half she was in was almost stable, rocking only a little. It was dark except for the erratic shower of sparks under the control console where small electrical fires were coming to life and dying as the Loteks' self-repairing "smart" circuitry searched for open lines, and closed down shorted ones.

One end of the room was wide open to the night. Jane walked to the edge and looked down.

The other half of the C-144's fuselage was tipped almost perpendicular, held onto the bridge by the electrical cable, but slipping even now as the cables stretched and snapped. It was falling, but slowly.

At the far end, where one wall had been blown open, Jane could see a figure swinging out into the darkness, howling with laughter.

Now she knew what the weird sound was.

Johnny.

He had finally lost it.

"Take my hand," Shinji said.

"Fuck you!" Johnny laughed.

Wrapping his legs around the beam, Shinji crawled farther out into the darkness, over empty space, reaching down toward the million-dollar mnemonic messenger.

"Don't be a fool," he said, trying not to look down. "We can make a deal."

Jane was amazed. The Yakuza, the one without the mask, the one they called Shinji, was crawling out on a beam toward Johnny, extending his hand, a rescuer now, no longer a destroyer.

213

She ran back to where the second Yakuza lay dead, and pried the dart gun out of his hands. It was empty, but she found a spare clip on his web belt and clicked it in.

Now.

She edged back toward the open end of the room. This was going to be complicated, but not impossible:

First let Shinji rescue Johnny.

Then take him out.

She was easing herself over the edge, where she would have a clear shot, when she felt the big, cold, ham-sized hand clamp over her temples. And squeeze.

She heard the voice just before she blacked out:

"Jesus time!"

"Dammit, take my hand!"

Shinji leaned out over the abyss, extending one hand as far as he could.

Johnny pulled himself up, and instead of grabbing Shinji's hand, reached over and grabbed his neck—and yanked, pulling so hard that the cables on which he swung popped, and snapped, and stretched like rubber bands.

But held. Just barely.

Shinji also held. He clung for dear life to the beam, so that it pulled out with him, balanced precariously, rocking like a seesaw, tipping. . . .

Then it, too, held.

"Damn you!" said Johnny. He was close enough to Shinji to kick him by swinging on the cable, swinging out to evade Shinji's return kick.

Only there was no return kick.

Shinji was holding on with both hands, turning himself around on the beam so that he was facing up. Johnny could feel the cables that were holding him popping and stretching. Just as they were about to give way altogether, he swung in and grabbed the beam above Shinji.

The beam slipped under his weight, and again held.

Just barely.

"A deal!" said Shinji. "Let's make a deal."

The roles were reversed. This time it was Johnny who crawled out on the beam, from above, and extended his hand.

Shinji reached up hopefully. Johnny took his wrist, just behind the thumb with the unscrewed cap. Shinji relaxed his grip, again hopefully.

But instead of pulling Shinji up, Johnny gave the wrist a little flick.

Shinji's eyes widened as he saw the bright flash of the filament, slicing through the end of the beam.

His eyes met Johnny's in a brief moment of cruel and total understanding as he began to fall. There was a long moment of silence, and then the night was loud with a single scream, dopplering from alto to tenor as Shinji fell.

Then silence again. Sudden and total.

A silence broken only by the soft dawn wind. The hawsers creaked, steel groaned, and Johnny realized where he was: hanging 110 feet over the Ratlands on a beam that was held only by a demolished tangle of cables, struts, and cross members.

Gingerly, he began to back up toward the comparative safety of the bridge structure, the ruined remnants of Times Square. The beam tipped and swayed dangerously, and there was a reddish tint in the air. Johnny looked behind him—just what he needed, another disaster! Was there a fire?

There was a fire, and it was a big one. The light from it was reddening the sky, flooding over the low ridge of the Palisades to the east.

The sun was coming up.

* * *

215

The girl was fast, but once caught she was easy.

Street Preacher was delighted at how nice she felt.

Street Preacher liked girls.

Their soft temples. Their narrow little heads.

He checked for a pulse. Didn't want to kill her.

Not like that.

Not easy.

Hooking one giant hand in the waistband of her tight black jeans, he dragged her across the tilted, buckled floor to the two timbers that had caught his eye.

They had been thrown up by the force of the missile into the form of a cross.

Perfect.

He slapped her up against it with one hand.

With his other hand, he searched behind him in the rubble.

Found a steel plate that would do for a hammer.

Finding the other was harder.

My kingdom for a nail.

Meanwhile, to the east, toward the south end of the bridge, another figure was being taken down from another cross.

Still alive, but barely.

J-Bone watched as the young crucified Lotek was laid on a blanket and taken away to the improvised clinic down under the bridge. It was more wishful thinking than serious medicine, he knew. Without Spider's expertise, what could they do? Get him stoned so he died without too much more pain. J-Bone forced his mind back to the business at hand. He had other, more pressing responsibilities. He had watched the missile pass through Times Square without exploding. The next one could take down the bridge, if he didn't stop it.

Judging by the trajectory, it had come from the south end of the bridge. Down by the parking lot where Spider's van had burned.

He fitted the laser sight onto his spring-loaded crossbow and headed south.

The hunter.

SEVENTEEN

—■—

Johnny pulled himself up the beam to the still-stable half of Times Square, stepped through the blown-out wall onto the floor—then jumped back in horror, almost falling.

Takahashi!

Johnny had thought he was dead.

And he almost was. The Yakuza executive's crisp white shirt was soaked through with blood from Shinji's darts. Takahashi staggered and reached into the pocket of his suit.

Johnny crouched down, expecting a gun.

Instead, Takahashi held out a piece of paper, torn from a fax.

"Yours . . ." he said. And toppled over, blood bubbling from his lips.

Johnny took the paper from his hand and unfolded it.

It was a riot scene, scanned from the *Beijing Evening News*.

"Number two!" Johnny said to himself. *Image #2 of the download code. But one more, still missing!*

218

Then Johnny heard singing behind him. A deep bass voice:

> "In the blood.
> In the blood,
> In the sweet everlasting
> Blood of the Lamb."

At first Johnny was not surprised. He was still a little dazed. It was gospel, and this was Heaven, after all.

Then he heard the scream.

Jane!

Then he heard the hammering.

Johnny recognized the white-haired man even though he couldn't see his face. He recognized him as the man who had attacked the stepvan outside Spider's. He recognized him by his movements: They were slow, deliberate, inexorable. Street Preacher moved like a tank, with neither intelligence nor hesitation, neither eagerness nor interest.

Thunk!

Thunk!

Street Preacher had torn a monitor bracket from the wall, and was using it to drive a nail through the fleshy center of Jane's palm.

Thunk!

Thunk!

After four hits he no longer needed to hold Jane's hand in place over the beam of his improvised cross. It was secured.

Thunk!

Thunk!

Jane had stopped screaming. Johnny was already on his way. He crawled under a section of dropped ceiling; he jumped over a smashed table that had once

219

held video switching relays and was now a mess of blasted, broken chips.

On his way across the room he picked up a four-foot section of pipe, and was already swinging it like a baseball bat as he hurled himself the last few feet across the glass- and rubble-littered floor.

The pipe connected with the back of Street Preacher's head.

Kkkranng!

Johnny's hands stung but he held onto the pipe.

Instead of going down, Street Preacher turned slowly, his skull ringing like steel, which indeed it was, since one of his myriad cyborg enhancements included a cranial protection rim.

His eyes were like tank headlights.

His steel teeth grinned a lethal grin.

Before Johnny could swing again, Street Preacher had plucked the pipe from his hand and hurled it, spinning, into the outer darkness beyond the shattered wall.

"Run, Johnny!" shouted Jane.

But it was too late.

Street Preacher had fallen to his knees, but not to pray. To fight. He had Johnny by the foot.

He stood up, swinging him like a rag doll, and swung him, spinning, toward the shattered wall, just like the pipe.

"Nooo!" Jane cried.

But Johnny didn't fly out into the darkness, like the pipe.

Instead he hit the wall. Head first.

Jane winced. Even though she was nailed to the cross herself, she could feel his pain. With the data overload crammed in his head, inaccessible. . . .

But the odd thing was that as Johnny slid down the wall, unconscious, he began to weep like a child, even as what might have been a smile was spreading, slowly, across his face.

* * *

It was curious. J-Bone had crept out over the south end of the bridge, expecting to see a tank or armored vehicle below; at the very least, a mobile rocket launcher.

Instead, all he saw was a woman in black, standing by a fire, holding what appeared to be a baby in her arms.

Caressing it. Kissing it. Talking to it.

Then she set it down to change its diaper, and he saw that it wasn't a baby at all. It was a Russian-made Thermidor shoulder-mounted recoilless heat-seeking anti-aircraft missile launcher.

She was reloading it.

By the time she picked it up, ready to fire, the red dot of J-Bone's laser sight was dancing on the swell of her left breast.

She kissed and caressed the Thermidor one more time as she pointed it up toward the central structure of the bridge. But she never got another chance to pull the trigger.

J-Bone's plasteel dart had already found its way into the muscular tissue of her motherly heart.

She fell face first into the fire, taking her four-foot metal baby with her.

Johnny was having another dream.

He knew it was a dream because his mother was in it, again, and his mother only existed in dreams.

In the dream, she sat at her desk, looking down. As usual.

He was approaching the desk and she refused to look up. As usual.

There was something on the desk, and he reached for it, reached up, too high. . . . Uh-oh! He knocked it onto the floor. It broke. *Oh no!*

"Bad boy!" Johnny's mother said in the dream. Then she did what he had been hoping she would do all along. She turned and looked down at him.

But there was no one there.

Her face was a blank.

Then J229ohnny remembered that he had erased her face, erased his memory of her. Even in dreams, it couldn't be recovered.

He felt a tremendous sadness, a sense of loss that he knew, even in his dream, was far too heavy a burden for a little four-year-old heart.

"Bad boy!"

Hoping to make it up to her, Johnny bent down to pick up the thing he had dropped. It was a picture frame. The glass was shattered.

He turned it over.

It was a picture of a woman with a baby in her arms.

But this picture had a face.

In the dream—or was it in the dream?—something in his brain took over, moving in on the picture in stages, like clicks: isolating the woman, *click,* the head and shoulders, *click,* the face. She was younger but he recognized the sad, searching eyes, the *yin* and *yang* earrings.

It was the woman who had appeared on the TV in Beijing, and just a few minutes ago, on the monitors, before Takahashi was killed.

"I've got it!" Johnny said.

"Wrong," said Street Preacher, moving slowly, inexorably, toward him. "It has got you." Street Preacher took the cross from the chain around his neck and flicked it open into a knife. "Salvation." The four-inch bowie blade gleamed. "He has made you the vessel of his mercy. . . ."

"I've got it!" said Johnny, getting to his feet, sliding along the wall, away from Street Preacher's knife.

"Got what?" asked Jane. She was using her teeth, trying to loosen the nail that pinned her hand to the beam of the cross.

"The third image," said Johnny, still sliding along the wall. "The rest of the download code. I have the whole thing!"

". . . as I am the vessel of his wrath," continued Street Preacher. The boxes and rubble that Johnny had to clamber over as he moved sideways along the wall, Street Preacher simply shoved aside, shuffling forward through furniture and broken beams as if they were water.

The nail was stubborn. Jane heard a splashing noise behind her, and she remembered Jones. He was thrashing in his tank. *Needs a fix,* Jane thought, *bad as I need a crowbar.*

"Where can the Sinner hide?" Street Preacher's knife led the way, unerringly, like a missile, a throat-seeking missile.

"Got it!" Jane groaned in pain and triumph.

"Got what?" Johnny asked.

"The nail." Her hand, pulled free, was smeared with blood; she clenched it to stanch the flow. One thing about puncture wounds, she mused: Little blood, much pain. The opposite of the slash that was being prepared for Johnny's throat.

No sense hitting Street Preacher. Like trying to stop a car. Jane had a better idea. She headed across the room for Jones's tank.

Street Preacher raised the knife. The throat-seeking missile.

Johnny took another step back.

The last one. He was on the corner.

He closed his eyes. At least he didn't have to watch.

"The cure," intoned Street Preacher, "is mine . . ."

Jones, too, was dreaming.

What he was dreaming cannot be described here, for our words are like hands, tools for grasping, and

223

language for Jones was a different thing entirely, a medium that slipped through and under and around concepts, observing rather than grabbing them. Jones had a soul, and like ours it was a soul that told itself a story, a continuous narration called consciousness; but in Jones's consciousness, the sea and not the swimmer was the subject. The soul was merely the storyteller. The story was a good one: It had gone on for a hundred hundred thousand years, since Jones and his kind had returned to the Mother Waters from their harsh exile on land.

Jones's dream, as usual, was of the old days.

The dream ended, appropriately, with a hand.

That five-sided starfish-looking symbol, the living token of the strange anxious creatures that had encountered, entrapped, intrigued, enslaved, and finally befriended him—tearing him away from his world and imprisoning him in a smaller one, of individual personality. They had taken his soul and given him a personality. Like it or not, Jones was now as much human as dolphin; he had two monkeys on his back, heroin and self.

He had a jones and he was a Jones. It was only in his dreams that he visited his old reality, but he still longed for it. The dream always ended when the hand appeared. The hand with food or heroin or orders.

This time it was a red hand. On the glass.

No, the hand was normal. The red was blood.

Jones knew blood. Like man, he and his kind were predators and prey as well. They were prey for only the largest, the hammerheads and the great whites: those whose stupidity was their strength because it gave them the simulacrum of concentration, single-mindedness:

Kill.

Kill.

Kill.

The stupid ones. They were in his DNA. Therefore, Jones knew right away what the red hand was telling him. When he listened he heard it. When he raised himself out of the water, he saw it. Moving slowly across the floor toward the man.

Kill.

Kill.

Kill.

In the old days, in the dreamtime, Jones and his kind were sometimes able to drive the stupid ones away with a concerted effort of mind that thrashed the waters with biologically created ultrasound.

Here, that was not possible. It took many minds, and here, there was only Jones.

But it was Jones with the SQUID. And with the help of the red-hand, the one who was standing on the rim of the pool, jerry-rigging the remaining ultrasound scanner, turning the cone until it found its target . . .

Johnny heard a whistling noise that rose to a scream, and then disappeared.

"Blessed are the Peacemakers," Street Preacher said as his knife waved through the air, homing in closer and closer to Johnny's throat.

His voice was strangely flat. The overtones were missing. Then Johnny saw why. Jones was quivering all over, standing on his tail on the water in a stop-action leap. Water was spinning off his articulated plasteel armor, singing through the air with inaudible vibrations.

Jane was standing on the rim of the tank, struggling with her blood-soaked hand to swivel the cone-shaped antenna of the single remaining ultrasound scanner toward Street Preacher. As she turned it, a thin trail of destruction traveled across the floor where it had been pointed:

A bottle melted.

A paper snapped into flame.

The plywood floor charred and smoked.

A fallen monitor heated, hissed and exploded.

The trail of ultrasound reached Street Preacher just as he was about to bring his knife down on Johnny's throat.

A black line, it moved up his back . . .

"What spawn of Satan . . . ?"

Street Preacher turned, and to Johnny's amazement began to dance. It was not a concession to sin; it was involuntary, as the silicon subdermals—the muscular augmenters, the myriad implants that had been embedded in his joints and muscles—began to explode. One by one at first, and then in a cacophony, like a string of cheap firecrackers on the Fourth of July.

"Dear Sweet Jesus!" Street Preacher lifted his hands to shield his eyes, but even his eyes exploded, showering his hands with glass. Then the hands themselves began to pop and swell and spray blood as they exploded from within.

Street Preacher lurched blindly, grabbing the end of a cut power line to keep from falling. Smoking from his empty eyes and ears, he was a fearsome sight. He lurched toward Johnny, one step, two . . .

Johnny tossed him the other end of the severed cable.

Street Preacher caught it instinctively, unseeingly; and he suddenly straightened, standing full height, as if at attention, as the blue-white current surged through him, popping in tendrils of flame off his shock of white hair.

Then, still gripping both cables, he fell to the floor.

Jane had also fallen. Weakened either from pain or exhaustion—or both—she slipped from the side of the tank, and caught herself on the ultrasound scanner. Her injured hand leaving a bloody trail, she slid down toward the floor.

By the time she had collapsed at the base of the tank, Johnny was at her side.

"Jane!"

"I'm okay . . ."

"You always were a liar."

"No, I . . ."

"What the fuck's going on here?"

Jane and Johnny both looked up, together.

J-Bone was standing in the shattered doorway like an avenging angel, backlit by the dawn, his spring-loaded crossbow in his hand.

Two other Loteks stood behind him. One was dragging a toolkit; the other had coils of wire.

"J-Bone! Where you been?" Jane asked.

"Taking care of business. What's with Street Preacher?"

"Gone to meet his maker," said Jane. "I hope, anyway. But what about . . . ?"

She ran to the tank and looked down. Jones was rolling from side to side.

"Looks like he needs a fix," said J-Bone, signalling with a toss of his head to a third Lotek, who was already rummaging through the drawers for the hero-in works.

"Hook me up," said Johnny.

"What?" J-Bone looked at him, surprised.

"Hook me up. I've got it. The rest of the code." He held out the fax Takahashi had given him, the image of the riots in Beijing captured from the TV.

"That makes two," said J-Bone. "But we're still missing the third."

"I have the third."

"Where? Let's see it."

"You'll have to wait and see it on the monitor. It's in my head. But now I know how to access it."

Twenty minutes later a certain rough calm, typically Lotek, had been restored to what was left of Times

Square. Jones lay peacefully on his back in his tank. Johnny was in the chair. Jane was beside him, holding his hand.

One Lotek was improvising a new stand for the second ultrasound scanner. Another Lotek was refitting the control console, stripping coaxial cable with a boxcutter, even as J-Bone fiddled to bring the monitors and the SQUID on-line.

"How many monitors we got left?" J-Bone asked.

"Three," came a voice from the top of a ladder, where still another Lotek was rewiring the working monitors, two from CNN and one marked GOOD MORNING AMERICA, in sequence. "I'm just turning them on."

The room lit with a new glow, but instead of snow, a face came up on the monitors.

"What the . . . ?" J-Bone began.

It was a woman's face. The woman with the *yin* and *yang* earrings. Everyone in the room now recognized her but no one knew who—or what—she was.

Johnny was the first to speak. "You're the third image!" he said. "Your face was captured from the TV in Beijing. Who are you? Why do you look so . . . familiar?"

"I'm your mother," she said.

EIGHTEEN

———■———

"You're my what?"

"I'm your mother."

A silence fell over the ruined room. There was no sound except the groaning of the bridge's rusted beams, the creaking of timbers and plywood against the ropes and cables that held the Loteks' "heaven" in place, the haunting whisper of the almost-dawn wind. J-Bone, the Loteks at the control console, even Jones rolling in his pool—all were watching the monitors; all eyes were fixed on the woman's face, repeated on the screens, cool and composed except for the unspoken plea in her voice.

All but one were watching the monitors. All but Jane. She stood beside Johnny's chair, her eyes fixed on his face, as if it alone contained the mystery she wanted resolved.

Jane was waiting for Johnny to speak, but he was silent. His face was closed like a fist.

"I am your mother. My name is Anna. Anna Kalman. I died six years ago, but before I died I had a neural scan performed, and my personality was imprinted into the neural net. Pharmakom arranged it."

"She was one of the founders!" J-Bone whispered loudly. "I remember because Spider and me, we did a global search on all this stuff."

"All what stuff?" Johnny asked.

"NAS. Anything having to do with NAS."

"It's true," Anna said. "I was head of Pharmakom. We were developing the cure for NAS. Among other things."

"And holding it back!" J-Bone said.

Anna nodded. "That, too. I'm not proud of that. In fact, I've done what I can to change it."

"How's that?" J-Bone asked, but Johnny shut him up with a wave of his hand. Johnny had more important questions on his mind.

"You're my mother," he said. It was the first time he had spoken directly to her. It was a statement, followed by a question: "And my father?"

Anna shook her head. "I got you at the bank. I wanted a child, thought I wanted a child. But I was too obsessed with my work, Johnny." Her image was flickering slightly.

"When you died. Did I . . . did I know?"

Anna shook her head. "You were already gone. It was my fault. I was obsessed with building Pharmakom. I took you with me everywhere, Johnny; you spent your youth in hotels around the world. But I had no time for you. I shoved you aside. When you became a teenager you ran away and I—I let you go."

Her eyes brimmed, overflowing with tears like the water from Jones's pool.

"Later, when I was dying, I found out you'd had your memory erased. It was too late for me."

"Too late," Johnny said.

"Still, I tried to look after you, Johnny! I arranged that they would choose you as the courier, Johnny. I have always tried to look after you . . ."

230

Johnny's anger was child-like in its sudden intensity. "If you're my mother, why didn't you let me know you were the third image?"

"Because I did not *know!* I had no *access.* That was just a mistake; the scanner must have picked me up off the TV screen at the Beijing hotel."

"What were you doing on that screen anyway?"

"I was in communication with the scientists. I helped arrange the theft of the data."

"Even though you are still on the board of Pharmakom?" J-Bone asked, skeptically.

"Yes. Even though. And Johnny, I arranged that they would use you to . . ."

"*Use* me? Is that what you wanted from me, to ease your conscience?" He turned away. "What *is* it you want from me, anyway?"

"Want from you?" Anna looked confused.

"Yeah. You said yourself, you never wanted anything from me before. What is it you want from me now?"

"I, uh . . ."

Johnny didn't wait for an answer. He turned his back on her. "J-Bone—"

"Huh?" The Lotek leader turned away from the monitors also.

"I'm ready."

"Ready for what?"

"The download. Let's do it. I have all three images now. I don't even need Jones. All I have to do is make an access run."

"It's not that simple anymore," J-Bone said.

"What do you mean?"

"Put the helmet on and I'll show you."

While Johnny put on the helmet, J-Bone pushed a toggle up on the console. Anna's face on one monitor was replaced by the cross-section view of Johnny's brain. The tentacles of the seepage were all through it,

231

like tendrils of a vine. The chip was no longer even visible.

"The data's still there," said J-Bone, "but it's corrupted all to hell. The seepage has linked it to every other part of your brain."

"Does that mean it's lost?" Jane asked.

"No. Not quite. That's the thing. If we loop it through Jones we can pull it out, but . . ."

"But—" Johnny prodded.

"It's the neurological equivalent of bungee jumping through a brick wall," J-Bone said, almost cheerfully. "It'll probably kill you."

Johnny looked at Jane, then briefly at his mother's image. "And if we don't?"

J-Bone shrugged. "If we take it out the easy way, the data's lost."

Jane took Johnny's hand. "Johnny, don't."

He noticed that her hand was shaking, just slightly. The NAS. And he was reminded that what was in his head was more than just data. It was the cure.

"Loop it, then," Johnny said.

Anna's face was frantic. "Johnny, I never meant for you to . . ."

"Loop it," Johnny said, leaning back in the chair. He reached out to Jane, and then turned to J-Bone.

"Hit me."

J-Bone nodded at the two Loteks on the console. They slid the toggles up to their max.

Jones began leaping in his pool.

On the three central monitors, Anna's face was replaced by three images: the riot, the Japanese cartoon superhero, and the still image of Anna's face.

"Bingo," said J-Bone. He reached out and pulled Jane to his side, holding her as if sheltering her against a sudden storm. "Here we go!"

He was inside.
Immediately.
There was no cruising through cyberspace looking

232

for the proper data node, no soaring around the spires and crystals of LANs and databases, looking for a way in.

He was in.

At first Johnny was disappointed: he missed the flying, the freedom of cyberspace. Then he remembered why he was here, and he was glad.

He was inside because he was riding the download code. He didn't need to look for access; he *was* access. He started where he wanted to be, inside Pharmakom's data.

As always when he was in the matrix, he had a form; a form he could both sense and, somehow, *see*.

He was a flat card with three sides, a creature of two dimensions, who somehow fluttered in and out of a third. The fluttering, and not the thing that fluttered, was what he was.

The dancer and the dance. Three sides. Three faces.

The download code. He *was* it and he *rode* it, down.

He was inside a great round hall, like a gutted skyscraper lit on all sides as if the walls were translucent. But dim. Dim as hell. Flying buttresses, scooped and scoured all over. Ornate, with Gothic curves. Flying things, like dust, great winged bits of dust. Bats of dust. White bats.

Down, down, he was going down. Or was the wall going up? Johnny knew not to look too closely, not to try and make too much sense of anything. Not here.

He was good as a "cowboy," a wrangler through cyberspace, because he was able to run on instinct, and his instincts were as loose as dreams. He understood that cyberspace was like dream space, seemingly illogical—though actually quite logical. Different rules. And the rules often changed a lot.

He fluttered and floated and fell, down through the tube, letting himself "fall" as the code carried him deeper and deeper. It was almost fun.

"Decryption sequence incomplete. Unauthorized interface attempt. . . ."

What was that? *Oh shit!*

"Warning. Intruder countermeasures arming."

That's the leakage, Johnny thought. *Has to be. The fucking program is so corrupted that it's arming its protectives. It's gone psychotic, doesn't even recognize its own download codes . . .*

"What's happening?" asked Jane.

Johnny had a strangely peaceful expression on his face. Jones was the only one working: thrashing from side to side in his pool, as if searching for space in which to swim. Making tighter and tighter circles.

"Johnny is riding the code in," J-Bone said. "It's an easy trip down. When he actually triggers the download, then . . ."

"Then *what?*"

J-Bone shrugged. "Then we'll see."

Jane shivered. She squeezed Johnny's hand, hoping he would respond.

He didn't.

"Meanwhile, Jones is multi-tasking like a motherfucker," J-Bone said. "He's keeping the loop open for Johnny, so he'll be able to help pull the data out. And he's making a satellite connection for me. I'm going to dump this data directly into the matrix as soon as we get it out. Unfiltered, unedited, and unfuckingcensored. Straight shot to a hundred million eyes and ears . . ."

"Speaking of which, you're on," one of the Loteks called out, passing J-Bone a set of earphones and a mike.

Forget the leakage . . . the debris. The almost-familiar images, probably from his own erased past, all mixed in. *Let it go.*

Drop. *Dreamride it on down.*

On the walls, in between and around the hideous Pharmakom logos that studded the walls like gargoyles, the data was weaving and dropping and running like wax in the sun: some of it numbers, some of it letters, some of it runes and glyphs and images that should have been familiar but weren't. Johnny knew better than to look too closely. *Glide on past.* Cyberspace was a world where everything shifted when it was examined, where consciousness had the brute force of a blow.

Johnny knew this world; he knew to move lightly here.

Truth was, he loved it here.

"Pharmakom Saigon Research, Project A87—slash —24—slash—9876239B."

That's better.

"Warning! Data overload. Incoherent sector on file. Intruder alert. Alert alert."

Damn! Incoherent is right.

Johnny floated, down, down down down. There was no turning back, anyway. The program was too fucked up to recognize him but too fucked up to keep him out. So far, anyway. Maybe when he initiated the download it would all sort out. And if it didn't? Not only was the data corrupt, it was mixed with his own mind.

I shouldn't even fucking be here . . .

But where else could he be? He was in his own mind, on a rescue operation.

"Johnny . . ."

He ignored the voice.

There. At the bottom of the shaft, which had somehow become three-sided, was the chip. It floated in, or on, a fog that was shaped like a brain, that hand-shaped curve, that fist that held worlds. He was here to open it. The chip was shimmering like a hot

235

coal, in and out of existence. *Unstable in the fucking extreme.* For the first time, Johnny could see how overloaded he was. The chip, like the walls of the shaft, was covered with vines reaching out, reaching in. Above it was a shower of particles, like dust in red, falling and rising at the same time. Data. Debris. Disaster.

"Johnny . . . !"

You?

"Of course."

What the hell are you doing here?

"I'm in the matrix. I live here, to the extent I live anywhere. I followed you in on the download. To warn you that . . ."

That the data is corrupted. I already know that. I think I can get around it as soon as I get to the chip.

"Not that. Something worse. There's a Trojan horse, Johnny. A destroyer virus."

How do you know?

"I helped put it there. It's set up to block a download, it'll . . ."

Destroy the data?

"Worse than that, Johnny. Destroy the carrier."

What triggers it?

"It's already triggered. The access code triggered it when you hit the bottom of the entry sequence. Look around."

And it was true. The walls, still covered with shifting runes and images, were beginning to ooze a white substance (or near-substance) like smoke, that dropped instead of rose, and then disappeared. This was not the spill, the synaptic leakage; it was something else, something with a different logic. A hunter. Johnny could feel it collecting in his "bones," in the interstices between the various phases of his virtual existence, for he was his own movements, and his movements were slowing.

It was invisible but not quite.

236

He spread two fingers and saw it glowing, white, a web.

ICE, said Johnny.

"Yes. It will lock up and then erase the carrier program, which means you, before you can get the data out, unless—"

Unless what?

"I have clearance. It can't touch me. I'm on the Pharmakom board. Go into the chip with me. Take me in with you. Same thing. Either way."

How?

"You know how. We have to meld."

"Listen up out there," said J-Bone, slipping into his best deejay persona. And in a hundred thousand hotels, in a million private homes, in huts in Asia and basement rec rooms in Canada, on 3.98 out of every ten of the world's 4.9 billion electronic video screens, J-Bone's image appeared, wavering only slightly, parceled and repeated by Jones's satellite intrusion code, shifting too fast for the interference filters to even identify it, much less block it. "Listen up out there!"

"Who the hell is that?" asked a banker in Japanese, a fisherman in Norwegian, a restaurateur in Tagalog.

"J-Bone!" breathed a boy in a Kansas video parlor and a girl in a board hut (with satellite) on the Goan coast of India.

"Listen up!" said J-Bone. "This will be your last blast from Lotek World Headquarters, and we're going out with a bang. Hit that SAVE button now, people, 'cause we have got something *hot,* which we intend to share with the world whether the world fucking wants it or not—"

How?

"Just do it. Don't think about it, just do it."

How do I know I can trust you?

"I'm your mother, Johnny."

But—

"Don't think about it, just do it."

Johnny didn't think about it, he just did it. Like everything else in cyberspace, it was easy enough if he just did it without bringing into play the Newtonian matrices that connected his macro-musculature to the micro-emergent CPU that was his brain.

Now he was still fluttering, but he was part of another fluttering, no longer moving with his will but with another, and that wasn't all.

There was something else. A feeling. The strangest feeling. Of wanting, like when he had wanted his mother to bend down and pick him up, but she never would. It was like wanting and having at the same time.

He felt as if he were wrapped in her arms *(And how do I know what that feels like?),* wrapped in her body, barely a being, a glowing spot. Home. He felt the heart that lay in him like a fist suddenly open, like a hand, and take another hand . . .

"Come on . . ."

And at the same time, the fluttering. He was the fluttering; he was moving toward the chip, around it—touching it—and it unfolded as chips do when he touched it, into a new universe, one that opened with him inside.

"AAAAaaggghhh!"

Sudden, unexpected pain. But not his pain: worse. How could another's pain be worse?

What's wrong?

"I don't know. I thought I had clearance. Maybe Pharmakom . . . pulled my clearance."

We should pull back then. Before . . .

"Too late. Open the chip, Johnny; open another window. We have to get to the download initiation sequence. Aaagghhh!"

More pain. A fierce, fluttering pain.

But it's hitting you instead of me!

"Don't think about it, just do it."
He did it.

"What's wrong?" Jane asked.

"Wrong?" J-Bone turned away from the mike for just a moment, dropping his deejay persona to look at Jane and then at Johnny, rigid in his chair. Johnny's ears under the helmet were leaking blood. His hands on the arm of the chair were shaking. He looked like a man in the last stages of NAS.

"Fuck if I know," said J-Bone.

Blue lights were flickering on the monitors and around the corpse of Street Preacher, who lay face up on the floor with a coaxial cable clutched in each massive fist. "Leave him," said J-Bone to a Lotek that was nudging at the body with a toe. "He's our main trunk connection."

Then J-Bone turned back to his microphone:

"Hang in there, people, for the direct download of the most valuable info in years. The cure for NAS."

In.

Every inside had another inside. Inside the chip was outside the data, all darkness now, but that was okay.

Johnny didn't have to understand the architecture of the chip; he didn't have to find the download sequence window. It would find him. All he had to do was open it.

But he couldn't open it. Something had him. Them.

Johnny tried to move toward the chip but it was as if he were moving through water. And slow water were moving through him. Heavy water.

ICE.

The virus wrapping itself around him, through him, invisible but impenetrable too. It would not only keep him from initiating the download, it would trap him here. Johnny had seen people frozen in cyberspace before, locked by a bad chip, an unexpected virus.

239

Eternity for them wasn't the soaring cyberspace of perfect freedom, but a dungeon beyond all imagining, where the mind was demergent, fixed on its last image. Conscious stasis. Eternity over and over, every second.

He tried to move and found himself spinning. He knew what it was; he was cycling in harmonic sequence with one of the Lotek CPUs. He was caught in a loop.

The pain of the ICE was like cold fire—it was not his pain, it was worse—and with every turn, every cycle, he saw his mother, Anna, Anna Kalman, further immobilized and beginning to fade . . .

"What's happening?" Jane asked.

Johnny was thrashing his arms about, slower and slower, as if he were underwater. Screams filled the air, getting higher and higher in pitch. Someone or something was screaming with him, in hideous concert . . .

"Jones!" said J-Bone, turning once more away from the microphone. He flicked a toggle on his earphones and listened as the gibberish got higher and higher, then faded into ultrasonic inaudibility.

"What does Jones want?" asked Jane.

"He wants to go in."

Mother! Johnny yelled.

She was almost invisible. Fading. Then on the event horizon, far above, Johnny saw a shape.

A white shape. Invisible/visible, in/out like a strobe, as Johnny cycled powerlessly.

Jones glided in, fast and smooth and powerful. Beautiful. Here in the electronic matrix he wore no gray armor, no US Navy stencil. Watching him, Johnny realized why Jones was able to live in his little prison of a pool. He spent most of his time in cyberspace, where he could swim. Where he could fly. Where he could soar.

And where he could kill. The SQUID parabolics implanted on either side of his skull could be used for reconnaissance—or destruction. Here in cyberspace no scanners, no antennae were necessary. The beams swept in front of Jones like twin headlights, and where they crossed and struck the ICE encrusting the four-sided cycling figure that was Johnny/Anna, the ICE morphed into rock solid visibility, then shattered into invisibility again . . .

Gone.

But where was Anna? Johnny had stopped spinning; he moved! and opened another window and he was at the chip; he was inside the final sector of the download protocol.

But where was Anna? Johnny felt she was with him but he couldn't make contact. The chip was glowing; here it was hot, covered with swarming tentacles. Johnny realized with a feeling very like horror that he had left the matrix and was inside his own mind. He had ridden the data cone all the way down into his own flesh, where the leakage was entangled with his own memories and consciousness.

He tugged, pulled, probed—and jumped back. The pain was root stuff, primordial, no longer mediated through nerve and spine and brain. It was pure cell pain and it was all his. It didn't even hurt. It *was* hurt . . . pure damage. . . .

He looked for his mother, Anna, but he couldn't find her; she was no more separate from him than an arm that had gone to sleep. She was with him but of no help. He was alone.

Or was he?

Jones was circling overhead, waiting, and Johnny knew what he had to do. Jones could loop it out but first Johnny had to cut it free.

241

He held his breath and pulled. He folded himself in on himself, in a matrix version of the slow-breath maneuver he had learned in Bangkok, and walked out of the pain, his eyes wide open, trying to ignore the screaming, knowing it was his own . . .

"My God!" J-Bone ripped off his earphones. "Can you shut him up?"

Johnny lay back in the chair, his palms together as if in prayer, his mouth wide open. He was screaming.

The download codes were gone off the monitors. Anna was back, but fading, being eaten by snow.

Jones was standing—literally—on his tail, his entire body out of the water, like a still picture from the water show.

And Johnny kept on screaming.

"Shut him the fuck up or something!" J-Bone said.

"He's okay," Jane said.

"What do you mean, *okay?*"

"I've seen this before," Jane said. "Something about the way he's holding his hands. Means he's got it under control."

Chip.
Found.
Opened.
Free.

Johnny cut through, watching the pieces of himself float upward, fall upward toward the light. Reached down. Didn't find the initiating macro, *was* the macro. He was the universe running a self-test.

Okay! Falling, falling up. And all around, peeling in great spirals off the walls, the data sweeping upward in perfect orderly streams, like a Tetris game in reverse. And even the "voice." Almost friendly:

Downloading Pharmakom data. File resolution restored. Data integrity restored.

It was the program speaking, and Johnny knew it

242

was all right, for as the space was emptied, the space itself shrunk, until there was just he/Anna riding a universe like a wave, but a tiny one. She was heavy, but he had her. She was no longer ICE-encrusted, but she was barely fluttering.

"*Let's go,*" said another voice. Jones.

The universe was bigger with Jones in it. He was a white sky to things. A powerful sky. He had looped out the data, pulling it free, and now there was Johnny to loop out.

"*Let's go!*" said Jones.

I'm trying, I'm holding on to her.

"*Can't loop you both. She stays here, in the matrix.*"

Can't leave her here. Too weak. Too much ICE.

"*Let's go!*" said Jones.

"*Go . . . !*" Another voice. Anna's.

No.

"*Johnny, I belong here. Besides, I'm dying, being erased.*"

No! I won't leave you here.

"*Don't think about it, just do it.*"

This time he didn't do it.

But it didn't matter.

This time it was Anna who pulled free and Johnny felt her falling, for they were still one—fluttering again, but it was a down flutter, a darkening, falling deeper into the matrix.

He called out, almost.

He looked back, almost. She was vague, dim, and his hand was still warm where she had stood in the center of his palm.

That was why Jane and J-Bone saw him smiling.

"Straight-out, folks, Pharmakom didn't want you to have it, but here it is, unfuckingstoppable, straight from the mouths of babes, the Lotek special, and the last one . . ."

And in a hundred thousand hotels, in a million

243

private homes, in huts in Asia and basement rec rooms in Canada, on 3.98 out of every ten of the world's 4.9 billion electronic video screens, a stream of numbers and symbols appeared, held in place by Jones's fast-shifting satellite intrusion code.

Followed by a voice-over: *"Downloading Pharmakom data. File resolution restored. Data integrity restored."*

"Hooray!" went up a roar from all the Loteks as the data went out.

"But it's just numbers and shit. Nobody can understand it!" protested Jane.

"People understand what it *is!*" J-Bone said. "And it's being recorded by enough folks who can read it. And create it. Bootleg it. Free it, all over the fucking world. Listen!"

The first thing Johnny saw when he opened his eyes was—

Jane.

Why did she look so familiar? So *right?*

She held out both hands. He took them and staggered to his feet.

"Did we . . . ? Did it?" he asked.

Jane nodded. "Come see!" She dragged him toward the far side of the room, where J-Bone and the other Loteks were standing at the blown-out wall, peering out into the dawn.

"Wait." Johnny pulled free. Above the console, the monitors were dim. Flickering. But the image of his mother, Anna, was still there. Just barely. She was smiling, just barely.

"Johnny," she whispered. "You made it. Did you get the data out?"

"We got it," said Johnny. "What's happening to you? The ICE . . . ?"

She shook her head. It moved slowly, her *yin* and *yang* earrings leaving a smear of loose pixels. "It's

Pharmakom. They're erasing me. Revenge. Just glad that—"

"Glad that what?"

But she was gone.

The Lotek on the control console fiddled with the gain, switched monitors on and off, then turned to Johnny to confirm it. "Gone," he said. "No signal."

Johnny felt Jane's hand on his arm. "She was—" she began. But she couldn't think of anything to say.

"It's okay," Johnny said. And strangely enough, it was. He searched briefly for tears, regrets, sorrow, but there was nothing there. It had all been used up years before.

And that was okay, too.

He followed Jane to the shattered end of the room, where the wall had blown away. He stood with her, looking over the shoulders of the Loteks, at the reddening sky.

In the distance, to the west and south, over Newark, rockets were rising. Flares. Car horns.

"What's going on?" Johnny asked.

"They're celebrating," said J-Bone. He stepped back and clapped a hand on Johnny's shoulder and one on Jane's. "They got the news. We did it. It belongs to everybody. It's DONE!"

"Done," said Johnny. He looked back at the monitors where his mother had been, and then down at Jane. He opened his hand over hers, and as he did he felt his heart opening. Like a fist. It was almost a new feeling. But familiar, too.

There was a sputtering behind them, and the lights flared—

"Hey!" a Lotek shouted.

Street Preacher was stirring. He stumbled to his knees, then to his feet, his dead eyes sparking with strange new energy as a surge from somewhere in the grid passed through the cables in his fists—

Then he fell backward as a bolt struck with a *crack*

245

in the center of his forehead. He fell to the floor with a crash, like a falling tree.

"Said it was *over!*" J-Bone muttered, putting away his spring-loaded crossbow. "Where you two going?"

"Down," said Johnny, pulling on a jacket from the pile by the door. "To see what's up. Come go with us."

"Why not," said J-Bone, signalling to the rest of the Loteks. "Can't hang around Heaven forever."